BUCCANEER BLOOD:

THE ADVENTURES OF DENIS BURKE

OTHER BOOKS IN THE
H. BEDFORD-JONES UNIFORM
EDITION LIBRARY:

Cyrano

D'Artagnan

The King's Passport

O'Brien, Buccaneer

The Sphinx Emerald

H. BEDFORD-JONES

BUCCANEER BLOOD:
THE ADVENTURES OF DENIS BURKE

H. BEDFORD-JONES

COVER ILLUSTRATION BY

PAUL STAHR

ALTUS PRESS • 2014

EDITED AND DESIGNED BY
Matthew Moring

PUBLISHING HISTORY
"Escape!" originally appeared in the November 7, 1931 issue of *Argosy* magazine. Copyright 1931 by The Frank A. Munsey Company. Copyright renewed 1958 and assigned to Steeger Properties, LLC. All Rights Reserved.

"Luck of the Sea Burkes" originally appeared in the January 9 & 16, 1932 issues of *Argosy* magazine. Copyright 1932 by The Frank A. Munsey Company. Copyright renewed 1959 and assigned to Steeger Properties, LLC. All Rights Reserved.

"Spanish Gold" originally appeared in the March 19, 1932 issue of *Argosy* magazine. Copyright 1932 by The Frank A. Munsey Company. Copyright renewed 1959 and assigned to Steeger Properties, LLC. All Rights Reserved.

"Buccaneer Blood" originally appeared in the September 10, 1932 issue of *Argosy* magazine. Copyright 1932 by The Frank A. Munsey Company. Copyright renewed 1959 and assigned to Steeger Properties, LLC. All Rights Reserved.

"Spanish Blood Is Proud Blood" originally appeared in the March 25, 1933 issue of *Argosy* magazine. Copyright 1933 by The Frank A. Munsey Company. Copyright renewed 1960 and assigned to Steeger Properties, LLC. All Rights Reserved.

THANKS TO
Joel Frieman, Everard P. Digges LaTouche and Gerd Pircher

Printed in the United States of America.

TABLE OF CONTENTS

I

ESCAPE!

To insult the haughty Louis XIV was to insult all France—but Denis Burke, bold Irish courtier, fought best against tall odds.

CHAPTER I

THE MAN WHO DEFIED FRANCE

DENIS BURKE, lieutenant-colonel of the Royal Irlandois, dismounted in the courtyard of the inn used as Paris headquarters by the officers of the Irish Brigade, and strode up to his own rooms. He had just ridden in from Versailles, and the storm in his eager eyes and bronzed, aquiline features was a reflection of the storm he had raised in the summer palace of Louis XIV.

It was June of 1703, and Paris was sweltering. The barracks and officers' quarters were all but deserted, for the brigade of Irish exiles had been ordered south to join the sixty thousand troops engaged in exterminating the revolted Camisards.

Coming to his own room, Burke strode in. Out of a chair jumped his lackey, old Malachi Halloran, who dropped his long clay pipe in his haste and broke it.

"Bad news, your honor?" he exclaimed at sight of Burke's face. The latter shrugged.

"That depends, Malachi. I'm done for, and you'll have to take your choice. Clear out, leave me; I'm running for it, and if I'm caught it means the Bastille."

"Faith, myself has served your honor since we were run out of Ireland together," said grizzled Malachi stoutly. "And what would you be doing in the Bastille without the likes o' me to be serving you?"

"Devil take you!" Burke clapped him on the shoulder. "I'm done for, I tell you. Do you stick?"

Burke's slip gave the vicomte *his opening.*

"Shame to me if I didn't, your honor. Did you pull the king's nose?"

"Next thing to it," said Burke cheerfully. "Quick, then! Saddlebags—take what we need, clothes on our backs. Saddle the best horses in the stables; my black, and Desmond's big gray. Desmond will be glad enough to let me use him. Off with you! Report back the minute you're ready. Have the horses at the little gate leading out to the Rue d'Enfer. Tell our own men to cover us if questions are asked. Understand?"

"Praise be!" exclaimed Malachi, and departed in haste for the other room to get the saddlebags packed.

Burke hurriedly flung off his court uniform, threw his star of St. Michel into the corner, flung his court rapier after it. From the wall he took down his campaign sword—a fine, long, plain blade of Toledo steel—and buckled it to his baldric. He stripped in haste, got into clean linen, from a wardrobe took out a traveling suit of stained brown velvet, from a chest took a magnificent cloak of blue stuff laced with silver, all but waterproof, and a beaver with floating golden plume.

"Faith, they'd not recognize the colonel of brigade in these citizens' clothes!" he said with a chuckle. He turned to the

shaving cabinet and seized on brush and razor.

NOT THAT Denis Burke would be hard to recognize, in any case. When the mustache and chin-tuft had vanished, his face leaped out differently, yet the same—imperious, handsome, keen of eye and nose and chin, a face born to command and to be obeyed.

He had just folded up brush and razor in a strip of linen when he heard clattering hoofs below, and looked from his window to see an officer dismount hastily and rush for the stairs. He grinned cheerfully.

"There's Desmond now, eh? I thought he'd be rushing after me with ncws!"

A moment later Desmond burst into the room and stopped short.

"Burke! Have you gone mad? The king's furious! What did you say to him?"

"I said enough," and Burke chuckled as he reached for his breeches. "I told him what I thought of sending the brigade to massacre peasants in Languedoc, and told him to go to the devil. He didn't seem to like it. And I had a nice meeting with that scurvy devil Baron Ravenel—you should ha' seen his face when I slapped his lean jaw!"

"So that's it! Man, I came to warn you," broke out Desmond hurriedly. "It means the Bastille at least! Ravenel is high in favor. He's got a commission to a ship at St. Malo, and it's a certainty that the king will clap you behind bars for this—"

"St. Malo, is it? Faith, I'm going that way my own self!" said Burke. "Anyhow, I spoke my mind to the king, God bless him!... Malachi! Will you be getting those horses?"

"Bags are just packed, your honor. I'm off now," floated back Malachi's voice.

"You're not running?" snapped Desmond.

"D'you suppose I'm going to stand on my dignity and go to hell for it? Not I," said Burke with a laugh. "I threw my commission in the king's face."

"But where the devil can you go?" exclaimed Desmond in dismay.

"To the devil. Back to sea, of course! I come from the sea Burkes anyhow, and I'm sick of soldiering. Will you go with me?"

"Not I," said Desmond. "I'm telling you that they'll be hot after you, Denis. Have you any money?"

"Some."

"Take this." Desmond hauled out a handful of gold. "I won heavily last night—no, take it, you rascal!"

"Thanks," said Burke, and waved his hand about the room. "If ye see anything here ye'd fancy, help yourself. Where are those riding boots? Ah!" He seized a pair of Cordovan boots, thigh high, and began getting into them. "And, Desmond! Spread the word, like a good chap, that I'm riding for Flanders."

"I will not!" exclaimed Desmond. "Would I be giving you away, man?"

"Spread that word, and you'll be saving me. Off with you, now!"

A handshake, and Desmond was gone.

Burke fell to work destroying letters, clearing out his personal belongings, taking what he must have—little enough at that. He chuckled anew at thought of the tumult he had raised at Versailles: insulting the king himself, slapping Ravenel's face, tearing his commission to bits and flinging it down, and then walking out.

And no wonder. Burke himself had been furious at being ordered to do butcher's work in Languedoc, killing and burning, exterminating poor devils of peasants who had been tortured into revolt. Impulsive, hotheaded, Denis Burke was a good soldier, but no courtier, and Louis of France was not accustomed to hear the blunt ideas of other men on the subject of honor.

His meeting with Ravenel delighted him beyond measure. From their first encounter the two men had been deadly enemies, for no particular reason except mutual dislike. Ravenel was something of a hero, for he had made a cruise with a filibustering ship from St. Malo and had brought back a small fortune. A Breton noble, he had come to court and been warmly received by the king, who delighted to honor his corsairs. And now Burke had slapped his face, to the covert joy of more than one in the throng.

If he had destroyed his whole future by this act, little Burke cared.

"Horses ready, your honor," said Malachi, flinging open the door. "Anything more to go?"

"This," and Burke handed over a small parcel of clean linen and toilet necessities. "Get out of that uniform, you omadhaun! Quickly! I'll meet you below."

"In two minutes, your honor."

Malachi departed again in haste. Burke went to the window, hearing a clatter below, and looked out to see an officer dismounting in the courtyard. He recognized the colonel of the Swiss Guards, one Lafoix—a man whom he had never met, a trim, precise martinet who was universally detested by his brother officers.

WITH A chuckle Burke jammed the beaver over his head, slung the cloak across his shoulders, picked up a pipe and stuffed it with tobacco, and then swung into a chair beside the table. He must give Malachi time to change costume, in any event. He worked over the flint and steel until he got a light for his pipe, and was just puffing it up when a knock sounded at the door.

"Enter!" called Burke jauntily, and Colonel Lafoix strode into the room.

"I am seeking M. Burke," he said abruptly. "He is not here?"

"I'm waiting for him myself," said Burke. "He's expected any moment. Come in, come in and make yourself comfortable."

"Thank you," said the Swiss, stalking forward. He looked at Burke without recognition, and pulled off his gloves. Putting them on the table, he drew a paper from his pocket and laid it with them, and drew up a chair.

"You are a friend of M. Burke?" he inquired.

"I am not," said Burke promptly. "I'm the rascal's worst enemy! You're a friend of his?"

"Hardly." Lafoix shrugged, and indicated the unsealed paper. "I have a coach arriving for him in ten minutes. Glance at that letter, if you like—since you're no friend of his, it may give you a bit of pleasure."

With a perfectly straight face, Burke picked up the letter. It was a printed form, filled in with the proper names, and was addressed to the officer in command of the Bastille:

IN THE NAME OF THE KING.

> Dear and well-beloved, we order and command that you receive in your house Lieutenant Colonel Denis Burke and keep him there until new orders come from us, at the charges of the pension which will be paid by our treasurer. Let no error be made, for such is our pleasure.
>
> Signed: Louis.
> Given at Versailles, June 3, 1703.
> Countersigned: Pontchartrain.

"A *lettre de cachet,* eh?" said Burke. "And what has the scoundrel done now, that he is to be put in jail?"

"Plenty. It is incredible!" exclaimed the Swiss stiffly. "He insulted the king himself! He slapped a nobleman in the precincts of the court! The man has gone mad."

"All Irishmen are mad," said Burke, laying down his pipe. "Well, my colonel, you'll put this fellow away where he'll make no more trouble, eh? He'll be back soon, I understand. That must be your coach now, eh?"

A thunderous noise arose from the courtyard, as a coach came rolling in on the cobbles. The Swiss arose and went to the window, shoving it out to gaze down. The minute his back was turned Burke slipped the king's letter into his breast pocket, walked out of the room, and closed the door silently. He slipped swiftly down to the small rear entrance of the hotel. There he found the two saddled horses waiting, and Malachi. The latter held his stirrup, and he swung up to the saddle.

"To Versailles, Malachi!"

"What, your honor?" The soldier, now garbed in sober civilian clothes, blinked at him. "Is it mad you are, and you fresh from there—"

"They'll not know me," and Burke laughed as he put in his spurs. "And we must go that road if we're to reach Brittany. Pistols at the saddle, eh? Good. Loaded?"

"Aye, your honor. We'll need a pass at the gates in order to get out o' Paris—"

"I have my own pass. What matter if they track us? We must outride the couriers in any case. Forward!"

They went clattering down the Seine, heading for the Porte de Versailles.

FULL WELL Burke knew the madness of his venture, increased a hundredfold by the use of his own military pass; yet it was so utterly mad that it might succeed. He could not hope entirely to outrun the post-couriers. Within an hour orders would be speeding out by every main highway to the frontiers of Spain and Italy and Flanders and Germany; the old king would spare neither money nor effort to apprehend the Irishman who had flaunted him to his face.

St. Malo was the one destination they would never suspect. It was distant, and offered no apparent hope of escape. Exiled from Ireland and under attainder of treason, Burke could not make for England. The shortest routes to the frontiers would be the ones chosen—they could not dream he would ride elsewhere.

Burke had a more personal reason for riding toward St. Malo, however, and once past Versailles he trusted to audacity to carry him through. Of this quality he lacked nothing.

"Faith, Malachi," he chuckled as they clattered along toward the Versailles Gate, "you should have seen the king's painted old face when I told him Irish gentlemen had better things to do than burn farms and massacre peasants!"

"It's true, your honor," said Malachi. "My regiment was in that business of the Waldenses, and what the lads told me of it was a sin and a shame. Will we be through Versailles by dark?"

"We'd better be, if we want to save our necks, Malachi! Praise be, we'll not have to use my pass there. Spur up a bit."

They quickened pace. Without incident they came to the Porte de Versailles, and amid a throng of country folk leaving the city, were passed out with only a glance at their papers. Spurs struck in, and they sent the horses ahead at a gallop—for here they had to make speed at all costs. Once past Versailles, Burke felt he might breathe freely.

The short twelve miles was nearly covered, and Versailles was in sight ahead, when Burke flung his companion a word and drew rein. A cavalier coming toward them had halted suddenly, as a little group of country women blocked the road. He was splendidly garbed, a lackey rode behind him, and Burke recognized him at once as the Vicomte de Clisson, an idler about the court, no doubt riding into Paris for an evening of pleasure and dissipation.

One of the women fell. Clisson laughed, leaned over in the saddle, and flailed her with his riding-crop.

"Run, animal, run!" he called brutally, just as Burke came up. The latter, flushed with impetuous anger, reined in abruptly,

"Man, my dear Clisson," said he, forgetting everything, "is the only animal who has the brutality to strike a female."

The noble eyed him in startled recognition.

"What the devil! I thought you were in the Bastille ere now, Irishman! What was that you said? Did you have the effrontery to insult me?"

"Faith, can you be insulted?" said Burke dryly. "It wouldn't take much effrontery to try it on you!"

Quick as a flash, Clisson leaned far over and his hand struck Burke across the face. Then he was out of the saddle, but no quicker than Burke.

"Malachi! Take the rascal lackey!"

Despite the edict against lackeys bearing swords, Clisson's man carried a rapier. Burke faced the *vicomte* and laughed a little as his blade rasped from the scabbard.

"By the saints, I'll give you a message for Ravenel!" he exclaimed gayly. "Or rather, I'll send him one by you—"

"En garde!" cried Clisson hotly and drove in a lunge for the heart.

The blades met, clung in mid-air, rasped and clicked in the afternoon sunlight. Dust rose from the stamping feet and hung in the air about the two figures. A laugh was on Burke's lips, his blue eyes were glinting eagerly—then his foot turned a stone and he fell to one knee.

An exultant oath burst from Clisson and he sent in a dastardly lunge. Burke wrenched himself sidewise and it missed. Next instant he was on his feet, smiling no longer.

"For that, you dog, you'll never see Paris again!" he said, and his eyes blazed as cruelly as the steel in his hand.

Clisson took a step back, and another. A gasp came from his

lips; a horrible pallor rose in his face as he met Burke's eyes, read the message in them. He opened his mouth to speak, but instead of words a gush of blood appeared.

Burke stepped back, watched him pitch forward in the dust, hand to throat.

"Shall I finish this fool, your honor?" asked Malachi, kneeling above the hapless lackey.

"Let him go," said Burke. "We'll take their horses—a spare mount for each of us. Forward!"

Malachi grinned as he caught the horses and brought them up.

"Now we'll have all France after us, your honor! This means the gallows."

Swinging up to the saddle, Burke snapped his fingers at Versailles.

"It'll take more than all France to bring Denis Burke to the scaffold! That for you, Louis the Sun King! Faith, you'll hear a word or two from me before you ever hang me! On our way, Malachi!"

And, his laugh ringing back at the dead man and the staring lackey, he put in spurs and was gone in a cloud of dust.

CHAPTER II

THE KING'S MEN

WHERE THIS merely the tale of a flight across France, it would have little point. However, it is the tale of an Irishman's audacity and imagination, which stopped at nothing; and you may still hear echoes of it in the archives of Maine and Brittany.

Denis Burke had defied all France; but he had certain advantages, of which he was well aware. First, he would be hunted in all directions, save the way he had actually gone. Second, he was seeking to save his neck, which was a powerful incentive. Third, he had his military pass and documents, which looked more valuable on second thought. Last but not least, he was well supplied with money; and in his pocket was the *lettre de cachet* for his own arrest.

Spurring hard, they reached Houdan toward midnight, and were lodged at the inn of the little town on the Végre, going on again at sunrise. They passed through Dreux without incident; then, barely a mile outside town, overtook a company of fifty horsemen. As they made out the glitter of arms on the road ahead, Malachi drew rein.

"The Maréchaussée, your honor!" he exclaimed in warning.

Burke nodded. He had already recognized the uniforms of this mounted body, who served as coast guards, highway police and general upholders of the law throughout France. This large force was evidently headed westward. Even if he passed them safely, he would have them at his heels the moment a courier caught up with them.

"Gallop, Malachi!" he cried, and put in his spurs.

They came thundering up with the column. Burke's voice leaped out.

"In the king's name!"

The ranks fell apart. When he came up with the captain in command, he drew rein and saluted.

"Monsieur! Your name?" he demanded with authority.

"M. de Roboise, in command of this company of the Maréchaussée."

"Good! Courier of the king!" Burke held out the *lettre de cachet,* or enough of it to hastily show the signatures of Louis and his minister. "I failed to catch you at Dreux, *m'sieu,* but well enough. You are ordered to abandon everything else, ride north to Evreux, and there stop all the roads leading to the west and north. Haste is imperative. A conspiracy has been discovered at Paris, reaching into the court itself. Marshal Villers is under arrest, the Duc de Berry in the Bastille, the Cardinal de Bouillon has fled. You are ordered to arrest all who seek the frontiers and to close the ports of Calais and Dunkirk; give passage only to those who bear the royal signature. Haste!"

The honest commandant turned pale at hearing this tale of conspiracy, involving the greatest names of France.

"Monsieur!" he exclaimed, aghast. "But the half-company of our force at Evreux—"

"Is placed under your orders," broke in Burke. "Back to Dreux quickly, and ride north as though the devil were after you! The officer in charge at Alençon will take over your duties. Ride!"

The commandant saluted, and turned to his trumpeter. Burke put in spurs and went away at a gallop, while behind him the column turned about and headed back for the city in all haste. A gay laugh broke from Burke as Malachi drew abreast.

"Faith, they're out of the way at all events!" he exclaimed. "And now for the Château de Verneuil, me lad!"

"I thought so," said Malachi grimly. "That's why we rode for St. Malo, eh?"

"One reason, at all events," said Burke cheerfully.

"But they'll know you there—"

"They'll know me better after I'm gone. Forward!"

Behind them the dust rose in a white haze across the sunlight, as their four horses went clattering down the road.

MORE THAN once had Denis Burke come riding this way, though never farther west than the little hamlet of Verneuil with its *château;* and he meant to reach Verneuil this same night. And truth to tell, this was his personal reason for coming west—but of a sudden it had all changed for him. As he pictured that girl, he saw her differently now. And he fell to talking with Malachi as they rode, for he had no secrets from this man who served him and loved him.

"Ye mind the daughter of the Marquis de Verneuil, Malachi? No need to look so glum about it. I know well ye don't like her."

"Eh? I never said a word to yourself about it!" protested

Malachi in hot alarm. Burke grinned at him.

"I know what you thought. Well, lad, I've been thinking. It's one thing to be courting a lass as a fine colonel, with a future ahead and all that; it's quite another to come as a vagabond and the police after him. She's not the lass to go adventuring under the shadow of the gallows with me. She's all powder and lace and brocade, brittle as glass."

"Duar na criosd!" swore Malachi in astonishment. "I never knew your honor felt that way about her! Sure, it's in love you were—"

"Until I realized how little she mattered. Love? Devil take it!"

"Then why go by the *château?"* demanded Malachi.

"D'ye mind, when the marquis was at Paris last month, two of the lads were sick of the army and their time up? He took them at my request to give them places on his estate."

"Sure, your honor doesn't mean the O'Rourke cousins, Phelim and Shamus?"

"The same, Malachi. Better men we'd never find in all France, and neither of them over forty, and if ye think they'd ride with us—"

"They'd go to the devil and get the keys of hell for your honor!" exclaimed Malachi, his scarred features blazing with excitement. "Truth, I'd forgotten them—and better men of their hands your honor would never find! I mind, Phelim was sword instructor in the regiment—praise be! I thought your honor was going there to get the lass!"

Burke laughed at that, and they spurred on.

They ate their noon meal at Nonancourt, and pushed on without delay; but now Burke was watching the road behind them. He was following the post road to the west, and calculated that at latest couriers would have left Paris during the night. A fast courier, changing horses at every post, would cut their riding time in half.

"And that will be bad luck for the poor devil," he reflected. "It's my life or his."

Mid afternoon. From a hillcrest, well this side of Verneuil, he sighted a rising trail of dust in the rear. He drew rein.

"On to the *château,* Malachi," he said. "Take the two spare horses with you. If the O'Rourkes are minded to ride with me, tell them there will be a storm of men in the west and the death of many, and perhaps no luck in it at all. Wait for me at the village inn."

Malachi cast an eye at the dust in the rear, saluted, and rode on.

"Prime the pistols afresh, your honor," he called back, and so departed.

Burke chuckled and obeyed the behest, priming the two brass pistolets at his saddle and then waiting at the hillcrest, resting his horse.

A storm of men! His heart lightened at the old Irish phrase, and his eye kindled: Why not, indeed? Luck was with him, and the luck of the sea Burkes was ever in the west and in the gray waves of ocean. This had been so all his life, and was the tradition of his family. Good! Head for St. Malo and the sea, and take what luck might fling into his lap! From this moment his confidence rose, and the mad game of escape became a serious purpose.

To all homeless men the sea afforded refuge, and he who had the readiest wits and the strongest hand might venture to set all law at defiance. So, as he waited on the hilltop, Burke looked to the west and dreamed great things, quite forgetting that he was a man without a country, hope or asylum.

THEN THE click of hoofs, and a horse laboring heavily up to the hillcrest, and a rider spurring his foam-white steed. Burke pricked his horse out into the road, pistol drawn.

"Way, in the king's name!" called the courier sharply. "Courier of the king!"

For answer, Burke fired point-blank. The courier rolled out of the saddle with a howl, his shoulder broken by the ball. Burke caught the horse, turned him around, sent him back again with a slap, and then, dismounting, leaned over the courier and stripped off his pouch.

"You'll be broken on the wheel for this!" said the man faintly.

"Not if I'm to be caught first," said Burke, and then knelt. "Here, give me your arm, fellow."

He bound up the hurt of the astonished courier, mounted again, and spurred for Verneuil.

On the way, he scanned the two documents in the pouch. One was the courier's warrant, under the royal seal, commanding that all aid and furtherance be given the bearer; and Burke pocketed this with a chuckle. The other commanded all the royal bailiffs, seneschals, governors and other officers to seize the person of the late lieutenant-colonel of the Royal Irlandois, Denis Burke by name, and send him in irons to Paris. This document Burke tore up and scattered in fragments as he rode.

It was sunset when he clattered into the hamlet of Verneuil, on the Eure, and rode into the inn yard to find three men awaiting him. He leaned over in the saddle and gripped hands with the two O'Rourkes—red-headed men both, Phelim a strapping big man, Shamus smaller and very keen of eye, a shrewd and crafty rascal.

"No time to sit, lads," he said, and turned to the hostler. "Feed the horses. Give me a cup of wine. Haste!"

"We ride with your honor," said Phelim O'Rourke. Burke eyed him keenly.

"Ye know what it means, Phelim?"

"What the devil care we? We're sick of being lackeys to a nobleman. Who should follow a Burke, if not an O'Rourke?"

"Well said." Burke seized the flagon brought him, and lifted it. "Here's luck!"

Shamus came close to his stirrup. "Your honor, we might leave the post road here. I know roads over the hills that will save a mortal lot of going and will head us straight for Rennes. There we can take the main highway again for St. Malo."

"Good." Burke produced a gold piece. "Here, buy a fowl or

two off the spit, with bread and wine. We've a long night ahead, and are on campaign."

Twenty minutes later they were splashing across a ford of the Eure, and ahead of them lay Maine and Brittany and the sea.

LIFE OR death now hung upon speed, and speed they made. With the next sunset, Rennes lay outspread before them—Rennes, capital of Brittany, a great and ancient city. But the horses were foundering beneath them as they rode.

Burke had considered well. Here at Rennes were regular troops, as well as cavaliers of the Maréchaussée. St. Malo and the sea lay a hard half-day's ride to the north. Escape might now be considered possible, but already Burke was thinking of other things.

As they approached the city, mist was gathering over the tree-clad slopes; for Rennes had the peculiarity of being subject to dense fogs, thanks in part to the river upon which it lay, and the low ground.

"Do any of you know this place?" asked Burke.

Malachi nodded. "I was quartered here three months, your honor."

"I'm riding ahead. You follow; your papers are in order. A meeting place in the town?"

"The Tavern of the Horloge, your honor. In the big market square they call the Champ Jacquier, close to the governor's palace."

"Excellent. Await me there."

An hour's halt at Châteaubault, a village two leagues away, had not only refreshed the horses, but had given Burke a chance to use razor and pen, making a slight but important alteration in the *lettre de cachet.* He flattered himself, too, that it had been well done, thanks to the fact that the royal governor of Rennes chanced to be of his own rank; M. le Comte de Poissy, lieutenant-colonel of the Royal Piedmont regiment.

Putting spurs to his flagging horse, he went dashing toward the gates. He was gambling everything now on his speed. If any couriers were ahead of him, then he was infallibly lost. If not, he had more than an even chance. He knew that Poissy was a vain and pompous noble, about whose intrigues with certain ladies of the court there had been some dark whispers.

"Courier of the king!" His voice drove at the throng crowding about the gates, and the folk fell away from his path hastily. "Sergeant of the guard! A guide to the palace. I have despatches from M. le Comte."

A soldier laid aside his musket and ran ahead of him, and Burke pressed on behind. The town astonished him, for the streets were extremely narrow, while the houses rose to six and seven stories in height.

Then, abruptly, they emerged upon the market square, and the soldier pointed to the ancient Presidial. Burke flung him a coin and spurred past, drawing up before the guards at the palace entrance.

"Courier from the king!" he barked. "Dispatches for M. de Poissy!"

A sergeant stepped forward and saluted. "Follow me, *m'sieu.* M. le Comte has but just returned from riding on the river, and is with his secretary now."

CHAPTER III

A BOLD TRICK

THE PALACE, like most of the houses in Rennes, was infernally damp. Thus Burke was not surprised at being shown into a cheerful room alight with candelabra, a fire blazing on the hearth. The governor sat at a large table, dictating to a secretary. He was a man of forty-odd, magnificently attired, whose flabby features and soft white hands gave Burke a swift and certain index to his character.

"What's this?" he exclaimed. "A courier from Paris?"

"From Versailles, *m'sieu,*" said Burke, stepping forward. "If I mistake not, I had the honor of meeting you last year. I am Lieutenant-Colonel Burke of the Royal Irish."

"Eh? Yes, yes, I think I remember you," said Poissy, rising. "But—you're not the courier?"

"I am," said Burke. He saw instantly that no news of him had reached here. The gamble was won. "I must ask you for private speech instantly, *monsieur!*"

"If you like, of course." The governor motioned to his secretary, who dropped his quill and departed. "A glass of wine, M. Burke?"

"By all means."

Burke poured wine from the decanter and drained the glass. The door was closed. He came close to the governor and lowered his voice.

"*Monsieur,* the king has learned everything."

The eyes of Poissy dilated. Burke tapped him on the chest gravely.

"What is more, I have here the order to conduct you to the Bastille."

He opened the *lettre de cachet,* that ominous printed form all too well known to members of the court, and held it out so that the other could cast an eye over it. Then he put it back in his pocket quickly.

Poissy dropped back into his chair, and his rubicund countenance was overspread by a mortal pallor.

"But—but there is some mistake!" he stammered. "His majesty has no more loyal servant than I—this cannot be—my relative the Maréchal de Boufflers—"

Burke caught at the word—precisely the one hint he needed.

"Exactly, *monsieur;* the marshal had a few words with me before leaving. Here," and he produced the courier's royal warrant and held it out before the staring, despairing eyes of the governor, "are my further orders, I am to send yon under arrest to Paris and relieve you of your command here. But—let us talk it over. Your relative, Maréchal de Boufflers, spoke privately with me at Versailles."

Poor Poissy leaped at this hint. He straightened in his chair and reached out a shaking hand for his wineglass.

"A chair, *monsieur*, a chair," he murmured. Burke sat down.

"I do not know the details of your disgrace," he said cheerfully, "but the marshal seemed to be aware of them. He said that his majesty had learned everything."

"Yes, yes," said Poissy gloomily. "He warned me—but go on."

"You are of course aware how these little matters are conducted with gentlemen of the court," proceeded Burke. "Believe me, no consideration can be too great for you. I am myself a soldier, I know the marshal quite well, and I think we may avoid all notoriety in the matter. In fact, no one need know of it."

The governor blinked at him. "But, *monsieur*—arrest! Disgrace! I am relieved of my charge here—-"

"Not so fast!" and Burke laughed, stretching out his legs comfortably to the fire. "Your great relative arranged matters with me. I will give you this *lettre de cachet,* upon your word of honor to present yourself at the Bastille within a fortnight. You will post direct to Versailles, and see either the marshal or, in his absence, Cardinal de Bouillon. By that time the order may have been rescinded by their influence. You understand?"

Poissy caught Burke's hand and pressed it, regarding him with such heartfelt gratitude that remorse all but swamped the Irishman's purpose.

"*Monsieur*, you—ah, how can I repay this kindness?" he cried.

"By keeping quiet about it," said Burke promptly. "Say nothing to any one, except that you're summoned to Paris by the king. Turn over affairs here to your deputy and get off in the morning. My faith, it's simple enough!"

"But you?" Poissy blinked at him again. "If you're to relieve me—"

"Time enough for that. I haven't arrived, officially. I have some private business to transact at St. Malo—in fact, I'm riding on there to-night. I have three companions with me, who are awaiting me at the inn on the square, yonder. I'll come back here in a week and see what's turned up."

The other again seized his hand.

"You have saved me! There is still hope, then? But come; you cannot depart at once. We shall dine here, privately. My family has gone to the coast for the summer, and I am alone. I must find some means of repaying you for your great kindness."

"Well, a good dinner might not be amiss," said Burke, "not to mention a pipe. I see you smoke tobacco, too. If I might send word to my friends to dine at the inn and wait for me, we may arrange matters at leisure."

FIVE MINUTES later, Burke sent a lackey with a verbal message to Malachi, and contentedly puffed a long clay pipe filled with the best tobacco. The governor was away, giving orders in regard to dinner and wines, and presently came stamping back into the room. Somewhat calmer now, he also filled a pipe and settled down.

"In twenty minutes dinner will be served," he said. "Now, I beg of you, tell me what I can do to repay in some part the debt I owe you!"

"For one thing, our horses are done up—"

"You shall have the best in our stables; which is to say, the best this side of Paris!"

"Who is in command at St. Malo?"

"The Marquis d'Aulette, colonel of the Roussillon regiment, a very good friend of mine."

"Indeed! Aulette, eh?" Burke shook his head lugubriously. "That's bad news, my dear Poissy, very bad! Just between ourselves, Aulette and I have had trouble over a lady, and my present business in St. Malo is—I confide in your honor, my dear fellow—to carry off a certain young woman who is expecting me. Now, if I show up and my name and rank are reported to the governor—"

"Peste! That is awkward, indeed," murmured Poissy, with every indication of lively sympathy.

At this moment the governor's lackey returned from his errand, bearing a note for Burke. The latter knew this must come from Malachi, the only one of the three who could write, and he opened the missive to find that it was so:

> Old comrades quartered here. If you want a dozen more men, say so.

Burke's decision was made instantly. With a laugh, he extended the paper.

"Read this, my dear Poissy! Is it true that you have some of my regiment here?"

"Eh?" The governor read the note, then broke out laughing. "You want a few men to help carry off the lady? Yes, we have twoscore of your Irish here, convalescents. Most of the town garrisons are formed from the wounded, you know. But let me warn you, my dear fellow, that this abduction of women is most dangerous! The laws are severe on this point."

Burke winked. "Trust me for that! Come, it looks as though I might be under obligations to you, instead of the other way around. If you could spare me a dozen men, and horses to carry them—"

"With all my heart!"

"And, perhaps, a letter such as is given officers on leave of absence, stating that I am the Sieur d'Argenton, traveling to St. Malo on the king's business—eh? I have already my royal warrant which will back this up."

The other hesitated an instant.

"Why not? Devil take it, you're doing enough for me! By the way, that *lettre de cachet,* curse the thing! You have my word, of course."

"Oh, certainly." Burke brought it out and handed it over. Poissy pocketed it with a grimace, after one hasty glance at the filled-in name, then reached for the decanter.

AN HOUR later, leaving the royal governor of Brittany comfortably drunk, Burke mounted a splendid horse and rode to the tavern, where he found fifteen more horses being admired by Malachi and a crowd of Irish, half in uniform. They surrounded him instantly.

"Quiet, lads!" said Burke in Irish, which none of the French around could understand. "Malachi, how many?"

"Fifteen of us all told, your honor. They know it's a wild game, and no matter."

"Good. Listen, lads! If ye ride with me, you gamble your necks and worse. Heed it well."

"Faith, colonel dear, hell's waited a long while for us!" said some one, and there was a roaring laugh of assent. "Say the word, and we're with you!"

"Mount and ride, then!" ordered Burke, and went clattering away across the square, with the governor's passes ready to show the guards at the gate.

Sunrise found them camped two miles outside St. Malo—a reckless, merry company of hellions who had heard Burke's plan with a wild laugh of delight, though it meant the death of many a man among them. A bite of bread and a draft of wine, and Burke mounted.

"Ye understand?" he said, looking down at them, his blue eyes twinkling whimsically. "The time and place understood? Good. No drinking, mind well! Any man that's drunk will get left."

And, with a wave of his hand and a rousing, ragged cheer behind him, he rode for St. Malo.

CHAPTER IV

RISKY PLANS

ST. MALO was built upon a rock in the sea, connected with the land by a long causeway. It was strongly fortified and heavily garrisoned. Its chief occupation was piracy, thinly veiled under other names. The Malouins were the best seamen of France, and bitter fighters. The chief men of St. Malo made a business of outfitting privateers and corsairs, which scourged the seven seas in search of booty.

Finding his entry unquestioned, thanks to the document provided by Poissy, Burke rode to the Place St. Vincent, halted at the best tavern, and engaged a chamber as the Sieur d'Argenton. It was still early morning, and he strode forth to the Platform of St. Francis, the great round corner of the walls overlooking the port and its entry. Here a dozen old seamen were sunning themselves, pipe in mouth. Picking out the most garrulous of the lot, Burke gave him tobacco in exchange for a light, and soon had him talking.

With the information already gathered from Poissy, he rapidly grew rich in knowledge if not in pocket.

"And where is this craft I've heard about?" he asked. "The one outfitting for Baron Ravenel?"

"Yonder." The ancient pointed to a brig opposite, where the little town of St. Servan sprawled its quays along the river mouth that held crowded shipping. "Outfitted and her guns aboard. When M. le Baron arrives, the crew's to be picked by lot; every one wants to sail with him, for he has luck. She's not painted yet, but that's a small matter. A good ship."

"How is she called?" asked Burke.

The other shook his head. "Just 'Ravenel's brig,' *monsieur.* She's not named yet; she was brought in as a prize three months ago, taken from the English. Ravenel is to name her himself."

Burke looked down at the brig, and his eyes glistened. Overhauled and fit, except for paint, she was not large, but still carried five guns to a side—culverins of sixteen-pound weight, he took them for.

He questioned the ancient about this and that; the quarters of the troops, the quarters of the various royal officers, the rules of the port, a thousand and one details that occurred to him. When he had finished he knew all that he needed to know, and with noon approaching, turned back to his inn for the best meal he could get.

As he made his way through the town, he met some of his men in parties of twos and threes, but none of them gave him a second glance. He came face to face with Malachi, and the veteran instinctively began a salute, only to check it and turn his back. Burke chuckled and went his way. They were obeying orders excellently.

"DENIS BURKE! By the saints, man—hold on!"

The voice struck at him when he was almost at the inn. He could see no officer in the throng around, yet some one had recognized him. He quickened his pace: next instant a hand clenched on his arm, swung him around.

"Denis! Is it too proud you are to talk with an old friend—"

Burke drew himself up haughtily, as he looked into the bearded features he knew so well.

"You mistake, *monsieur*," he said in French, then switched quickly to Irish. It was risky enough here in St. Malo, where seamen of every nation abounded, but he must chance it.

"Follow me and join me inside. Have a care!"

He turned and went on, and once in the tavern picked out a table in a dark corner near the hearth where spits were turning. What luck, to meet Brian Garf O'Malley here—"Rough" Brian, as he was known in the west of Ireland, once a captain of ships and a great man! He had been as a brother to Burke in early days, for the Burkes of Mayo and the O'Malleys were ever close in kin and loyalty.

Presently Garf came into the tavern, a great hulking figure, black-bearded, violent in looks as his nickname indicated, and sat him down at the table across from Burke. He put out his hand, and their fingers clenched.

"In trouble?" he said. Burke's eyes lighted warmly.

"Not after the sight of you, O'Malley. Ten years and more since we met—what do you here?"

"I was lieutenant on a Malouin corsair, but the English caught us off Guernsey and knocked us to smithereens. We got away in a fog and crawled into port three days ago—forty men dead and no luck. And you, Denis? Not in the army?"

"Don't breathe my name, man! Will ye take a venture with me, Garf O'Malley?"

"That will I," said the bearded seaman, unhesitating. His stormy gray eyes were straight and level, joyous at the sight of Burke. "But I've no money."

"Have ye blood? And a sword?"

The other whistled. "So that's it, eh? Well ye know I'll go with you to the farther side of hell! Speak it out, lad."

"It's the luck of the sea, meeting you—the luck of the sea to the Burkes! Have you any men ye can lay hand on? Irish or English?"

"A score or more, mostly English Jacobites."

"I've fifteen, scattered about the town. Forty, eh? That's not so bad. What time are the gates closed, and the port? Is it six sharp?"

"To the minute."

With his forefinger dipped in wine, Burke drew on the table-top the outline of the granite island, with its harbor and the town of St. Servan opposite, in the river-mouth that Served as shipyard and anchorage.

"I noticed your ship here, badly damaged. Just outside her is another, a brig."

"Aye, Ravenel's brig."

"No. Burke's brig."

The wild gray eyes flashed up to meet the whimsical blue ones. Then Burke nodded.

"My men will pick up any others they can trust, and leave the gates at five, crossing the Sillon, as they call the causeway, to the mainland. They'll straggle into St. Servan. You get your men and do the same. The meeting place is that water-front tavern in St. Servan, called the Inn of St. Aaron, at six o'clock. At that hour the tide's on flood, I find. We'll get off with her easily enough."

"Think ye so?" said the other grimly. "Then listen. There are two ships o' war lying in the channel—a fifty-six and a forty-two."

"At six o'clock they'll be over the horizon."

"Is it joking you are, Denis?"

"No." Blue eyes held gray eyes steadily. "If those fighting ships are there at six I'm a dead man, Garf. All France is after me this blessed minute."

"More power to you, then! I'm with you. But another thing—no vessel can leave port without a permit from the royal governor. There's cannons enough on those bastions to blow her out of the water in two minutes!"

Burke's eyes twinkled. "And what if the Marquis d'Aulette is on her quarter-deck?"

The bearded seaman threw out his hands helplessly.

"It's mad you are! Stark mad!"

"Not a bit of it. Merely in a tight place and working a way clear, Garf. After all, ye don't risk much. If I don't show up by six, you'll know I'm a lost man, and you and the others can separate and go your ways. Well, give me an answer, man! Are you for the gamble or not?"

"Devil take ye, haven't I said I was with ye?" growled O'Malley angrily. "Mad or sane, I'm for you if we hang for it!" He brought down his fist. There was a crash, and the oaken table split asunder, spilling wine and pewter over the floor. In no time a marveling crowd began to gather, and tongues rose high.

Burke hastily shoved gold into the seaman's hand, and slipped off unobserved.

HE STRODE away, wondrous light-hearted. By sheer chance, the arrangements made with Malachi, which he had anticipated changing according to necessity, were almost exactly suited to tide and stress. The greatest danger lay from the king's two ships in the estuary, but he had discounted this, and at six o'clock hoped to have the way clear.

The unexpected blessing of Garf O'Malley made his pulses leap. Here was what he needed most of all—a skilled seaman, and a pilot who knew these waters. He could guess that O'Malley, like many another Irishman, had fallen upon evil days and cared little about the future; it could hold no worse than had the past.

"And now for it!" thought Burke, turning his steps to the great *château* whose massive towers defended the entry to St. Malo. "Two o'clock—no time to lose, but time enough to hang me!"

Despite his words to the hapless Poissy back in Rennes, he had never met the Marquis d'Aulette, had never heard of him, and knew nothing whatever about him. Not that this daunted Burke in the least. His ready wit, his superb self-confidence, usually carried him through any emergency on the spur of the moment. He well knew, however, that in this strongly garrisoned city he might at any instant encounter officers who knew him by sight or personally, but whether they would recognize him was another question. Booted and spurred, beaver pulled low, cloak flung around him, he looked very different from the Irish Brigade officer of other days.

Striding up to the entrance of the *château,* Burke briskly saluted the officer in charge of the guard.

"Lieutenant! Will you have the kindness to announce me immediately to the governor? I am Sieur d'Argenton, post-haste from Versailles, with messages of the highest importance. Has any other courier preceded me today?"

"None, *monsieur,*" replied the lieutenant, turning. "Will you have the goodness to accompany me? I believe M. le Marquis has just finished the daily review."

Burke, with his warm and genial smile, took the officer's arm familiarly.

"One moment, *mon ami!* Is this M. d'Aulette the gentleman of that name who is a close friend of Mme. de Maintenon?"

The other smiled. "Heaven forbid! He is a soldier and no courtier. It is well known that his sole friend at court is the Duc de Chevreuse, who is his godfather."

"Thanks, thanks," said Burke. "A mistake in the name, eh? Say nothing of it, I beg of you."

"I have already forgotten it," returned the lieutenant politely. "I will take you to the private library, and advise M. le Marquis of your presence."

Together they passed into a long corridor. An officer was approaching them, a tall, long-jawed man whom Burke recognized instantly with a subdued groan. Twice ere this he had clashed with Major du Chambon, a martinet of the most disagreeable type, reputed the best swordsman in the army, a man who bore the Irish mercenaries a fixed and vivid hatred for causes unknown.

Du Chambon halted suddenly, staring at Burke.

"Ah!" he exclaimed. "Is it not M. Burke of the Royal Irlandois?"

Burke surveyed him coldly. "You mistake, *monsieur.* I am Sieur d'Argenton, with dispatches from the king."

He passed on, leaving Du Chambon to stare after him with a puzzled frown. This meeting, however, staggered him badly. He knew at once that it threatened him most vitally unless he were still ahead of all couriers.

The lieutenant, after a word with guards in the corridor, ushered him into a large room whose paneled walls were half-concealed by shelves of books. Plans of fortifications were heaped upon a large central table, and the place had an air of being much used.

When the lieutenant had departed, Burke stepped forward to the table and coolly surveyed the papers there, but found nothing to interest him. Clearly enough, he had a very different man to deal with here from the governor at Rennes—and of this he was assured a moment later, when two soldiers stepped in, presented arms, and announced the governor.

M. D'AULETTE came briskly into the room. He was a man of forty, his features long and serious, his gaze deep and severe. At first glance Burke gave himself up for lost; then he noted the energetic, proud lips, caught a sudden flash from the deep eyes, and his spirits rose as he judged his man more correctly. He bowed, and the marquis held out his hand.

"Your dispatches, *monsieur?*"

"They are verbal, M. le Marquis." Burke produced the royal warrant he had taken from the courier he had shot outside of Rennes. Fortunately, the warrant specified that all aid be given the bearer, without mentioning his name. The other glanced at it and returned it with a curt salute, then turned to the guards.

"Leave us. No one to enter without my permission." He indicated a chair. "Sieur d'Argenton, will you be seated? You have ridden in haste, I gather," and his eye took in Burke's travel-stained costume.

"In the greatest haste, I assure you," Burke lowered himself into a chair with a grimace by no means assumed, for he was saddle-stiff. "I have come, M. le Marquis, upon a certain mission from his majesty, for which you have seen the warrant. It is of no great haste or importance. I am charged, however, with another errand of the greatest urgency and of the deepest gravity, on behalf of M. le Duc de Chevreuse."

Aulette transfixed his visitor with a searching gaze.

"Do private affairs come ahead of his majesty's business, *monsieur?*"

"When they threaten his majesty's realm, I believe you will

agree that they do," said Burke coolly, all his assurance returning. He knew enough court gossip to avoid possible pitfalls, and now he plunged suddenly and wholeheartedly.

"You are aware, no doubt, that M. le Duc is favored with private advices from abroad? In this case he has received the most startling news, which is entirely authentic. Unluckily, he is not on the best of terms with M. de Pontchartrain, who has not yet learned of the matter and who might refuse to believe it. In short, *monsieur*, an English fleet is to make upon Mont St. Michel on the tenth of this month."

"The tenth!" Aulette started. "But that is—"

"Close at hand; exactly. M. le Duc has received warning from London. There it is known that our fleet is largely occupied elsewhere. Two English frigates are convoying a number of troopships. The plan is to seize Mont St. Michel, and from there to attack St. Malo both by land and sea. M. le Duc prays you to send out whatever force you may have here, on the instant, to cruise across the Bay of Cancale—"

"But they are not under my instructions! They receive orders from the Ministry of Marine!" exclaimed the marquis. "True, a word with the captains might effect something."

"It would settle everything," said Burke earnestly. "If it did no more than frighten off the English, a short cruise of a day would perhaps save France untold danger, *monsieur!* Ships leaving here now, at once, would be across the bay long ere morning."

Decision settled in Aulette's face.

"These officers are here now in the *château.* I shall speak with them at once; your other affairs can await my return?"

"They can, *monsieur*," said Burke.

"Is there anything I can send you—food, wine?"

"I desire nothing, thank you."

"Then, I pray you, pardon my absence." With a ceremonious bow, the marquis turned and strode from the room, slamming the door behind him.

Burke chuckled and stretched out comfortably.

"Double six the first main!" he murmured. "The fool saves France—and never asks a scrap of writing from his precious godfather! As I thought. He's so much the soldier that he'd give his very soul to have a footing at court! So far, so good. If we—"

There was a sudden trample of hasty feet. The marquis reëntered the room, tearing open a sealed paper. Behind him came a reeling, dust-covered man, whom Burke knew at the first glance to be a courier. The marquis turned, after tossing the document on the table.

"Very good, *monsieur*," he said. "No other despatches? Come. I shall have you given a room and made comfortable. Your pardon once more, M. d'Argenton. One of these accursed Irish of ours has turned traitor, it seems."

Burke thought the worst had happened—but he was wrong.

CHAPTER V

A SUSPICIOUS MAJOR

BURKE WAS aroused from his reflections by the shattering boom of a heavy gun from the battlements.

He darted from his chair and went to one of the high windows, which overlooked the Sillon and the port beyond. Undoubtedly signals were being made from the *château*. From one of the two frigates, then from the other, a gun spoke in a billow of white smoke; activity seized upon both ships, men running aloft, canvas being shaken out.

"They're off, then!" murmured Burke, complacently. "Now perhaps Garf O'Malley won't think I'm such a madman, eh?"

He turned from the window, and his eyes fell on the open document. Going to the table, he found it to be as he thought, a duplicate of the one he had taken from the wounded courier. No use destroying this now; the harm was done.

Burke sat down abruptly at the table. Here were sheets of paper and vellum. He seized one of the latter, drew it to him, dipped a quill in the inkwell, and began to write very rapidly. His blue eyes glittered whimsically—if they only gave him a chance to finish!

Before him he set the royal warrant, regarded the signatures of Louis and Pontchartrain carefully, then dashed them off; he did not make the mistake of copying them with slow pains. He eyed the result approvingly and sanded the writing.

"It wouldn't pass any critical examination, but who's going to be critical?" he said cheerfully, and folded over the vellum. Pocketing it, he rose and went to the window again.

The two frigates were standing out of the channel. Burke grinned at this, and then swung around as the doors were thrown open. Aulette and two officers came into the room. Striding up to his table, the governor caught up the order regarding Burke and handed it to the officers.

"Show this to the officers of the guard at the gates and let word be passed around," he ordered. They saluted and strode out. He dropped into his chair. "Well, M. d'Argenton! The vessels are sailing."

"I congratulate you," said Burke. "And now for the less important business. Perhaps you know the Baron Ravenel?"

"Naturally, I do," said the other without any warmth. Burke chuckled.

"He is suspected of having falsified the accounts of his recent successful cruise, and of thereby having cheated his majesty of the sixth part due the crown. At least, such is the charge made against him; by whom, I know not. In this connection—"

He produced the folded vellum and Aulette spread it out, glancing over it frowningly. He looked up at Burke, his face pale and streaked with sweat; obviously, he was ill.

"You know the contents of this letter?"

"More or less, yes. You are requested to go aboard Ravenel's new vessel with me, make search and seizure of all documents which may be found, and forward them to Versailles in my charge. I believe that is all?"

Aulette nodded and laid aside the document without closer examination.

"Very well," he said. "Are you pressed to go aboard at once?"

Burke shrugged. "At your convenience, *monsieur*. When the heat of the day has passed, if you like."

The other's face cleared. "Excellent! To tell the truth, Sieur d'Argenton, I am subject to a tertian fever, and to-day it has gripped me most damnably. With your consent, I shall retire for an hour or so of rest."

Burke bowed. "By all means, *monsieur*. Hm! It's close to three—"

"Shall we say, five o'clock? You might care to rest yourself."

"I'm not weary, thanks," said Burke, who dreaded inaction at such a crisis. "I rested at Rennes, and am hard enough not to mind a bit of a ride."

"By the way, you left M. de Poissy well, I trust?""

"Drunk," said Burke, with a grin. "I might walk about and see a bit of the town, eh?"

"By all means," said Aulette. "I'll turn you over to one of my officers. Orderly!" The doors opened and a guard saluted. "Send Captain Sainterre here. Also M. du Chambon."

This name struck upon Burke with numbing effect. He opened his lips to speak, then checked himself. At this instant, he perceived, the wrong word might spoil everything. For once his ready wit failed him completely, and before he could rally, the captain who had been summoned appeared and saluted.

"Take thirty men," ordered the governor, wiping the sweat from his face, "and go aboard that brig of Baron Ravenel's. Put ashore all of her crew, workmen and guards, and allow no one aboard till I arrive later with this gentleman. Nothing to be taken ashore."

The captain saluted and was gone. Burke, staggered by this unexpected result of his diplomacy, tried in vain to think of some plausible protest. Then Major du Chambon came stiffly into the room, and the chance was gone.

"Ah, M. du Chambon!" said the governor, rising. "Allow me to present Sieur d'Argenton, who comes on an errand from his majesty. I will ask you to place yourself at his disposal and see that he lacks for nothing, and return him to me at the main portal at five o'clock sharp. You will excuse me, M. d'Argenton—name of the devil, this fever is going to my head!"

By this time, indeed, the man was in pitiable state, eyes bulging from his head, his face purpled, his hands shaking. He stayed not on ceremony, but left the room hastily. Burke looked at Du Chambon, who bowed gravely to him as the doors closed.

"*MONSIEUR*," SAID the long-jawed major, "I regret exceedingly the mistake I made upon meeting you. I am entirely at your service; if you have a taste for wine, I shall be happy to accommodate you with some excellent Chambertin, the pride of our officers' mess. Eh?"

"With all my heart," said Burke, at once assuming a manner entirely foreign to him, of grave severity.

The other opened the doors, and they passed together from the room. While Burke was by no means anxious for the company thus forced upon him, it was regrettably true that he had two hours to kill; and he flattered himself that Du Chambon was convinced of his mistake.

"There may be one or two other gentlemen in my quarters," said the major. "Captain Servaut and I have the whole tower to ourselves, and it is something of a central point. If you prefer to rest, or to look about the town, pray command me."

"Not at all," rejoined Burke. "A glass of wine and a chat are most attractive."

They crossed the little garden of the *château,* to a tower on the seaward side—a small, round tower of two stories. It held two large rooms. Coming to the lower chamber, Chambon flung open the door and found it empty, but the noise of laughter and talking floated down the narrow winding stairs, and he started upward. Burke followed, reflecting that if his changed appearance had fooled Chambon it would certainly fool any one else who might have met him in other days.

The room at the top of the tower was large, low-ceiled, and the furniture had been cleared away to make room for half a dozen officers seated and standing about a table, casting dice and drinking. One swift glance showed Burke no familiar face; then Chambon introduced him.

"Gentlemen, M. d'Argenton, who has brought dispatches from Versailles. Achille! Where is that rascally lackey? More wine! A dozen bottles of the Chambertin, and fresh glasses!"

Burke was agreeably surprised to find himself welcomed by the party. He settled down at once to make himself at home, and after a bottle of the Chambertin, which was really excellent, his spirits mounted. From time to time officers departed or others dropped in, and the stakes ran high at the table.

The time passed swiftly. Burke did not miss an occasional puzzled look from the closely set eyes of Chambon, but found no warning in these glances. Word had spread about the lieutenant colonel of the Royal Irlandois, and one of the officers appealed to him, asking what the offense of Burke had been.

"I know nothing of it, *messieurs,*" rejoined Burke with a shrug. "Is it my throw?"

So the matter passed, and more wine was poured.

Under the sparkling influence of the Chambertin, Burke gradually lost his assumed manner and reverted to himself. He grew interested in the dice; the stakes mounted, his winnings became considerable, and it was with a start that he recollected the time, to discover that it was four thirty, the afternoon nearly gone.

AT THE moment there were four others in the room besides Chambon. The latter made a signal to the other four, who drew back from the table, then went to the door and turned the key in the lock. He swung about, to fasten a dark gaze upon Burke.

"M. de Beaudry," he said, still watching Burke but addressing a captain at the table, "will you have the goodness to tell me whether you recognize our friend, Sieur d'Argenton?"

One man after another looked at Burke, and in their eyes he read a strange message. Like a flash the truth came to him.

"Certainly, gentlemen," said the captain addressed. "I never met Lieutenant Colonel Burke, but I saw him on two occasions, and remember his face distinctly."

"And I," said Major du Chambon, "have been certain of it from the first." He reached beneath his coat and produced a pistolet. "Sieur d'Argenton, your sword."

Burke laughed a little, and refilled his glass with wine. Then he rose and bowed to Chambon very politely. He knew now that he was a lost man, but he refused to admit it.

"My dear Du Chambon, you shall have it, with the greatest of pleasure," he said, and drew the Toledo blade from the scabbard. "Faith, you played a very pretty game! I suppose you'll unmask me to M. le Marquis?"

"That is my duty," said Du Chambon stiffly. Burke, still holding the rapier, turned and picked up the wineglass in his left hand and raised it. His eyes swept about in a laugh, from face to face.

"Your health, gentlemen!" he exclaimed cheerfully. His eyes twinkled at Du Chambon. "Faith, major, you would not put a bullet into me, would you really?"

"I'll shoot you like a dog," snarled Chambon, "if you don't hand over that sword!"

Burke chuckled. "Then it's yours without further argument—point first!"

The wineglass shot its contents forth, deluging the pistol, wetting the priming—and as the flint clicked vainly Burke's rapier drove into Chambon's throat.

The other four were on their feet instantly with startled cries, swords flicking out. Burke whirled and faced them, his blue eyes all ablaze.

"So, ye dogs!" he cried sharply. "Thought ye had me trapped, eh? Aye, and I heard the talk among you; the best swordsmen in the garrison, are you? Then prove it! By the luck of the Burkes, prove it!"

"You murdered Du Chambon foully!" shouted one of the four, and with that they flung themselves upon him.

He did not await their assault, however. As they drove at him, Burke slipped sidewise and kicked a chair at them, then hurled himself forward. Beaudry, the captain who had recognized him, took the steel through his body, and Burke wrenched it clear just in time to meet the thrust of another blade and parry it.

Three of them now—their rapiers converging on him. Suddenly Burke became deadly cool, drew back before them, his face set like ice, every nerve and sense on the alert. The clang and click of the blades filled the room. The Toledo moved, flickered in and out, seemed like a wall of steel in front of Burke; eye could not follow its glitter and gleam. A laugh came suddenly to his lips, a laugh of disdain and arrogant confidence.

"So three of you fine gentlemen would talk foul murder, and yet try to beat down a single foe, eh?" he taunted them. "Aye, that's your French style of fighting. Well, here's an Irish blade to bite on—and that's two left—"

A swift, savage lunge in tierce. One of them cried out, gripped at the air, and fell across the table and overturned it with a crash. Burke leaped aside, swerved, caught a rapier on his own blade, and faced the two remaining.

As he fought, his brain was clear enough, reaching out beyond the present scene. If he could best these other two men—why, he had a chance, sure enough! Nothing except pistol shots would draw any attention to this tower or what happened in it, obviously, and none of those present had pistols.

SHARPLY HE jerked to attention. One of the two who faced him, driving in savage lunges from either side, was gasping hot words at the other.

"The door, André—open it! Chambon had—men waiting—below—"

Burke whistled to himself. The others were panting; breath was coming hard to him, but he was good for a long while yet. They separated, trying to occupy him from each flank, but swift as light Burke leaped at the man on his right, the man André. His blade stabbed in and stabbed again, under the other's guard, and André was down, groaning hideously.

"So!" Burke faced the last of them and saluted with a gay laugh. "Five of the best blades in the army, eh? Four of ye done, and ye haven't touched me! Now for your lesson, *monsieur*—a short one, a sharp one! Your blade's too flat and straight, my captain. I'll show you what is called the *'coup de fouet'*—an interesting stroke."

The Toledo gave a smart, abrupt touch on the outside of the other's rapier, and knocked it down, clean out of his hand. Burke chuckled and drew back, as the dismayed officer stood all awkwardly.

"Pick it up, pick it up!" he exclaimed. "You'll not get off so light, I promise you, but I'm no murderer. I'm going to show you the 'counter in tierce parade'—a simple little thing. Not three men in France can use it effectively."

He paused suddenly. There was a beating upon the door at his back, voices there were upraised. As the officer picked up his rapier and stood on guard, Burke calculated swiftly. Not more than two or three men outside, probably.

He reached back, turned the key so that the door was unlocked, and then engaged the rapier awaiting him.

"Quick and short, *monsieur!*" he said. "In the shoulder, a deep, sure thrust that'll let the blood out of you in no time—ha! Poor wrist you have! Observe carefully—the head well back from your point, the nails downward—there!"

He sprang back, just as the door was flung open so that, for the moment, it concealed him from the sight of the three men who stumbled into the room.

The officer staggered back, clapping hand to shoulder whence the blood gushed, crying hoarse, incoherent orders at the three men. These were soldiers, muskets in hand. Too late, they turned; Burke was already upon them. His blade drove through the first man, and he wrenched it loose as a musket swung for his head. That blow he dodged, and his point flicked through the musketeer's throat.

The one who remained screamed something and darted for the door and the stairs. Burke was after him instantly, out of that chamber of death and blood, and ran him through from behind, at the head of the narrow stairs. The man rolled down, sprawled over the stairs, his musket clattering.

Burke stepped back into the room, caught his cloak and hat, saw his last antagonist slumped against the wall, and shut the door again. It must be close to five o'clock, he knew. If no alarm had been raised, he still had a chance—a bare chance! He leaped across the body of the soldier on the stairs, came to the door of the lower chamber—and it was flung open almost in his face.

An officer, half dressed, stood there sword in hand.

"What's going on up above?" he cried out. "Is it fighting—what the devil? Who are you?"

"The devil," said Burke, lunging at him, blade clinging to blade, forcing him back into the room. "I regret, my dear fellow, that your curiosity—ha! A good stroke!—is stronger than your discretion."

The other's blade touched his very throat, pricked his skin, but the thrust went no farther. By so little the Frenchman failed of closing Burke's career, and in the lack, ruined his own, for Burke's riposte drove through his body.

A moment later, his rapier sheathed, Burke stepped from the doorway of the tower and carefully closed it behind him. He jammed his hat on his head, threw the cloak about his shoulders, and with a deep breath settled his panting lungs. A soldier was approaching, and he beckoned the man, drew a gold piece from his pocket, which he held up.

"Major du Chambon and his friends are settling a serious argument. The major desires you to remain on guard here and let no one enter the tower, for an hour if possible. Can you do it, my man?"

The soldier gaped at sight of the gold piece, seized it, saluted, and took his post. Burke departed to his rendezvous with the governor, humming a gay air as he strode along.

CHAPTER VI

ABOARD THE BRIG

WITH ONLY two orderlies for company, M. d'Aulette was waiting at the main entry of the *château,* mounted, a saddled horse awaiting Burke. The latter strode up with a wave of his hand, and flung himself into the saddle.

"My apologies, *monsieur,* if I kept you waiting," he said. "The hospitality of M. du Chambon was a trifle pressing. You have, I trust, recovered from your attack?"

The marquis shrugged. "Well enough to attend to duty, *monsieur,* thank you."

Burke glanced back as they went; no sign of alarm! They came to the Sillon without incident. This long, wide causeway was thronged with folk who drew apart to give them passage, and ahead, Burke saw Garf O'Malley striding along with half a dozen men around him. The bearded seaman gaped up at him with fallen jaw, and Burke winked jovially. A few steps farther, d'Aulette uttered an exclamation and spurred up alongside two of the men from Rennes, who still wore their regimentals.

"Who are you?" he demanded sharply. "Whence came you?"

"From Rennes, with some comrades, on leave," was the answer. "Only today."

"You have leave of absence? Show it me."

They produced their passes, which, thanks to M. de Poissy, were quite in order. D'Aulette nodded and rode on again.

"These rascally Irish are everywhere!" he exclaimed. "And

mad, all of them. To think of the fools coming here from Rennes, no doubt walking all the way—devil take them! Well, there is St. Servan ahead, M. d'Argenton."

Burke looked back, not ahead, and was relieved when he discerned no sign of commotion. No alarm had yet been given, though it might break at any moment now. They reached the end of the causeway, and the buildings of St. Servan opened out ahead. An impatient exclamation broke from the irritable governor, and he drew to one side to question another group of the Rennes recruits.

Seeing Malachi just ahead, Burke went on and spoke sharply to him in Irish,

"It's touch and go, Malachi. You'll be joined by Garf O'Malley and a score or more men. Come aboard instantly they're all up, and you see me aboard. No pistols. Cold steel."

He twisted his horse about and fell in again beside D'Aulette, who had not observed the incident, and who broke into further irritated talk about the Irish mercenaries. Burke chuckled to himself, as they turned toward the quay of the marine, reserved for the royal forces. An officer appeared with a smart salute, and calling men from the long storehouses close at hand, had a boat put into the water.

With six men at the oars, D'Aulette and Burke were speeding out toward the brig within another five minutes. But, as he eyed the thirty soldiers spread along her rail watching them, with Captain Sainterre at the gangway, uneasiness seized upon Burke. There could be no question of surprise here; before his own men could pile into boats and pull out to the brig, those muskets would be loaded and ready.

However, no sign of his real dismay appeared on his face as he followed D'Aulette up the ladder to the deck above. Sainterre saluted them.

"As ordered, *monsieur*," he said. "The agents of the owners threaten protest."

"Let them threaten," said the marquis disdainfully. "You will remain on guard. Come, M. d'Argenton! We can find the cabins, I think."

As they entered the main cabin in the high poop, by the passage leading from the waist, Burke looked at the shore. He saw a throng of men pouring down to the waterside, where the boats of fishers lay drawn up, and then closed the door behind them.

Another ten minutes and all was won—or lost!

THEY CAME into the main cabin, and here Burke shut the door at the end of the passage. The key was in the lock, and he coolly turned it. At this instant came a dull reverberation from somewhere in the distance. D'Aulette swung around.

"What was that?"

Burke flung off cloak and beaver, shook the hair out of his eyes, and whipped out his rapier. His voice leaped out in eager exultation.

"The alarm, *monsieur.* Sit in that chair, and quickly! D'you hear me?"

"Eh? Are you mad?' exclaimed the governor, starting back. Then he saw the blood on the long rapier, and his face changed. His hand went to his own sword.

"Fool! You'd force me to kill you?" snapped Burke angrily. "No, I'll not do that—on guard, then! On guard!"

D'Aulette, bewildered and dismayed, drove in a lunge. At the second pass, the rapier was torn from his hand and sent whirling across the cabin. Burke came up to him, shoved him heavily, and sent him backward into a huge armchair.

"Now be quiet!" he commanded, sword-point to throat. "Arms back of you—that's it!"

Another cannon sounded from the *château.* Burke worked swiftly, tying the wrists and ankles of the hapless marquis to the oaken chair, while D'Aulette shouted and cursed impotently. From the passage came a pounding of feet, and the voice of Sainterre. Blows thundered at the locked door.

"There!" Burke rose, picked up his rapier, and laughed. "Now for the end of it!"

With a leap, he was across the cabin, and unlocked the door. Into the room stumbled Captain Sainterre with an excited cry.

"*Monsieur!* There is an alarm at the *château,* and a mob of men are coming off in boats—"

He broke off and stared. Burke faced him, blue eyes blazing.

"My men, M. Sainterre! You are my prisoner. Yield!"

"Cut him down!" roared the marquis from his chair, where he struggled vainly.

Sainterre did neither. He half lifted his arms as though in surrender—then suddenly caught the hat from his head and hurled it into Burke's face. With the same motion, he flung himself sidewise, and was gone down the passage, shouting at his men.

"Captain dear, you've had your chance—bad luck to you!" said Burke, and plunged after the officer.

The outer door slammed in his face. He struck against it full force, burst it open, found Sainterre shouting and drawing his sword. Burke fell upon him like a whirlwind. Next instant, Sainterre collapsed as the Toledo blade drove through his body.

Burke whirled.

"Below with you!" His voice blared at the staring, excited soldiers, who were loading their muskets. "Surrender, and you'll not be harmed."

A musket smashed out response, and Burke staggered, jerked half around by the ball. A wild, shrill yell arose from the waist, as over the bulwarks poured wild figures, and steel flickered in the sunset light.

Garf O'Malley had come aboard, with Malachi at his heels.

For an instant there was a wild mêlée there in the waist, as the soldiers gathered to repel the assault; then other boats were alongside, Irish yells shrilled up, and more men piled over the rail. Now musket after musket banged out and powder smoke drifted down the deck, and in the gray pall men died with shriek and curse as the steel clove them down. The soldiers broke, fled for refuge from these wild men, and were driven below like sheep—what were left of them.

Of all this, however, Denis Burke saw little, for he clung to the rail and darkness was upon him. Then he felt himself lifted, and wakened to the voice of Garf O'Malley in his ears.

"Denis, lad! She's ours. Is he hurt, Malachi?"

"Not to death," said Malachi stoutly. "No more than a letting of blood, if I can stop the cursed wound. Hold steady, your honor! You'll be on your feet in a minute."

"Take her out, Garf," murmured Denis Burke, and the bearded seaman was gone, with a thunderous command to his men.

Already boats were putting out from shore, but too late. Her cables cut, the brig's canvas fell; with tide and wind she headed for the sea. Those who crowded on the bastions to watch saw two men beside her great helm on the poop, and presently a third was led to join them—a figure known to all, recognized by all. At sight of it, the gunners were halted abruptly.

It was the Marquis d'Aulette, governor of the town.

Without a reply to the storm of hails, to the signals, to the small craft racing out, the brig held seaward. The officers on the walls knew not what to make of it, and dared not fire; those few moments of paralyzed hesitation were all that Burke needed, all he had counted upon. They marked the very crisis of all his flight from Paris, the culmination of all his audacity and daring.

Then, as the brig drew out abreast of the town and headed still seaward, with the chief batteries behind her, Burke turned to his captive.

"*Monsieur,*" he said quietly, "I trust that you will not be late for dinner. A boat is being made ready; a number of soldiers will go into her, and take you ashore unharmed."

D'Aulette's eyes drove into him with hatred and bitterness. "This is past my understanding, *monsieur,*" he said, "but I am certain of one thing. For this madness, you will be broken on the wheel or hanged! I shall myself hang you."

Burke bowed slightly, wincing from the pain of his hurt.

"Impossible, *monsieur*. I was born to be drowned. May I bid you a safe journey home?"

White-faced with helpless fury, the governor was presently escorted down into his boat. The brig paid off, the yards were squared away, and she leaned over to the thrust of the wind. Malachi came up to Burke, and saluted, a grin on his scarred features.

"Ye've done it, your honor—more power to you! But you'll have to let me bind up that hurt more securely. Praise be, after a week yourself will be all right, for the bullet's out of the flesh."

"Time enough, Malachi," said Burke, and glanced back at the city. "It'll be dark in half an hour or less—aye, we're safe enough. All well, Garf?"

O'Malley came striding up, with a wild roar of exultation, and seized Burke's hand in a grip of iron.

"All well, cap'n! It's a proud man I am to be sailing with you!"

"You're my lieutenant and master—and friend," said Burke, the warm smile touching his face and transfiguring it.

"And the horizon's clear!" said O'Malley, sweeping a glance around. "The frigates are out o' sight."

Burke stood looking back at the city, and the words lingered with him. The past was dead and gone, yes, though there would be echoes of it in the future; and a chuckle broke from him as he wondered if M. de Poissy had reached Versailles yet. Then his head came up and he flung a salute back at the shores of France and the city lessening in the distance.

"Farewell to the lot of ye!" he murmured. "The horizon's clear—aye! The horizon's clear, and the luck of the sea Burkes lies over it, waiting for me!"

II

LUCK OF THE SEA BURKES

Denis Burke, Irish swordsman and buccaneer, was to find more perils on the rich Spanish Main than cold steel and cannons.

CHAPTER I

PLUNDER

ALL THAT morning the guns had thundered down the rolling seas upon an empty horizon, while the brisk wind sent the whitecaps dancing and whirling on toward Hispaniola and Cuba. The great Spaniard was in agony on the face of the waters, but she was well armed, as all Spaniards needs must be in this year of 1703, when all Europe was at wild war; and her captain fought her with splendid skill and courage.

The little ten-gun brig that had waylaid her, flying a strange green flag, would have gone to the bottom from any of her broadsides, had one ever landed. Her sailing master, a great bearded man, was too wise for that, far too wise to exchange shot for shot with the towering Spaniard; too wise even to board her and have his men shot and piked out of the high mats and netting stretched up above her bulwarks.

To all appearance, the strangely uneven battle was singularly lacking in effect. True, a few shots had smashed into the brig, but no shot at all had marred the carved and gilded decorations of the high Spanish stern and poop. Five guns at a time, the brig reeled and staggered as her broadsides poured into the Spaniard; those guns were loaded not with ball, but with scrap iron and bags of bullets.

Suddenly the result of this strategy became evident. The rigging of the frigate, already much cut about and weakened, was touched in a vital place. The great fore-yard came down with a splintering crash across the forecastle, bringing canvas and tophamper with it. Over the decks were strewn spars and sails, dragging alongside, hindering every movement, bringing down in their wake the after tophamper as well. The frigate fell away; until the mess was cleared up she could not be handled.

"Good!" said Denis Burke, standing beside his bearded skipper at the tiller of the brig. His voice rang down the decks. "Ready, gunners! Full broadsides, rake her decks only!"

"Stand by the braces!" roared Garf O'Malley, his beard blowing in the wind.

The brig came about. Deliberately, while the frigate could bring no gun to bear upon her, she tacked back and forth under the bows of the great ship. Her guns thundered in repeated broadsides. A frightful storm of missiles swept the decks of the Spaniard, striking down her crew and soldiers. Her captain and a few men endeavored to cut away the wreckage, but few of them stood beside the captain after another broadside.

"A brave man, that," said Burke. "What think you, Garf?"

"Take her," said Garf with a nod, and headed straight for the frigate.

The two ships crashed together, but lightly. Grappling irons caught the high bulwark above, and men went up like cats—a hundred and fifty of them, wild Irishmen who followed Denis Burke down the trail of the buccaneers to gold and glory. This was their first prize, this stalwart Spanish ship homeward bound from the New World, and it was likely to prove a rich one.

FIRST OVER the rail was Burke himself, carefully dressed as though for a court ball, in his hand gleaming the gold hilt of his Toledo rapier. The Spaniards were already running to repel boarders. Burke parried a pike-thrust, and his point drove into the soldier's throat. Then his men were jumping down around him, leaping in with the cold steel while pistols flashed in their faces and pikes lunged to bring them down, and musketeers hastily loaded their cumbrous weapons to hail them with bullets.

So sharp, so brutally ferocious, was the rush of the Irish, that

Expertly the Spaniard crossed rapiers with Burke.

it burst clear through the Spanish ranks. Another minute, and the whole forward deck and waist was a wild confusion of fighting figures. Through them darted Burke; with a score of his men he came to the poop ladders and was up and on the musketeers before their loading was done. And there men died fast on the long sloping deck rising to the poop itself and the cabin doors. Not all of them were Spaniards who fell. The captain of the frigate, a tall man with red hair and a handsome breastplate, cut down man after man, drove forward to reach Burke, and the Irishman turned to meet him. Already the ship was taken, for by now the Spaniards were rushing below or crying for quarter.

"Yield!" ordered Burke sharply in Spanish, as he came face to face with the captain. "Your ship's taken. You'll have quarter."

"Devil take you!" shouted the other, and sent in a lunge that all but finished Burke.

Then the blades crossed, and Denis Burke knew he was fighting for his life. Splendid swordsman as he was, with all the training of years of exile that had brought him to the rank of colonel in the Irish Brigade, he had here met one who was close to being a match for him.

In the midst of it all, somebody hurled a belaying pin that struck the frigate's captain behind the ear and stretched him out, senseless. Burke was glad enough of this. He had the measure of his opponent, and would have killed the man in another moment or two. Now he could afford to spare him.

"Bind him and all the other prisoners," he directed. "Bose! Take charge of the decks. To me, Malachi!"

"Coming, your honor."

Old Malachi Halloran, who had been Burke's soldier servant for years past, came up the deck sheathing a red sword, and saluted. Burke turned to the closed doors of the cabin. They were closed from inside, close fastened. Catching up a musket, Malachi beat on the port door with the butt.

"Open!" commanded Burke in Spanish. "Open, and you shall have quarter, good treatment, safety. Refuse, and we burst down the doors."

"Señor!" came the response. "Do you swear to give quarter?"

"No prisoner shall be harmed or molested," returned Burke.

A glance showed him that Garf O'Malley had cast off and was holding the brig a little away from the frigate, because of the rolling seas. Burke had been very anxious not to do this splendid ship any harm, having need of her intact.

The door before him was opened and a monk appeared. Burke saluted him, with a cheerful smile into the stern eyes.

"We don't war on priests, women or helpless folk," he said reassuringly. "Bid them all outside here."

Numbers of his men had gathered to watch, but seeing that they were obviously well under Burke's control, the monk called to those inside the cabins. These ventured out into the sunlight and blowing wind, looking down the bloody decks, gazing with terrified eyes at Burke. There were half a dozen women, numbers of monks, several officials, and a number of servants or slaves, black and white.

Burke turned and spoke to one of his own men.

"Signal O'Malley to come aboard here."

One of the slaves broke forth and came running, and caught at his arm—a stooped, gaunt man with shrewd eyes.

"English, master?" he cried out eagerly. "Set me free, then—say I'm free, master!"

Burke laughed. "Aye, you're free, and those with you. Who are you?"

"Cotton by name, sir; Jeremiah Cotton o' Bristol, ship's master. A slave I've been wi' the dons these four years and more. Filibusters, are ye? I'll join! A cutlass—give me a cutlass! By the gods, I'm going to let some o' this damned Spanish blood!"

In wild jubilation he went running to where a fallen cutlass lay, and would have flung himself murderously at the priests and women, but Burke stepped in front of him.

"Stop," said he.

"Out o' my way!" yelled Cotton. "Sink me if I don't—"

Burke made a sign. Two of his men, who had stood ready, seized Cotton, and as he fought against them, one struck him senseless.

"Take him away and tie him up until he learns obedience," said Burke.

This they did, and Master Cotton learned obedience. More came of this matter, later on.

THE SLAVES were freed, and in chains below were found a dozen filibusters, prisoners being sent to Spain for torture and execution. These were mostly French, and by the time they had also learned something of their new leader, big Garf O'Malley had brought up the brig again and was aboard, striding aft.

He was less astonished than were the filibusters at what he found. Many of Burke's men were soldiers out of the Irish Brigade, who had come from France with him, and others were from Galway, where he had halted to recruit his crew. They obeyed him promptly, with no more leaning to license or liquor than if they had been men of the royal navy; and this, for buccaneers, was a new and strange thing.

Certain of them were caring for the wounded and disposing of the dead, others were repairing the shot rigging and getting up the bullet-torn canvas; the ship was being put into shape, with no plundering or disorder, while the prisoners in the waist and the staring group aft stood watching in astonished wonder.

Burke turned to O'Malley.

"What say you, Garf?" he demanded. "Here's a good ship, well found, able to fight anything that sails. She's undamaged, provisioned for Europe. We've a little brig yonder that must run from any king's corvette that pokes her nose over the horizon, with precious little provision and water remaining—but enough to take these dons into Santo Domingo."

"Rough" O'Malley, as his nickname was translated, met the dancing eyes of Burke, and his teeth showed as he grinned in comprehension.

"Why not?" he rejoined. "You'd sacrifice speed for strength, that's all. Best be sure of the strength before we go farther. Shall I take a look?"

"Aye," said Burke. "Go over the ship and guns, and I'll abide by your decision."

This, to tell the truth, had been in his mind from the first; this was why he had done the frigate no damage. If she were as good a ship as she seemed, then he might well sacrifice speed, and a good bargain!

Now he turned to the captives and bowed to them very grandly.

"*Señores,*" he said in Spanish, "you will be sent away unharmed. Your personal belongings are yours to take with you. Get them, you and your servants, such as wish to go with you. The slaves are freed. Only what you wish to take from your cabins, mind! Get it all, bring it out here on deck. Forward there, bose! Bring me the Spanish captain."

While the delighted captives scattered into the cabins again, with numbers of servants who remained with them, the red-haired captain was led up to where Burke stood.

A bold-eyed man he was, hard of feature, heavy of jaw, wide of shoulder.

"Your name?" asked Burke.

The other grinned at him wolfishly. "Aguilar. Don Sancho de Aguilar, my buccaneer."

"You fought your ship well, *señor* don."

"She was not mine to fight. Our captain was slain at your first discharge. I am a soldier, and took charge. Will you grant me a service, *Señor* Buccaneer?"

"What is it?" asked Burke, thinking the other meant to challenge him to a duel.

"Keep me with you," and Aguilar lowered his voice, with a glance around. A savage flash showed in his dark violet eyes. "I'll explain to you later, *señor.* Keep me with you, presumably as a prisoner. I'll show you where there's a fortune, a fabulous treasure, that you can get with a bit of fighting!"

"So!" Burke surveyed the man keenly. "And your motive?"

"Revenge, *señor*—revenge, and the most beautiful woman in the world for myself! For you, the gold!"

With his customary swift decision, Burke nodded.

"Good. I'll send you into the cabins yonder under guard."

He sent the two men who had brought Aguilar, telling them to keep him bound and to remain with him in the main cabin.

He turned, to find Garf O'Malley striding up.

"The finest of guns, Denis!" exclaimed the seaman eagerly. "And a good sound ship, not long careened and scraped."

"Then get out collision mats aboard the brig and lay her alongside," said Burke. "Get all our own stuff out of her, and change flags. I'll see to things aboard here."

FOR THE next half hour he was a busy man indeed. The Indian ex-slaves, the French filibusters, and some of the Spanish themselves, were not loath to join him. He ordered them to one side for later decision, found that a master's mate of the frigate had survived, and gave him charge of the brig. In no long while, his own men had all their stuff out of her, with most of the powder, and the Spaniards were going aboard. As he passed Burke, the lean, dark friar halted.

"*Señor,* the Conde de Aguilar is not dead?"

"A count, is he?" Burke chuckled whimsically. "No, he is a prisoner for ransom."

The monk's face darkened.

"You'll get little ransom out of him. Do you know that he has been disgraced and was being sent back to Spain in this ship for trial by the king?"

"Then tell the king how he redeemed himself by fighting us," said Burke. "What sort of disgrace came upon him?"

"He was vice-governor of Santo Domingo, *señor,*" was the response. "He was accused of taking bribes. His plantation and goods were confiscated, so your ransom—"

"Will be my affair," said Burke, and watched the friar depart.

Presently all was done. O'Malley gave the master's mate a course for Santo Domingo and the brig filled and stood away with her wounded and living cargo. Burke left his men at their job of repairing the running rigging, and strode into the main cabin. Here he found O'Malley and old Malachi Halloran, who had served him in many a campaign, going over the ship's papers.

"Sit ye down and sample this wine, Denis," said Garf O'Malley. "She has a rich cargo. Cocoa and sugar from the islands, with a shipment of silver and some boxes of gold bars for the royal treasury, besides emeralds, gold plate and other trinkets. A health to her!"

"Not bad for our first capture," and Burke laughed. Then he looked at the others, and his blue eyes became keen. "Listen to me, now! Well you know that with the brig we were safe in no French port. We took her out of St. Malo under the noses of the king's men, and all France wants to hang Denis Burke, late lieutenant-colonel of the Irish Brigade. The English want to hang him as an Irish Jacobite. Now the brig's gone, and Denis Burke's gone with her."

"Eh?" Garf O'Malley stared at him. "What mean ye?"

"This." Burke quaffed the wine and leaned back. "We'll never see County Mayo and County Galway again; Ireland's back of us forever, and the sea horizon lies ahead. Well, then! From this day on, I become Captain Mayo, d'ye understand? Pass the word among our own men. Let this name be the one given to the Frenchmen aboard here. I'll not disgrace the name of Burke by having it applied to a buccaneer."

"Faith, it's not a bad notion at all," said Garf delightedly. He clapped down his silver goblet, and the metal flattened out under his hand. "The devil! I forgot myself. Right you are, cap'n! Here's a health to Cap'n Mayo, and the foul fiend take all who gainsay him! It will pass for a Spanish name, likewise."

"Exactly," said Burke. "It's in my mind, Garf, to head up for Le Cap. Ye know, Cape François, which is usually shortened to Le Cap, is a resort of all good buccaneers. It is at the north end of Hispaniola and close to Tortuga, and we'll have a quick market there for our cargo. Then, with the ship lightened and in ballast, with a change of rig here and there, we'll be ready for business."

"And the men will have some fun spending their money, eh?" O'Malley nodded. "What label will ye clap on our new ship? We must get rid of this Spanish name of Madre de Dios."

"No, leave it for this cruise at least—we may have need of it." And Burke told about Aguilar, and what the friar had said. "What think ye, Garf? Shall we talk with him, now?"

"No better time," said O'Malley. "They'll not have the rigging in shape for another hour. Malachi, go you and take charge of the deck. Serve out rum all around, pass the word to our men that Denis Burke is dead and gone, God rest him, and that our cap'n is named Cap'n Mayo. And have that Spaniard fetched in here."

SO AGUILAR was brought in, relieved of his bonds, and the men dismissed. Burke found some clay pipes and excellent tobacco, and made himself comfortable. He calculated that his captive was not above twenty-five.

"So," he said, as Aguilar drank down some of the good wine, "you're a count, eh? And a bit red for a Spaniard."

"So?" The other grinned. "The best Spanish blood is fair, *señores.* It is that of the Goths, the 'old Christians' as they are called."

"True, but I never heard it was red like yours," said O'Malley. "If I had my own say in the matter, I'd put you down for a red O'Donnell, no less."

Aguilar broke into laughter. "Shane O'Donnell," he said in Irish, "and it's a true word yourself has said, Garf O'Malley! Shane O'Donnell, out of the old family, and now Conde de Aguilar. Here's luck to you!"

Big Garf swore in his beard, and Burke's blue eyes narrowed a trifle.

He knew, of course, that since the flight of the Earls of Tyrone and Tyrconnal in 1620 many O'Donnells and others had won name and fame in Spanish armies. He was by no means sure about this Aguilar, however. Whether the man meant them good or ill, was a question.

"Let's have it out, then," said he bluntly. "You've told me there was a yarn of gold and a woman. I've heard there was more to it; that you're accused of taking bribes and were being sent to Spain in this ship."

"True for you," said Aguilar coolly. "With whom am I speaking?"

"With Captain Mayo, the buccaneer," said Burke. "And this is my lieutenant and friend, Garf O'Malley."

"Right. If I heard your men talking of you by another name, then I'll forget it," and the other's eyes twinkled at him. "I was vice-governor of Hispaniola, then. Some of these plaguey royal officials conspired against me, brought false charges, had me arrested while I was down with the fever a month ago. The governor was, of course, sharing in the dirty work, and chief of the rascals was Don Jaime Salcedo—may I meet him soon again! He seized my castle and plantation, fifty miles down the coast from Santo Domingo, as his part of the spoils.

"We left Santo Domingo three days ago, and on the day we left, came word that one of the Plate fleet had put in at my castle, above a little bay, for repairs. Six hours out, a short and sharp hurricane separated us from the fleet and we were trying to pick up the other ships again when we sighted you. There's the story."

"Brief and to the point," approved Burke. "And this ship that put in at your castle—she has the gold you spoke of?"

Aguilar nodded. "Plenty of it. Don Salcedo has the castle, also, and his niece is with him. The woman I spoke of. You have this ship, plenty of men, my help and advice. If you're minded to run down there direct, we may all obtain what we most desire."

"There may be other ships there, sent to her help from Santo Domingo."

"Not ships of war, at least. A ship would probably go down with carpenters and other workmen, or they might go overland."

"H'm! And the woman's in love with you?"

Aguilar smiled, and his sharp, white teeth showed.

"If she isn't, she should be. Leave her to me."

"Very good," said Burke. "Then leave us to talk it over, by your leave. Either you'll go in with us fully, or not at all."

"And you with me, on the same terms," said Aguilar, as he rose, and he laughed as he looked at them. "Until soon, *señores!*"

When the cabin door had closed behind him, Burke looked at the frowning O'Malley.

"Well, Garf? What d'ye say to it? We'd have to go there straight off, carry through the business, and then head for Le Cap. We've got treasure enough as it lies."

O'Malley nodded. "We've got gold enough, if it's gold we're

after, Denis. And yon man is a rascal if I ever saw one—but he's no fool. Better a devil than a fool any day, as my old mother used to say. If it's gold you're after, I'd say no. But—"

Denis Burke broke into a laugh and clapped the seaman on the shoulder.

"But! We think alike, old friend. There's more to this than appears on the surface, eh? Then let's gobble up the bait and see what the luck of the sea Burkes holds for us, eh? Aguilar is a bold rascal, but we'll be bolder. Agreed?"

"Aye," said O'Malley, as he met the reckless, dancing eyes of Burke. "But remember, your luck lies in the sea, not ashore!"

"And sink me if I forget it," said Burke.

So was taken the mad decision, and an hour later the canvas of the Madre de Dios went bellying up, and her head was turned south for Hispaniola, and Aguilar wore his sword again.

CHAPTER II

IN DISGUISE

THE CASTLE of San Isidro was no more than a stone-walled fortalice large enough to contain four long brass cannon. Its huge value lay altogether in its location, on a knob of rock fifty feet high.

Upon one side of this knob lay a small but perfectly sheltered harbor, into which a tiny river discharged. The knob was directly above the river mouth, forming, indeed, one side of this mouth. Opposite, across the river and around to the other side of the knob, was all lower ground—rich plantation land, green with waving cane for a huge distance. Opposite the knob, too, and across the river mouth, was the long, comfortable, spacious plantation house, with its slave barracoons behind.

A soldier's eye had seized on this spot. The castle on the rocky knob, whose sides were steep and scaled by a difficult road, impossible even for mules, completely commanded the little harbor. It commanded, with equal completeness, the plantation house opposite and all the lower ground around. In older days this had been a favorite watering place for brethren of the coast and other gentry who dared not enter Santo Domingo, but the guns on the knob had changed all that long ago. Those four long brass cannon could spew forth bags of bullets or heavy shot with impunity, for no ship's guns could be elevated sufficiently to be brought to bear on the crest.

San Isidro, situated at the eastern end of the island, was isolated. San Domingo was fifty miles to the west, Samana far to the north. Mountains cut it off from the interior. Here one might well be a petty king, ruler of all he surveyed.

Aguilar piloted them truly and well. In the three days that elapsed ere they raised the coast, Burke had studied the man. He judged him to be unscrupulous, cruel, a splendid campaigner, a typical soldier of fortune, a man who would betray every one around him to serve his own ends. Burke was by no means blind in this affair.

They sailed into the little harbor to find two small coasters lying there, come from Santo Domingo, and half-careened on the white beach under the knob was a demi-galleon—a huge, unwieldy craft. Aguilar had warned them that the Madre de Dios, which had come from Mexico and had lain for three weeks at Santo Domingo, would be known to Salcedo and others here; so they sailed in with Spanish colors flying, and with every man aboard dressed in the Spanish garb provided abundantly from the effects of the departed ship's company. Aguilar remained out of sight.

Burke, who spoke Spanish perfectly, picked out half a dozen of the French filibusters who could also handle the language, and lowered a boat. He could count implicitly on these men. Reckless to a degree, delighting in the part they were playing, knowing no law save the will of their commander, these filibusters were a welcome addition to his complement of men. As they had no share in the plunder of the frigate, but would share in any takings here, they were more than eager to serve in the venture.

There was a low wharf here, with sheds beyond, on the side of the river opposite the knob. As he was rowed in to meet the throng coming down to the wharfs, Burke noted the glitter of helmets at the little fortress and the camp of men up the river bank—all obviously from the galleon, which would carry both soldiers and seamen.

Burke, who was by no means indifferent to costume, had come upon the chest of some grandee with huge delight.

At his side was his own gold-hilted Toledo; his deep-blue Genoa velvet, pricked out with cloth of gold, his heavy lace at throat and cuffs, his crimson Cordovan hip-boots, the star of St. Jago on his breast, the huge emerald rings on his hand, the wide hat with a superb plume, all became him well, lent his keen aquiline features a touch of splendor and created a magnificent setting for his air of distinction.

AS HE bowed to the assembled noblemen, Burke's spirits rose to his usual high audacity when confronting the unknown. This group of half a dozen men was composed of officers and grandees; in the center was a man of fifty, handsomely dressed, with a gray-brown beard and close-set, furtive eyes that oddly belied his grand air.

This, as Burke guessed, was Don Salcedo.

"Gentlemen, a very good morning to you!" said Burke cheerfully. "I am Don Agusto Mayo y Cabello, in command of a frigate just arrived at Santo Domingo from Cadiz. As my ship was badly battered by the recent hurricane, and most of the officers of the Madre de Dios were down with fever, I took charge of her and came to this port to see if I might be of service to you."

"*Caballero,* you are welcome, in the name of God!" said the stately don. "I am Don Jaime Salcedo, and these gentlemen are officers of the Santa Trinidad, whom you see here on shore in evil case. You say that Don Diego Gutierrez, the captain of the ship, is ill with fever? That is sad news. He is a very gallant *caballero.* But come, accompany us up to the house; it is entirely yours, with all its contents, and it is ill talking here in the hot sun. You are new come from Spain, Don Agusto?"

"Aye," returned Burke. "And then from some years of captivity among the Moors. I give you my word, *señor,* that when I escaped and arrived safely in Ceuta, I could scarce speak two words of Castilian! However, all goes well, and campaigning here in the Indies with a good ship will be better than slaving and starving under a Barbary sun."

"It will be," said one of the officers, "if the accursed buccaneers leave you alone!"

Burke laughed. "How should they bother a great ship, *señor?*"

"The devils run in under our broadsides and board; they are like ravening wolves, half starved or else drunk with rum. Not even the glorious soldiers of Spain can stand before them once they get a foothold on your deck! Our soldiers are seldom accustomed to a ship's deck, and of course our rogues of seamen are not good for fighting. The best chance if you meet a buccaneer is to cripple him with your guns before he gets alongside."

So, talking of one thing and another, they all approached the cool house. These men were most of them long absent from Spain; they demanded news avidly of the homeland, and Burke, nothing loath, provided it. What he did not know, he invented. There was news of the war to give also, and here he was more at home. He noted that Don Salcedo cast frequent glanccs out at the frigate, and as they drew near to the house, the Spaniard took his arm and spoke familiarly.

"Don Agusto, have you a gentleman aboard who was to be taken to Spain by that ship—one Conde de Aguilar?"

"I think he was taken ashore when the sailing was postponed," said Burke. "I am not heading for Spain now, you comprehend—I was asked by the governor to come up here and see whether we could be of any assistance to you."

The other nodded, satisfied, and bowed him into the house with stately courtesy.

HERE HE was conducted to the cool and shady patio, where the wide fronds of huge banana trees fended off the afternoon sun, and a fountain plashed softly among soft green orange trees. The party resumed their interrupted diversions—a lazy enjoyment of tobacco, chilled wine, and the talk which Spaniards loved. All were from the mainland, except Don Salcedo, with tales of gold, of Aztecs and Peruvians, and with privations and fever written on their faces. There had been no women aboard the Santa Trinidad, as it chanced.

Burke, his greeting over, said little and heard much. The galleon, it seemed, had run foul of a reef, considerably damaging her rudder and bottom, but was now nearly repaired. Her nominal captain, Don Balthazar Olivares, appeared supremely uninterested, leaving such matters entirely to his sailing master and seamen. He and his officers had been out that same morning with Don Salcedo, running down some maroons, as the Indians of the interior were called, to increase the labor supply of the plantation. They had brought in a dozen or more, and had killed thrice as many in the savage extermination practiced by the Spaniards. When Burke heard of Indian children cut down, of women tortured, his face went a little white and his eyes lost their warmly whimsical glow and became like chilled steel.

The maroons, he gathered, were not unmixed with blacks, many of whom had escaped from the plantations to the inaccessible portions of the mountains. At times they were hunted down in numbers and kept in a state of subjection, for outlying plantations such as this were always in danger from their raids.

The two small coasters had been sent from Santo Domingo with carpenters and artisans to work on the galleon. The latter's complement of two hundred soldiers was in the camp up the creek, with the exception of a few guards. Her guns, stores, and much of her cargo had perforce been landed; she would not be ready to take to sea again for a week at least, thanks to this necessary reloading, and Don Balthazar was already vastly bored with San Isidro. And fever threatened him.

"Perhaps," suggested Burke suavely, "you and your friends, *señor* don, would all come out to dinner aboard the Madre de Dios? Let us say, at sunset. The sea is calm, we can put out to sea for a few miles and obtain a cool breeze, and I have some excellent wine aboard. Perhaps Don Salcedo can provide us with a few cattle and some fresh fruit—unfortunately I neglected these matters at leaving Santo Domingo."

The suggestion was welcomed with great acclaim. Every one sat up straighter, and jaded eyes became bright again. Don Salcedo not only accepted the invitation to join the party, but promised to send aboard fresh meat and fruits within an hour's time.

Then came the one thing Burke was burning to discover, as one of the officers addressed Don Balthazar.

"Think you it will be safe for us all to leave, *señor* don? You know, the gold was fetched ashore here—"

"Nombre de Dios!" ejaculated the haughty Spaniard. "Who is going to steal it, then? I'll set a dozen men on guard here about the house, and Sergeant Ruiz will be an excellent man to leave in command of the place. Do you fear the maroons will attack, then?"

There was a burst of laughter, and under cover of this, Burke withdrew. Don Salcedo accompanied him down to the wharf and saw him off with much stately Spanish courtesy. As he was rowed out to his ship, Burke questioned the French filibusters at the oars.

"What of these maroons? Is there any way one can reach them?"

"But yes, *m'sieu!*" came the quick response. "Those slaves we freed, the Indians! We have but to land them anywhere on the coast, and they can reach their people swiftly."

"With a message?"

The stroke oar grinned at him. "They know the filibusters,

mon capitaine! We work with them often. If you want to bring down the maroons on these Spaniards, we can talk with the Indians in their own tongue and arrange everything."

Burke nodded, well satisfied at this. "Very well. Talk with them. If I set them ashore somewhere near by, before sunset, see whether they can bring down the maroons to attack the camp yonder at dawn."

He went up the side of the frigate, whose decks were carefully staged for benefit of those ashore with men in morion and breastplate, and clapped O'Malley on the shoulder.

"On to the cabin, Garf! All's well. Malachi! Come you and listen."

In the handsome main cabin they found Aguilar, eagerly awaiting them. Burke dropped on a seat and laughed.

"They're coming aboard at sunset or after—all the officers, and Don Salcedo! We're giving a grand dinner, and are putting out to sea for the cool evening breeze. Don Salcedo is even sending oxen aboard and fresh fruit, for the feast!"

He described his visit ashore. Aguilar broke in swiftly.

"And Doña Inez? You met her? You gave her the message?"

"Eh?" Burke stared at him, then chuckled whimsically. "Faith, I forgot all about her! No, I didn't see her. But I'm sending out men to fish, in a boat. We must put the Indians in her, covered over with a tarpaulin—here, I'll tell you the plan."

He spoke rapidly, eagerly, and Garf O'Malley listened with kindling eyes, but Aguilar scowled, and a bitter twist curved his lips, and the look he fastened upon Burke was keen and dark with unuttered thoughts.

Nor did Burke miss the look, though he appeared to take no heed.

CHAPTER III

SPANISH "GUESTS"

SUNSET WAS approaching when boats put out and the guests began to come aboard.

Burke had gleefully worked getting the frigate in readiness. The Indians were gone long since, and the boat had returned after landing them a couple of miles up the coast. A file of supposedly Spanish soldiers stood on the deck; the frigate was redolent with the odors of cooking meat; Burke and O'Malley stood by to receive their visitors; the after mess cabin was laid out with all the silver and gold plate found aboard—an entire service of it, made in Mexico for the King of Spain.

Don Salcedo and Don Balthazar came aboard, the former thin-visaged, furtive of eye; the latter haughty and listless. After them came the officers of the galleon, the lean, hard, fever-bitten veterans of Mexico and South America. When they were all over the rail, the bo's'n's whistle blew, the anchor came heavily up, and the topsails were shaken out. The stately frigate gathered way, passed the two little coasters, and headed out to sea.

The Spaniards thought it very singular that Burke had no officers here aboard; but in truth only the French filibusters had any great smattering of Spanish, and none of these could pass for a Spanish *caballero.* Burke laughed and laid it to the fever which had stricken most of the frigate's complement, and presently led his guests down to the mess cabin. The ports were all open wide, the sea was smooth, and the grateful coolness of the evening delighted them all. Lanterns and candelabra were lighted, and amid no little laughter and merriment the wine was poured, and Burke ordered Malachi to serve the dinner.

One place, at the foot of the table near the door, remained empty.

The wine was plied, toasts were drunk, the food was brought

in and the banquet got well under way. Then Burke, who sat at the head of the table with Don Balthazar on his right and Don Salcedo on his left, made a signal. The supposed servants departed. Unostentatiously, others slipped into the long cabin—men half naked, kerchiefs about their heads, steel at their waists, a pistol in each hand. And, coming to the chair at the foot of the table and bowing ceremoniously, was Conde de Aguilar.

There was a moment of stupefied, incredulous silence, while Don Salcedo sat with a terrible pallor creeping over his face. Then Burke rose and lifted his silver goblet.

"*SEÑORES!*" HE exclaimed upon the silence. "The comedy is played out, and now the drama begins; allow me to acquaint you with the facts of the case. I must introduce to you the Conde de Aguilar, whom some of you already know. He is my guest aboard this ship. I am Captain Mayo the buccaneer, and I captured this ship some days ago. *Señores,* you are all my prisoners, and if one man of you draws a weapon or leaves his chair, my men have orders to shoot. See to it!"

They sat in paralyzed silence, until a breath passed among them; the name of Aguilar. He caught it, and a thin smile touched his lips as he sipped his wine, looking from man to man.

"What, *caballeros,* no greeting for me?" he said derisively. "And you, honest Don Salcedo, no word for your old friend? Ah, yes, I forgot. You accused me of taking bribes, eh? You had me placed under arrest, all my property confiscated. Well, I am going to hang you in five minutes, so make your last prayer."

Don Salcedo pulled himself together.

"Aguilar," he said slowly, a level bitterness in his voice, "you are a scoundrel. Now I perceive this is no jest, but sober earnest. So you have become a traitor, a thorough rascal, combining with outlaws of the sea against your own countrymen?"

"*Señor* don," put in Burke, who did not intend to let Aguilar assert too much authority, "let us do him justice.

"He, and he alone, fought us, made us pay dear for the ship.

When all was lost, when he had been struck down and captured—then he said a word to me, and joined me."

"None the less, he is a scoundrel," said Don Salcedo.

"And now you hang!" cried out Aguilar fiercely, and gestured to the men around. "Take out that old man and hang him! Quickly!"

None of them made the slightest move to obey.

A furious oath broke from Aguilar, until he saw Burke's, quiet smile and realized the truth.

"Oh! They need the order from you, do they? Give it quickly, my friend!"

"Not at all," said Burke in Spanish, that all might understand. "*Señores,* I regret to say that the wishes of my friend Aguilar cannot be entirely complied with. It desolates me to remind him that I am master here, and you gentlemen are my guests, not his; my prisoners, not his. I do not betray my hospitality—beyond certain limits. As Spaniards, you are prisoners. As *caballeros* and soldiers, you are my guests. No harm shall come to you, no ransom shall be demanded; you'll be set at liberty when I've taken what I wish from your ship's cargo—"

Aguilar leaped to his feet, snarling a wild oath.

"Are you a traitor to your given word?" he demanded hotly, "You bargained with me for everything!"

"Not at all!" and Burke laughed a little. "For gold and a woman, remember. Nothing was said about the murder of a helpless man."

"Well, then, I'll bargain with you now!" flamed out Aguilar savagely at Burke. "I have gold of my own hidden in that house ashore. Plenty of it, enough to make any one rich for life, do you understand? You shall have a full half of it; but I want to see this goat-bearded rascal hung at the yard of this ship!"

Burke smiled whimsically down the long table, and only the icy glint in his eyes gave any hint of his hidden anger. Every one remained silent; the tense interest had been switched to these two men facing each other, and the Spaniards had for the moment forgotten their own plight in watching and listening.

"I see plainly," said Burke in a gentle voice, "that you are not accustomed to dealing with Irish gentlemen, my friend. I do not sell the blood of any man for gold. If you have a quarrel with this *caballero,* that is not my affair. Don Salcedo, you will pardon my discourtesy in neglecting to set the matter before you. Do you desire that I should turn you over to Conde de Aguilar, or do you prefer to remain as my guest?"

"Eh? Eh?" Don Salcedo blinked. "Why, *señor,* as—as your guest, of course!"

"Then the matter is closed," said Burke, with a wave of his hand.

"It is not closed!" cried out Aguilar fiercely. "I mean to have this man hung!"

"Either it is closed one way, or another if you prefer," said Burke. "If you are not content, my friend, my men will take you out and hang you. Choose, here and now."

Aguilar stared at him, and saw that Burke meant his words, as indeed he did. With an effort Aguilar dismissed the matter entirely and sank back into his chair.

"Very well, *señor,*" he said. "I withdraw my demand."

"That is very wise of you," rejoined Burke, smiling slightly, and rose. "If you will now join me on deck, I should like to discuss plans with you.

"*Señores,*" and he glanced around smilingly at the dismayed, stupefied faces, "pray continue your meal. There is no haste, as you must remain confined to this cabin until daylight, possibly longer. Accept the situation with grace, I beg of you, for otherwise you will certainly be killed. I shall rejoin you presently."

WITH A bow he passed down the length of the table, took Aguilar by the arm, and led him out to the ladder. When they had gained the deck, the other stopped short.

"*Señor,*" he said, his voice vibrant with repressed passion, "by the saints, tell me whether you spoke in jest or earnest down there!"

"Entirely in earnest," said Burke coolly, as Garf O'Malley strode up to them and halted. "No harm shall come to any of those men, unless they try to escape, which is unlikely. For the love of the saints to whom you appeal, can you not realize that I am a gentleman?"

"I thought you were a buccaneer," sneered Aguilar.

"One can be the other, my friend. All well, Garf?"

"All well," responded the bearded seaman.

"Good; let us discuss plans. Aguilar, it appears, has a large sum of gold hidden at his house ashore. He'll want to get that; it belongs to him, and he should have it. Also, he shares as we agreed in the loot of the galleon. We can't be sure that those Indians will get the maroons down upon the place by dawn, so we'd better make our own plans. First, that rocky knob holding the cannon. We'll have to seize it."

"You and I can do that," spoke up Aguilar, with an air of sneering challenge. "The two of us won't arouse any suspicion. We can take care of the sentry at the little gate, and hold it open until your men can rush up from below."

"Agreed," said Burke promptly. "Then turn the guns on the camp and hold it quiet, eh? If the maroons don't show up, we'll be playing safe that way. Garf, send us ashore with a dozen men in one boat—our best gunners. Once we're landed, you tumble out every one ashore. A score of men can seize the galleon. You lead the rest to the house and make sure of it, for the gold is there. Better send Malachi with me. All this, half an hour before daybreak. With dawn, we'll get off our hatches and load aboard the best of the galleon's cargo, with the gold from the house. We haven't room for much, so take only the best. Understood?"

"Right," said O'Malley. "By the way, that English shipmaster has been asking for you. He wants to speak with you."

LEAVING AGUILAR to his own devices, Burke accompanied his lieutenant into the waist, where they came on Jeremiah Cotton, smoking a clay pipe and leaning on the bulwark. The frigate was floating calmly, her canvas furled, some three miles offshore.

"Well, Cotton?" said Burke, as O'Malley passed on. "You wanted speech with me?"

"Aye, master," and the other turned to him. "I be main sorry, cap'n, for what I said and did the day of our meeting."

Burke clapped him on the back.

"Nonsense, man! Say no more about it. The leap from slavery into freedom is enough to unsettle any man's wits. If you want to join us when we reach Le Cap, say the word and we may arrange an officer's place for you aboard."

"Thank'ee, sir," returned Cotton. "But there was summat else I had in mind to say, cap'n. About this Don Aguilar, it is. I heard a mortal lot o' talk, about him since we took him aboard at Santo Domingo, and he bain't what one might call an honest gentleman, cap'n. He's a proper devil in a fight, but a main bad 'un at all times."

"Thanks, Cotton," said Burke quietly. "Never fear, I have his measure."

"Very good, cap'n. And if so be as there was a reward give me, I could show you where some o' them women aboard hid some jewels, sir. I heard 'em speak of it as they was put aboard the brig. You see, cap'n, they didn't trust you; they thought as how you meant for 'em to get out all their personal belongings, and then rob 'em to the skin."

"So?" Burke chuckled. "They've repented, then, ere this! Right. If you know where any loot is hidden, let's look it up. You'll get a third of it. Agreed?"

"Aye, cap'n!" Eagerness filled the gaunt man's voice. "It's in the larboard side after cabin, the one Cap'n O'Malley has taken for himself!"

"Get a lantern, then, and come along," said Burke. He looked around for O'Malley, but the latter had gathered the men in the forward waist and was telling them the plans for the landing, so Burke forbore to bother him at the moment.

Cotton obtained a lantern, pinched the wick of the candle

to make it burn brighter, and joined Burke on the quarter-deck. They passed into the poop cabins, and so came to that which O'Malley had taken—a large cabin lighted by one of the huge stern windows and highly ornamented with carved and gilded work.

Holding up the lantern, Cotton pointed to a framed saint's picture built into the wall at one side.

"There y'are, sir—behind that picture there's a secret place hidden. I don't know the workings of it, but—"

Burke went to the picture, tapped it and the frame, looked in vain for any means of discovering the secret place behind it.

"If you'll take the light, cap'n," said Cotton, hauling out his knife. "I'll cut the picture out o' the frame and we'll be at it that way."

Unsuspecting, Burke took the lantern. The gaunt man leaned forward and drew his knife about inside the frame, slitting through the heavy canvas of the picture. He jerked the canvas square away and thrust his face into the opening.

"It's there, cap'n, it's there!" came his muffled voice. "I can see the jewels shining and glittering, a whole heap of 'em!"

"Well, get away and give some one else a chance!" exclaimed Burke, amused by the man's eagerness. He came closer, holding up the lantern. "Here—"

Cotton drew back sharply, caromed into him, knocked against the lantern and plunged the cabin into darkness.

SOME SIXTH sense warned Burke, just as the awkward by-play happened. Like a flash he threw himself sidewise, falling against the cabin wall. Cotton's arm passed across his chest, the knife driving into the oak, then wrenching loose. A panted oath, and the gaunt man was on top of him, stabbing furiously.

"By the gods, I'll earn the money now!" rose his voice, as his left hand caught Burke's throat and the knife drove in for a finishing blow.

The blow did not land.

Anticipating it as the bony fingers found his throat, Burke fetched up his left arm sharply, deflected the knife, gripped the wrist of Cotton. For a moment the two men struggled furiously in the darkness. Cotton's breath came in hoarse panting surges; he fought like a madman to free his knife arm, was hard to hold as an eel. Then the two came breast to breast, and Burke had the grip he wanted, regardless of Cotton's free hand that flailed him with blows.

Turning swiftly in the darkness, putting out his strength, Burke flung the man bodily over his hip, flung him with a surging lift that picked him up and heaved him through the air. There was a crash, a wild and frantic cry; a moment later, Burke realized he stood alone in the darkness. Cotton had gone plunging out through the thin wooden lattice-work of the stern window, whose stout wooden doors stood ajar to let in air.

By the time Burke reached the deck and gave the alarm, some moments had passed. From the dark sea overside came no voice to answer the hails, nor did the lanterns lowered on ropes show any sign of Cotton. The man was gone, with that one plunge.

But Burke wondered whose money Cotton had been trying to earn, and had no answer to his mental query—none, at least, for the present.

As for jewels behind the picture, there were none. That had been a lie, pure and simple.

CHAPTER IV

THE ATTACK

MIDNIGHT WAS past, as the frigate turned in toward the coast, three or four miles away. A light breeze, barely ruffling the water, was sending her along at rippling speed. Burke, who had been snatching an hour or two of sleep, came hastening out on deck in response to the summons that had roused him, and joined O'Malley on the high poop. Two of the French filibusters stood there, also.

"What's up?" asked Burke, yawning. "Ships, you say?"

"Two vessels bearing down on us, Denis," said Garf O'Malley, and pointed. "There they are. Friend Tout-en-Muscles here says they're filibusters."

Burke saw them now, in the clear thin moonlight, for the moon was nearly at full and had come up late. Two small shapes indeed, but coming straight for their prey like wolves at the kill.

"Malachi! Get the bo's'n. Summon all hands, but quietly. No lights, except on the lower gun deck; all ports tight closed. Load the guns. Stand ready to trice up the ports when I give the word. No noise, no lights, remember!"

Tout-en-Muscles, a burly, knotted Frenchman, plucked at his elbow,

"M'sieu! They'll think to catch us napping and lay aboard us. If they know we're buccaneers, they'll not fight. Hail them when they come closer. If English, they'll fight anyway; but they may be French."

"Aye," said Burke. "Stand by to back up my hail. It may be some one you know."

Fast overhauling the heavy-laden, lumbering frigate, the two sea wolves came slipping along, canvas bellied out full, but no lights showing. Burke had long previously established aboard the huge frigate a system of messages, so that within a moment his orders could be sent to every quarter of the vessel; already he heard the stir of wakening men, the tramp of bare feet rising from the lower decks, and from the companionway came the acrid tang of the slow-matches being lighted. A man came up with a speaking-trumpet, and Burke waited at the starboard rail. The larger of the two sea wolves was closing in from that side.

"Cap'n!" exclaimed Tout-en-Muscles, after a brief word with his companion. His voice was excited. "Devil take me if I don't know that craft! It's the ship of Captain Roland, the filibuster!

I've sailed with him aboard her. He carries three hundred men at the least, and—"

Burke swung up the long cone to his lips, and sent his voice vibrantly across the moonlit, dancing waters in French.

"Captain Roland! Ahoy, there! Brethren of the coast!"

Then, swiftly, to one of the waiting men:

"Ports up, battle lanterns showing—quickly!"

The order went droning down the decks. A sharp yelp of astonishment came from the buccaneer, then a deep, heavy-throated voice.

"Who calls?"

"A friend," responded Burke. "Captain Mayo, the buccaneer! This is my ship, you comprehend? If you want to attack, you'll have a fight on your hands, Roland!"

"C'est vrai!" And Tout-en-Muscles leaped to the bulwark and shouted his name. "Remember me, *mon capitaine?* Here are filibusters French and Irish and English, and all the Spaniards are prisoners. Come alongside and talk, or fight if you so desire!"

Now the ports of the Madre de Dios were triced up, and the long guns run out on their carriages, so that the Frenchmen could see the gunners standing ready by the light of the swinging battle lanterns. The ship they had taken to be an unsuspecting Spaniard was abruptly seen to be manned by sea wolves like themselves, fangs bared, ready for a fight.

Quick, sharp orders passed between the two buccaneering vessels, then the larger one sheered in closer, the other stood away.

"Diable! We come as friends, in that case," shouted Captain Roland. "Heave to and I'll come alongside."

Burke laughed harshly. "No, no, my friend! You don't catch me so easily as that. Mind your helm and run alongside us, but you're not invited aboard."

The two vessels were close now, almost within biscuit-toss, and looking down on the other ship, Burke saw her captain standing in the shrouds.

"Bah! Don't think I want to dispute your bone," returned Roland. "We're loaded down now with plunder and making for Le Cap. Since you are no Spaniard, but a brother, I welcome you. Captain Mayo, is it? I never heard of such a name."

"You'll hear it often enough in future," and Burke chuckled. "If you're heading for Le Cap, I'll be there myself a few days after you. I'm standing in now to take San Isidro. Come along and join me, and share what we find there!"

"San Isidro? Name of the devil, but that's suicide!" yelped the bearded Roland. "They will blow you out of the water! Stay away from there, my friend."

"Nonsense," replied Burke. "Join your force to mine and we'll take the place easily."

"Name of the devil!" came the answer. "We've plunder enough now, and I'll not jeopardize it by running my head into a trap! If you attack San Isidro, you'll lose your ship and all else, I warn you!"

"Last chance to join me, Roland!" shouted Burke. "There's a galleon ashore there, and gold for the taking!"

"To the devil with her and you too, madman!" cried the other, and leaped down to his own deck. Next moment his ship stood away, and the two sea wolves sheered off to the northward and left the frigate to her own course.

Burke laughed a little, but made no other comment.

AN HOUR before dawn the frigate was standing in for the San Isidro entrance, half a mile distant. "All hands stand by!" ordered Burke. "Pikes and cutlasses; no muskets. Where's Aguilar?"

"Here, *señor.*" Aguilar appeared, wearing helmet and breastplate.

Openly, with lanterns on her deck, the frigate came into the little harbor and resumed her old position. A sharp hail drifted down from the rocky knob, although those in the battery must have recognized her, and Aguilar made response.

A boat was lowered. Presently Burke and Aguilar were going shoreward, with the men selected to assault the battery.

Instead of heading for the wharf, they crossed the estuary toward the rocky knob and landed on the beach below it. Aguilar called up, giving the names of two of Don Balthazar's officers, saying they were mounting for inspection. A listless assent floated down.

The very boldness of it all, the open, unhurried mounting of the two men, gave no cause for alarm to the unsuspecting sentries. They did not see the men below, scattering in the shadow, coming as far along the path as they dared. Other boats were going ashore from the frigate, heading for the wharf; voices were floating lazily over the dawn-darkness of the water. The long, cool night was past, another torrid day was at hand. If only those two accursed officers were drunk enough to make a careless inspection and cause no trouble—

"First blow to me," said Aguilar, with a laugh, as he and Burke came to the open gate in the stone wall, at the top of the path. A sentry stood there, musket on shoulder, breastplate glittering faintly in the dim moon of dawn.

Burke fell back. Aguilar, still laughing, drew his rapier, and without a word, without a hint of warning, drove it through the throat of the watching sentry. Burke could scarce repress a savage oath of horror at the black murder. The useless cruelty of it revolted him.

Another sentry, not a dozen paces away, saw the deed, uttered one shrill cry, leveled his musket and put a match to pan. To the roar, Burke heard the ball whistle overhead, and saw Aguilar run in through the smoke. That sentry died as the other had. Then Aguilar was back, with a short, exultant laugh.

The two stood side by side just within the shadow of the gateway. Men came running, an officer waving his sword, shouting at them in angry surprise, too impetuously eager to draw back and use muskets. Eight or ten men followed him in a torrent, not knowing what was going on, their pikes glittering in the wan light.

The officer flung himself at Burke, who coolly engaged his blade for an instant, then lunged. The Spaniard fell; his men poured forward, the two blades striking aside the pike heads, thrusting beneath them.

Men began to cry out and fall. Shouts rose loudly. From the path outside came a scuffling scramble of feet, hoarse panted voices. Burke could not but admire the address and agility of Aguilar in this critical moment, as he fought with weapons darting and licking around him, and death answered his thrusts.

Then a bursting yell, and the men from below poured in, and the rest was slaughter. Burke cornered one of the Spaniards, held him helpless, disarmed him, lowered his blade.

"I give you life, *señor*," he said rapidly. "Go to the camp yonder. Say that Captain Mayo, the buccaneer, has captured the guns here, the ships, the plantation. If any men leave the camp, these guns will open on them. Otherwise, there will be no attack. Go!"

In fear of his life, the man slipped from the gate and departed hastily toward the camp.

BURKE LOOKED down across the little river.. In the gray dawn-light men were streaming up in a dark flood from the wharf and sheds toward the plantation.

A shot rang out, and then another; a wild, shrill yell made answer.

"Taken, my captain!" Tout-en-Muscles appeared, waving a reddened cutlass, before Burke. "Shall we man the guns?"

"Aye," said Burke. "If the Spaniards start to leave their camp, open on them. Otherwise, send one shot over them, then wait. I've sent them word to bide quiet."

The filibuster gathered his men with shouts. Aguilar came to Burke hurriedly.

"Ready, *señor?*" he cried. "All awaits us, yonder!"

"Come, then."

They descended the path together, Aguilar, fired with eagerness to reach the plantation, telling of the ford below the camp where they could cross the river easily. Cross it they did, while the daylight grew, and from the great house ahead the noise of conflict died down and ceased. In the Spanish camp drums beat and trumpets shrilled. One of the cannon on the knob thundered out its warning message, and the drums ceased abruptly. There was no movement from the camp.

Aguilar went dashing ahead, and Burke, smiling at the man's impatience, followed more slowly, content to let the daylight grow. A screaming of women reached him, but it died away almost at once, and he perceived that Garf O'Malley was in full control. A cursing soldier, his face all stove in and bloody, went staggering toward the beach to bear witness that Garf's hand was heavy.

As Burke came up to the front of the house, where men were plundering unhindered, he perceived that a detachment was freeing the slaves in the barracoons, while others had seized the beached galleon and the two coasters. All fighting was at an end.

"The place is ours, Denis!" roared O'Malley, emerging from the house. "Orders?"

"Leave a dozen men here with me," said Burke. "Take all hands otherwise, and get the gold aboard, and anything from the galleon's cargo that we might want. Let the men plunder her at will, since there are no women, aboard."

"Malachi and six others are on guard over the women's quarters here," said O'Malley. "You'll find 'em inside, across the patio. I'll send six more to join you."

The bo's'n's whistle rang out its summons, as Burke passed on into the house.

His men had turned it into sad wreck and ruin, while here and there the bodies of Spaniards showed that those on guard here had not surrendered tamely. He went on through into the patio; the first spears of sunrise were reddening the eastern sky.

Malachi Halloran was on the far side, standing sword in hand. He saluted respectfully as Burke approached.

"All well, your honor. The men are inside, guarding the rooms. Aguilar just went in."

Burke nodded and passed on. He wanted to find where Aguilar's gold was hidden and get it safely aboard for the man. He came into a long passage where a number of his men were lounging, and at the same moment, heard a suppressed scream and a rising sound of angry voices from one of the rooms.

"Aguilar?" he asked, and his men nodded.

Burke advanced to the door, shoved it open, and stood looking at the scene before him.

A NUMBER of candles were burning dimly, struggling against the new daylight. Aguilar stood in the center of the room, bowing mockingly to a girl from whose face and head he had just torn a black lace shawl. She faced him angrily—a girl whose beauty struck Burke all amazed; she was dark and lovely, and her anger had heightened her color. Two older women half crouched at her side, moaning, but there was no fear in her face.

"You misapprehend, Doña Inez," said Aguilar, throwing aside the remnants of the black shawl. "Buccaneers have seized this place; your uncle, the others, are all prisoners. I am here to rescue you."

"I want none of your rescue," she said disdainfully. "I have no trust in you, for you are a liar and a rogue."

"None the less, you are mine," said Aguilar, "and you go with me, my pretty one."

She looked over his shoulder, and her eyes widened on the figure of Burke. Perhaps the whimsical smile in his eyes, the warm friendliness in that keenly aquiline face of his, reached out to her. A new light came into her eyes, and she drew herself up straighter.

"How now, *señor?*" said Burke quietly. "Perhaps there is some mistake here."

Burke remained silent at the insult.

Aguilar wheeled, threw him one keen scowl, then laughed.

"Not so, my friend. There is no mistake. This is the lady whom I sought here, and who belongs to me, as we agreed."

Burke bowed, with stately courtesy, to Doña Inez.

"Nevertheless, I think there is a mistake," he said amiably. "Or am I wrong, *señorita?* Of course, if you love this man, then I'm the last person on earth to stand in the way."

"Love him?" Her lip curled in scorn. "I would rather love a snake, a reptile!"

Aguilar laughed a little.

"She will change her mind soon enough, my captain," he said jauntily. "By the time she reaches Le Cap, you'll see."

Burke shook his head. "I fear she is not going to Le Cap," he said.

"Eh?" Aguilar straightened slightly. "What mean you? Did you not agree? You can't deny it, as you denied the other."

"My dear *señor,*" said Burke coolly, while the girl looked from one to the other with swift hot eyes, "I never deny my word, nor give it hastily. You gave us to understand that the woman you sought was in love with you. Now, for a love affair I have sympathy of the greatest, I assure you, provided it is two-sided. But you know the orders given my men; any ravishment is punished with death. Remember, my dear *señor*, I am a gentleman, and such an idea goes against the grain."

Aguilar's face went red, then became deathly pale, chill as cold clay.

"*Señor*," he said haughtily, "I desire this woman. It was to obtain her that I brought you here, gave this place into your hands."

"Betrayed your own people to buccaneers, eh?" struck in Doña Inez.

"None the less, she wants none of you," said Burke, and turned to her. "Do you desire to claim my protection against this man?"

"You are a *caballero*," she returned quickly. "Yes!"

Burke bowed, and then looked at the Spaniard.

"You have heard, my friend. There is no more to be said. This lady is not to be molested by you or any one else."

For an instant Aguilar looked at him with bitter, venomous eyes, then shrugged.

"Very well," he said, and turning on his heel, strode from the room. Burke looked after him thoughtfully, for he had expected the man to draw sword upon him, at the least. Then, as Doña Inez came to him and caught his arm in impulsive thanks, he bowed over her slender fingers and laughed softly into her dark eyes.

"Fear not, little dove," he said in Spanish. "You'll not be harmed; my men are guarding the doors."

So, turning, he strode out of the room.

CHAPTER V

BETRAYED

BURKE STRAIGHTWAY forgot Aguilar; a confused tumult of yelling, pierced by the explosions of musketry, reached him, and he left the house, to stand appalled by what he saw.

About the Spanish camp by the river, men were darting through the cane. The level sunlight glinted upon arrows, while the musketeers were sending bullets at their assailants, a cloud of powder smoke veiling the tents from the sight of Burke. The maroons had struck, suddenly and swiftly, burning the cane fields and the outer buildings as they came, so that a huge cloud of black smoke was billowing up from the fields beyond the camp.

Garf O'Malley, busily sending the last of the galleon's gold down to the wharf, came up with a question; but Burke shrugged.

"It's none of our affair, Garf. The Spaniards are soldiers. Those poor devils of maroons are ill-armed, but just as anxious to fight. Let 'em fight if they like. They'll probably get sufficient plunder to make the game worth while, too. You're all through here? Then if any of the maroons come to talk with me, I'll send them on to the galleon to get powder and arms. I'll want one of the French filibusters who can talk with them, unless they speak Spanish. Go ahead with the galleon's cargo, and I'll keep an eye on things."

So O'Malley departed, and Burke, drawing most of Malachi's men outside the house, broached a barrel of wine and remained ready, like a good general, to act where most needed. Aguilar, meantime, passed down to the wharf and stepped aboard one of the boats that plied out to the frigate with gold and plunder. None gainsaid him; every one knew he had joined them and helped place San Isidro in their hands, and all were now desperately busy, for the work ahead would consume the better part of the morning. Aboard the frigate, Aguilar went up to Long Dan O'Neill, one of Burke's Irishry who had been given temporary charge.

"The cap'n wants you to send the prisoners ashore," he said coolly, and pointed to the strip of beach beneath the knob of the battery. "Land them there. They're to be placed under guard up above. I'll go down and see that they make no trouble."

He turned and went below to the mess cabin where the hapless officers, now wide awake, crowded at the ports to see what was happening ashore. The guards passed him into the cabin at once. He closed the door and looked at the Spaniards, whose scowling faces were turned toward him.

"Señores!" exclaimed Aguilar swiftly. "The time is come! I had to act as I did last night to throw these buccaneers off guard. Now, *caballeros,* we strike for Spain! They are sending you ashore; your swords have not been taken from you. Let me lead the way to the battery. When you gain it, you shall see that I am not deceiving you. Be ready, strike hard, spare not! Don Balthazar, make your own arrangements. The landward guns you must turn on the Indios who attack the camp. The seaward guns, turn on this ship and her men. Careful, now! Not a word, not a look, or they'll suspect something!"

He left the cabin abruptly and went on deck again, whither they were presently led and sent down into an empty boat, with rowers to land them. It was true that Burke had not taken their weapons, wishing to spare them this indignity. Aguilar followed into the boat, and she put off for the spot indicated.

FIRST TO land, Aguilar set off briskly, climbing the path to the knoll above. They followed him more slowly, by no means sure of him, incredulous at his words. The camp beside the river was surrounded by leaping, yelling maroons, who discharged arrows at the tents and were gone before the muskets could reach them.

The wind carried the smoke from the burning huts and cane fields well away to landward.

"How goes it, *señor?*" demanded Tout-en-Muscles, as Aguilar reached the gate in the stone wall. "Who are these Spaniards?"

"The prisoners from the frigate," answered Aguilar. "The captain has ordered them to come here, yield their arms, and remain tied up until we have departed. Have you a pistol? I'm to signal him the moment they are safely stowed."

"Aye," said Tout-en-Muscles.

Drawing a pistol from his belt, he handed it to Aguilar.

The file of officers was now approaching the gateway. Aguilar coolly inspected the priming of the pistol; turning, he lifted the weapon, placed it against the broad back of Tout-en-Muscles, and pulled the trigger.

With the explosion, his sword leaped from its scabbard. He ran a second Frenchman through the body and hurled himself with incredible agility upon a third, while the Spanish officers came bursting into the place, swords out. The startled, amazed buccaneers were taken completely off guard. Some were cut down before they could draw weapon, the others were driven back into a corner of the walls. There, fighting to the last, they died.

The guns, already loaded, with matches alight in their stocks, had but to be aimed afresh. To the staff above the battery, the flag of Spain was run up; then, with a thunderous crash, the first gun spewed a hail of lead over the camp, among the figures of the maroons in the cane field.

Gun after gun spoke out, crash after crash reëchoed as the brazen throats roared forth their message of death. Lead hailed among the men who thronged about the galleon, the boats and wharf. The water spurted. Cries broke out from the frigate as the shot from two of the guns poured into her, raking her decks.

"Reload, reload quickly!" shouted Aguilar. "Now, if those fools in camp will take their chance—"

"Trust them," said Don Balthazar. "Sergeant Ruiz is an old soldier and needs no orders—Look! Look!"

The flag of Spain above the battery, the murderous discharges of those guns, had made everything clear enough to Burke's men. The buccaneers thronging the shore were seized with dismay and panic, and those aboard the frigate likewise, who perceived that those guns would soon shatter their ship or dismast her. Already they were shaking out her canvas, swarming aloft.

Swiftest of all to act, however, was Sergeant Ruiz. Almost before the thunder of the guns had died, his veterans were streaming out of the camp and pouring straight down upon the wharf and galleon, full two hundred of them, with morions and pikes glittering in the morning sunlight, while the seamen from the galleon made shift to defend the camp itself against the demoralized maroons.

Another thunder-roar, and another; the officers, working like mad, were getting the guns reloaded and laid. Bags of bullets spewed down upon the boats and water and frigate. A third gun roared out, and a solid shot smashed into the poop of the frigate with fearful effect. Men were swarming aboard her now, piling out in boats, swimming frantically.

Caught in that wild rush of despairing men, Garf O'Malley was struck down, flung into a boat, and came to himself aboard the frigate to find her cable cut. She was drifting out with the tide, her topsails slanted to catch the wind and drive her faster. Behind her came another boat or two from shore, half filled with men, and the guns in the battery above plumped down shot at her, gun after gun, in a vain effort to dismast her.

Not at once did O'Malley realize that Burke was not aboard the frigate.

BEFORE DENIS BURKE, at the plantation house, could realize what was going on—he was at the moment conferring with two of the leaders of the maroons—the worst had happened. Hidden from his sight, the Spaniards pouring down the river bank toward the shore struck upon the buccaneers there.

Burke, gathering his men from the house, starting for the shore, saw then that he was cut off. The steel Spanish helmets were around the galleon, on the wharf, more of them flooding forward into sight. Men were cut down as they scrambled into the boats. Some fought; a little knot of them checked the soldiery, let most of the boats get away safely. Then the pikes thrust them down. And the frigate was sailing out.

Glancing around, Burke found Malachi and ten men with him. The maroons had fled. Their attack on the camp was abandoned. Swiftly he perceived that there was no chance of escape now. They were entirely cut off from shore, and already parties of the Spaniards were bursting up toward the house as though to attack them.

"Back!" ordered Burke calmly. "Malachi! Get those muskets and pistols we found in the house and post the men about the wall."

"At once, your honor," said Malachi, and went to obey.

Burke followed them slowly back to the house, and there paused, watching the Madre de Dios slip away from his sight, out of the harbor. Something must have happened to Garf O'Malley, else the bearded seaman would never have thus deserted him. He, himself, he knew, was utterly lost. Yet, despite the chagrin that consumed him, despite the terrific force of this blow that had fallen in the very moment of triumph, he remained cool, collected, his brain working fast.

Aguilar! Now he knew why the man had gone away so quietly. Somehow, Aguilar had seized the battery, which was the key to San Isidro.

"That Spanish lass in there had the right idea of him," thought Burke bitterly. "I should ha' taken warning then and there. Well, it's all my own fault! Serves me right. Aguilar no doubt put that rascal Cotton up to killing me; that's what the fellow meant about earning the money. Aye, Aguilar had treachery in his mind, one way or another, from the first! Well, praise be, Denis Burke dies clean when he comes to the end o' the road. And this is what I get for leaving the sea, eh? There's no luck ashore for me. The luck o' the sea Burkes—"

His shoulders straightened a little. The dancing flame came back into his blue eyes, the touch of laughter to his lips. He was himself again, his agile brain darting ahead, making plans, resilient in disaster as in victory. At least, he reflected, most of the galleon's gold had gone aboard the frigate ere she put out; Garf O'Malley, if he still lived, would have that much more freight of fortune aboard!

SO THE Spanish soldiers, drawing near, halted and looked in wonder at him as he stood there, not heeding their approach, unmindful of them; they knew not whether he were friend or foe, in his fine Genoa velvet and Mechlin lace, his smiling unconcern, his immobility. Behind him, Malachi had distributed his men about the low wall which surrounded the front portion of the house—a little wall, built for ornament and to inclose a garden, rather than for defense. The Spaniards had no muskets, and could see the matches smoking along the wall, so they prudently waited.

"*Señor,*" said one of them, lifting his voice to Burke, "are you of the filibusters?"

"I am El Capitan Mayo," said Burke, and his fluent Spanish told them nothing. "Is that Don Balthazar I see coming?"

The soldiers stood irresolute. It was indeed Don Balthazar approaching from the beach, with one or two of his officers, and Don Salcedo, and Aguilar at his elbow. At this, Burke perceived readily enough what had taken place, and could not but feel a grudging admiration for the man whose quick wits and soldier's eye had quite wrecked him.

Seeing already that Burke was in his grasp, Don Balthazar strode grimly on and stopped a little beyond the reach of bullets.

"*Buenas dias, señor,*" he called to Burke, and bowed in his stately Spanish fashion, quite gravely. "As you see, it has pleased God to destroy your hopes. I trust you will surrender at once, before we fetch up musketeers to work upon you?"

"Gladly, *señor,*" returned Burke. "On condition that I go free with my men, and that you give us a boat with water and provisions."

"That I cannot do, *señor,*" replied Don Balthazar. "You and your men must go to Santo Domingo to be tried as filibusters and pirates."

Burke bowed. "In that case, *señor,* we do not surrender."

Now Don Salcedo cried out suddenly, and caught the proud Spaniard's arm, and spoke to him. At the man's concern, Burke remembered Doña Inez and the other women inside there.

"There are ladies in the house," spoke out Don Balthazar abruptly. "You are, no doubt, holding them as hostages? That will not avail you, Captain Mayo—"

"Devil take you!" exclaimed Burke angrily. "What do you take me for, then? No, I don't save my neck by hiding behind women. Ho there, Malachi! Send out the women in the house, and hurt them not."

The Spaniards stared at him in no little wonder, and Don Balthazar bowed gravely.

"*Señor,* you are a true *caballero,*" he called. "It is a great regret that I must kill you."

"Faith," said Burke whimsically, "it'll be sorrow to me if you do!"

So presently Doña Inez, her two attendants, and three other frightened women were brought out of the house, and Burke bowed politely to them as they passed him, and felt the clear eyes of the girl rest upon him for a moment. Then he turned and strode up to the heavy gate of the house, which was already flung shut and barred.

"Ready, Malachi!" he called.

CHAPTER VI

GUN SMOKE

THERE WAS some little delay in making the attack, for Doña Inez had a story to tell, and begged hard for Burke's life. Aguilar, however, had a word or two to say about this.

"Señores," he said, glancing about the little group of officers, "you know what happened there aboard the ship, how I was forced to pretend that I wished to hang Don Salcedo? Well, it was the same here ashore. My intention was to get Doña Inez out to safety, until I perceived that this Captain Mayo meant her no harm. I played a part, *por dios,* and I played it well! Now you have seen for yourself where the truth lies. Your very presence here displays it."

"That is, indeed, indisputable," said Don Balthazar.

Doña Inez broke in hotly, telling of Aguilar's words and actions, but Aguilar's hearty laughter, his amused explanation, was more than sufficient to convince them all, save possibly Doña Inez.

With no further argument, the Spaniards decided to attack at once, and the women were sent on down to the cool shade of the sheds by the beach.

At this moment a single musket was discharged from the house wall, and Aguilar fell forward as his knees loosened. The group scattered hastily. Two men picked up Aguilar, and it was seen that the heavy ball, nearly spent as it was, had struck him over the right eye, giving a nasty wound and stunning him, but nothing worse.

A trumpeter came up, his clarion shrilled, and muskets began to speak. The Spaniards were attacking the *hacienda,* either distrusting their own officers now, or not knowing of their presence.

That twelve men should attempt to defend all that house against hundreds, was of course sheer madness; yet for a little they did defend it with musket and pistol, most of them being old soldiers who knew their business. The serried lines of Spain moved up against them, with volley after volley of musketry that chipped the bricks and plaster, but did no hurt, while dead and injured men lay ever more thickly strewn out in the white sunlight. Again and again the glinting helmets came up to the very wall itself, only to have keen swords stab out at them from men beyond their reach, while pikes lunged up in vain.

But presently an end came to this, for the Spaniards got in at the rear of the house and others at windows, so that Burke and his men were driven into one corner of the place and bullets were hailed at them thickly. Powder-smoke filled all the rooms and choked them, darkening everything before their eyes.

In this obscurity the battle became a frenzied madness, and all sense of order, of direction or friend or foe, was clear lost. Spaniard fought Spaniard; there was a wild, fierce chaos of dark sweeping shapes, of exploding pistols, of glinting weapons. Burke, swept away in a rush, came staggering out into the patio and found that he was alone there among the enemy, and retreat cut off.

The fresh air cleared his brain and he flung himself at them with a wild shout, and they broke before him. One man, an officer, flung up rapier and met his attack stoutly; for a little they fought, until the golden-hilted Toledo went through the Spaniard's throat. Then appeared pikes, ringing him round, holding him hemmed into a corner, and Burke was offered once more a chance to save himself.

He laughed at this, knocked up a pike, and the man who held it fell to his thrust. Almost he broke them, but a wounded man caught his ankle and he fell forward—and then they were on him in a heap, dragging him down, beating him into insensibility with their hands.

AFTER A time Burke wakened, to find himself in a room

with Malachi Halloran and four others of his men, all of them much wounded, yet none so hurt as to be disabled. Their wounds had been washed and bound up—by order of Don Balthazar, as Malachi informed him. Food and wine were on a table, they were free to move about; but an iron grille closed the window opening and the door was barred shut. The afternoon was partly gone; time had passed.

There was little talk; the six men ate and drank, sat listlessly in the heat, cursed their wounds and the Spaniards. Presently one of them went to the grilled window, and Burke realized that the sun had died out.

"Storm," said the man. "The sky's all dun gray. Hurricane."

The same unspoken thought was in all their minds. Burke had been thinking of Garf O'Malley and the frigate. Garf would undoubtedly hang off and on the coast, make some attempt at a rescue. Hurricane would end all that, however; with a ship all foul and sailing sluggishly, this coast was dangerous in the extreme.

"Most of the gold went aboard," spoke up Malachi suddenly. "I watched it."

Burke chuckled. "I'd like to change places with that gold—eh? That's an idea, lads. Ransom! Why not?"

They were still discussing this chance, which looked very slender in view of the coming hurricane, when the door was unbarred and opened. An officer and a number of guards stood there, and the officer addressed Burke somewhat formally.

"Captain Mayo, Don Balthazar wishes to invite you to dinner, provided you will give your parole of honor not to attempt escape or aught against him."

"With all my heart! Agreed," said Burke eagerly. "Dinner? At this hour?"

"Thanks to you, *señor,*" and the other smiled, "we have not eaten this day. Come."

"I'll do what I can, lads," said Burke to the others, and so departed.

In the large dining room of the house, now arranged for dinner with such furniture as had escaped pillage and breakage, he found Don Balthazar, Don Salcedo, Aguilar and four other officers, who greeted him with grave bows. Burke saw that Aguilar wore his beloved Toledo blade, and a pulse hammered at his temple, but he controlled his anger and made courteous response to their greetings.

"You entertained us yesterday, we entertain you to-day, *señor*," said Don Balthazar. "Storm draws down; what matter? Let us have lights."

The sun vanished altogether, even while he was speaking. Ten minutes later the hurricane was sweeping around, threatening to hurl the very buildings into the sea. With fresh dismay, Burke perceived that it was from the south, which meant that the frigate must be blown far out into the Atlantic.

In any case, Burke presently learned that there was no hope whatever of ransom. Politely but firmly Don Balthazar refused to consider the matter, stating that he was in duty bound to send his prisoners to Santo Domingo for trial, then turned to Aguilar.

"Señor Conde," he said, "since you have asked for this mission, it is granted you. The letters will be prepared this evening. We have your word that you will rejoin us here, if the Council still desires that you be sent to Spain for trial, though in my opinion the letters which I will give you will pardon you entirely. Your services have been so valuable that they must certainly overbear all else. This tempest will soon be past. I think you may count on leaving at dawn with the smaller of the two coasters."

"Thank you, *señor* don," returned Aguilar, giving Burke one mocking glance. "Then I shall go aboard and make ready for the reception of my guests, as soon as this wind has blown out."

Despite the temptation, Burke put away the desire to exchange plain speech with Aguilar. In the eyes of these Spaniards, he himself was treated as an honorable enemy, a gentleman of their own caliber; restraint was here more powerful than hot words, which would effect nothing. Aguilar had fooled them very neatly, and would probably upbuild his shattered fortunes again upon the death of Burke. For trial at Santo Domingo could have but one end. A buccaneer was an outlaw, and if he failed he paid the price for inefficiency.

So they feasted, while the storm quickly blew itself out. An hour or so later it was gone, and the splendid glow of sunset took its place, bringing back the daylight. Burke saw nothing of any woman, although Don Salcedo thanked him with great courtesy for his consideration in sending Doña Inez to safety; the wine was passed, the pipes were filled with tobacco, and another hour was passed in talk of campaigns. Burke had reason to thank Aguilar for but one thing—silence as regarded his true name. But perhaps Aguilar forgot this altogether.

Before Burke was taken back to his comrades he heard a report brought in that, just before the hurricane broke, the Madre de Dios had been seen far out at sea, and afterward had not come in sight again. So he knew that Garf O'Malley was utterly beyond giving him any help.

COURTESY HAD an end, however. When Burke was led into the room where Malachi and the other four awaited him, soldiers trooped in bearing cumbrous chains and padlocks for wrists and ankles. In vain did Burke protest, offer to give parole for the night at least. The officer in command was inflexible, stating that this was done by order of Don Balthazar, and one by one the six captives were ironed and padlocked. Men foredoomed to death could not be trusted against temptation, and only too well did the Spaniards know of what such men were capable in extremity.

"Faith, my lads," said Burke when they were alone again, "there is no help for us now. No ransom will be considered, and there's none to give it, for Garf O'Malley has been blown far out to sea, and with morning we'll be gone to Santo Domingo under that devil Aguilar. Sorry the day you ever met a luckless man and took service with him!"

"Cheer up, your honor," said old Malachi stoutly. "Many's the time we have been in worse places than this. And what of it, after all? Sure, no man lives forever."

"And we die in good company," said another, with a laugh. "Who could die better than with a Burke of the MacWilliam blood to show the way? Few men have had such honor."

Burke laughed at this, and his spirits rose. "Faith, lads, we're not dead yet, so let's get some sleep while we may!"

He stretched out, but for a long while the discomfort of the irons and chains kept him from any sleep. Also, discouragement sat heavily upon him; the uselessness of his futile life weighed in keenly on his spirit. The years passed in somber review before him. Ireland in the old days, the stern battle for worthless King James, exile, confiscation of all he had and attainder for treason.

A new life begun in France with the Wild Geese, and well begun. Lieutenant-colonel in the Irish Brigade, Chevalier of St. Michel, honors and fame before him—and all flung away in one reckless moment when King Louis would have him do service he accounted dishonorable. Now he was homeless, a man without a country. In one blow he had gained a great frigate, wealth immeasurable, only to lose everything by the vilest treachery. And ahead was the garotte in the hot sunlight of Santo Domingo and his comrades dead around him; the execution of a criminal, a felon. This would be the end.

He squirmed uneasily, tortured by the thought.

"CAPTAIN MAYO! *El señor capitán!*"

Upon the darkness of the room stole the words, a voice soft and fearful breathing them. Burke came to one elbow, looked around. At the open window, against the iron grille, bulked a shape dark against the stars. He rose, holding the chains to stifle their clinking.

"One moment," he answered. "I come."

Sudden wild hope thrilled in him, hope of the impossible. A messenger from O'Malley after all. Perhaps an Indian, with word that the maroons were coming to the rescue. Even as these thoughts darted through his brain, he realized how wild, how utterly beyond reason they were. He came close to the window and saw a hooded shape there, head and shoulders dimly visible in the gloom.

"Who are you?" he asked.

For answer, the hood was pulled aside, and he looked into the dimly seen face of Doña Inez.

All hope was shredded away from him in the instant.

"I had to see you," she said softly. "Aguilar—that beast! He has fooled them all, but he has not fooled me. Even my father believes he speaks the truth. But I know! I have not given you thanks, *señor,* for all you did—"

"It is nothing," murmured Burke in the conventional Spanish response.

"It is a great deal," she went on quietly. "You are chained, *señor,* is it not?"

"Chained," said Burke. "And the chains are padlocked, as is done with slaves."

"Yes, they are the padlocks used for the slaves," she responded. "I know, because my uncle gave Don Balthazar the key which unlocks them all. But there was another key also, and this I stole out of my uncle's room to-night. He will think it has been lost. Here it is, *señor.* It is all that I can do for you, except to pray for your safety. Hide the key, for I heard them giving orders to search you when they took you out to the boat in the morning. They are afraid you might have weapons. *Adios, caballero! Adios!*"

She was gone before Burke could speak or thank her. He heard the clink of iron striking the floor, and, finding her indeed clear gone, stooped to retrieve the key. His fingers closed on it after a moment—a small bit of iron, as keys went, but still too large to be conveniently hidden in a pocket.

Hope flamed in him for a moment, then died again as he considered. There were guards outside the barred door; the grille at the window was too strong to be easily broken, and certainly could not be broken without noise. They could not escape from the house, reach the shore, and get hold of a boat—no, it was hopeless, would only cause them to be shot down in the attempt.

Burke tucked away the key and lay down to sleep again, and this time slumber came to him at once. Neither Malachi nor any of the other men had been awakened.

CHAPTER VII

BURKES SURPRISE

WITH SUNRISE, the prisoners were wakened to a hearty morning meal, and immediately afterward were led out under close guard.

The morning was fresh and clear, all signs of storm had vanished, and the sea appeared gentle. The Spanish soldiers had gathered in groups to stare at the captives, but none of the higher officers appeared.

Marched down to the wharf, Burke and the other five were embarked and taken out to one of the two coasters lying at anchor—a small craft, whose crew of half a dozen men had been augmented by as many soldiers to act as guard. Aguilar met them as they came over the rail, and bowed ironically to Burke.

"Good morning, *señor!* So our honest Captain Mayo is about to take his last voyage, eh? Being somewhat acquainted with you and your men, my friend, I think we'll just make sure that you have no means of avoiding your destiny. One at a time, guards!"

Burke was seized by two of the soldiers, who searched him thoroughly and efficiently, turning everything out of his pockets, tearing the jeweled star from his breast, not leaving him so much as the pipe and packet of tobacco he had obtained the previous night from Don Balthazar.

Malachi and the other four men suffered the same fate. When all was finished, Aguilar escorted his prisoners aft and down the companion to a stuffy little main cabin, barely large enough to contain them all.

"Here you are, *señores!*" he exclaimed genially. "Not as large, perhaps, as your late roomy quarters aboard your frigate, but large enough to contain your blasted hopes for a day. And ere night comes, we shall be in Santo Domingo, the wind being fair. Your ship, let me add, has not been sighted again, so dream not that she will rescue you. You are content, my honest Captain Mayo?"

Burke merely nodded. Then Aguilar came close to him and peered into his face, with savage violet eyes that burned hot.

"Fool!" he said in a low, tense voice. "You thought me helpless, you thought that you could prate and put on fine airs at my expense, balk me of all you had promised—and that I would accept it with impunity! You should know Irish blood better than that. This time to-morrow you'll be stretched on the rack, do you hear? They torture gentry of your kidney in Santo Domingo, let me tell you!"

Burke looked at him hard, blue eyes flaming into violet, and an angry flush mantled his cheek, but he said no word. Aguilar, he perceived, bore him all the virulent hatred cherished by one man toward another whom he had deeply wronged. Then, with a short laugh, Aguilar lifted a hand and struck Burke across the face.

Still Burke said no word, uttered no sound. Aguilar turned away and spoke to the soldiers at the door, in the passage outside.

"Two men remain here all the time, awake and on watch. See to it, corporal! I'll keep the key of their irons myself. They're not to be allowed on deck or to leave this room until we're in Santo Domingo harbor."

"*Si, señor* don," replied the corporal. "You need have no fear."

So Aguilar went away, the door was closed, the six were alone. Malachi Halloran gave Burke a queer look.

"Why did not your honor tell that dog what we think of him?"

Burke looked at him, smiled a little, but made no answer. He waited, listening. From the deck above came the *thud-thud* of feet, the voices of men and creaking of sheaves as the canvas was let out and the yards swung around; other voices from alongside rose in farewell. Then the little ship was moving through the water, and presently began to heel over a trifle, signifying she was out of the cove and leaning to the drive of the morning breeze.

THEN BURKE opened his mouth, thrust with his tongue, and something plopped out into his lap.

"The devil!" he exclaimed ruefully. "I all but swallowed it when that hound struck me!"

"Eh?" said Malachi, while they all stared at him. "What is it, your honor?"

Burke chuckled. "What should it be, but the luck of the sea Burkes? Lean forward, you rogue, and hold out your hands to me!"

His blue eyes were dancing merrily, and he fumbled in his lap until the iron key came into his fingers. A low word broke from the others at sight of it, and Malachi leaned forward, all agape with incredulity, until Burke got the key into the padlock and turned it easily. The padlock opened and the chains fell away.

One by one they were freed of their bonds, and sat rubbing at their wrists in grim silence, while Burke told how he had come by the key.

"Now, my lads, we've no time to lose," he continued cheerfully. "Every league we sail toward Santo Domingo puts us into greater jeopardy. Luck of the sea Burkes is it? Faith, we'll need all the luck there is! Two of you get over by the door. Malachi, stay with me. Ready, now? Throat and sword-arm, men! Not a cry, remember, not a shout nor sound!"

"Soldados!" He lifted his voice to the guards outside. *"Soldados!* We perish of thirst! Give us water, for love of the saints!"

He cocked his head, listening, then grinned at Malachi as a gruff order sounded outside. One of the guards had gone to fetch water.

Two of the men had moved over close to the door. The others sat beside Malachi and Burke, chains draped loosely about their wrists, heads drooping. Steps sounded, and the door was flung open. One soldier halted in the doorway, while his companion came forward, bearing an earthen jar of water.

"Thanks, *caballero,*" said Burke, lifting his head. The water-bearer jeered down at him.

"Thank me not, dog! If I had my way, I'd see all of you roasted alive here, as you will be in hell. Thank soft-hearted Juan yonder, if there must be thanks."

"Well said, well said!" returned Burke, and laughed a little. "For that, the life of Juan shall be spared, and you shall go very quickly to hell yourself."

"Say you so, indeed?" The soldier kicked at him viciously. "Well, here is your water, dog, and you'll get no more, so make the most of it."

With this, he leaned over to set down the earthen jar; Malachi's hands flew up, gripped about his throat, dragged him down. Burke caught at his arm, tore the poniard from his grasp, and buried it in his heart.

Then, leaping erect, Burke saw the other guard down and struggling. As he had ordered, the man's life was spared; a moment later he was securely bound and gagged, after the breastplate had been unbuckled. One of the men donned it hurriedly, caught up the fallen helmet, seized the fallen pike. There was a swift distribution of the captured weapons, pikes and daggers. Burke took none of them, but signed the others to remain quiet, and stepped out into the passage. This was short and narrow, the doors of cabins opening off it, with the companionway at the end.

Quietly, Burke opened one door after another, and so came upon that which he sought, in a small cabin that caught the sea wind in its open port. Aguilar lay stretched out in the berth, sound asleep. For a moment Burke regarded him, chuckling softly, then stepped in and caught up his own gold-hilted Toledo and belt from the pile of clothes beside the berth. In the door was its cumbrous key. Placing it on the outside of the lock, Burke slipped outside and drew the door shut, then turned the key and left it.

A moment later he had rejoined his own men.

"All right, lads!" His voice rang out vibrantly. "Up and at 'em! Cut down the soldiers, but spare the poor devils of seamen if they surrender. Come on!"

On the quarter-deck were grouped four soldiers, with their corporal and the ship's sailing-master and helmsman, throwing dice. The seamen forward were all watching a school of porpoises trailing along at a little distance. The coast was three or four miles away; no other sail was in sight.

A TERRIBLE thing these men saw as from the companionway burst Burke, sword in hand, and the other captives following him—free, armed, ready to come to grips! The soldiers caught at their weapons, saw Burke's rapier transfix their corporal, then were rolling on the deck, the buccaneers at their throats. The master of the ship drew out a dagger and was in the act of plunging it into Malachi's back, when the Toledo passed through him from breast to back, and he fell sprawling.

Brief and savage was that fight, sharp with ferocity, a struggle for life or death. None of Burke's men died there; of the Spaniards, one alone begged for quarter, and it was given him. While they took him below and left him with the other, Burke looked at the seamen, who had not offered to join them in the fight, and beckoned them aft.

"This is now my ship," he told them. "Hand over your knives! Work her for me to Le Cap, and you shall go free and be well rewarded. Refuse—"

"Señor, we do not refuse!" cried one of them, falling to his knees. "More, we wish to join your crew and take to filibustering!"

"Is this true?" said Burke, looking at them. One and all assented, and what was more to the point, swore on the cross there at the poop that they would serve him faithfully. None the less, he took all weapons from them, then sent them forward, and Malachi headed the ship about to the north.

A cry came from aloft, whither one of the men had mounted. Hearing it, Burke leaped into the shrouds, stood for a moment staring off to starboard, and caught sight of a fleck of white there to seaward. He passed the word, and one of the seamen came and joined him, also looking at the distant sail.

"Señor," said the man soberly, "she is undoubtedly a ship of Spain."

"Not my ship?" asked Burke.

"No, *señor.* Your canvas was brown, especially the topsails. This is white. And if we hold to the north, she will assuredly cut us off."

"Very well," said Burke coolly. He leaped back to the deck, and Malachi, from the helm, gave him an anxious look. "A Spaniard, Malachi. Hold steady for the north. Here, one of you! Go below and unlock the door of Aguilar's cabin, and let him come on deck."

"YOUR HONOR," said Malachi, "that ship yonder looms up fast. She is speedy and a great ship."

"But she hasn't the luck o' the sea Burkes, Malachi!" and Denis Burke's laugh was gay as he glanced over the rail at the white fleck. "She's a Spaniard, and she can outsail us two for one—this sorry ship moves like a tub in the water. She can outfight us. But, Malachi, she hasn't a Burke aboard her! Well, there comes my man. Stand back, all!"

"But how do we steer, your honor?" howled Malachi, as Burke started away at sight of Aguilar emerging on deck.

"Head straight for her!" flung back Burke.

Conde de Aguilar, who had been born an O'Donnell by his own word, stepped out coolly on deck and glanced around. He perceived instantly that he was a lost man, but gave no sign of the dismay and stupefaction that must have seized him, after the first involuntary gesture of angry incredulity.

When he faced about to meet Burke, however, the laugh on his lips was belied by the desperation in his steady gaze.

"You are a man of surprises, *caballero!*" he exclaimed negligently. "I see that I should not have gone to sleep."

"I think," said Burke, looking at him, "that I am closer to liking you in this moment than ever before, although that is not very close."

Aguilar shrugged. "A pox on your likes, and you, too! Well, I am empty-handed. What shall you do now? Hang me?"

"By all right, yes." Burke's gaze grew icy. "If you only possessed a weapon—"

"But I have," said Aguilar. "There's a rapier in the stuff I fetched aboard—my own old weapon."

"Send one of the seamen for it," said Burke, and beckoned to one of the men. Aguilar told him where the sword was, and the man went below at a nod from Burke.

"You are in earnest, then?" said Aguilar, looking curiously at him. "Yes, you are that sort of a fool. You should have been a knight-errant, a sprig of chivalry."

"I am something better," said Burke calmly. "An Irishman."

Aguilar laughed sneeringly at this, and looking out to sea, saw the fleck of white. A change came into his face, and he flung Burke a glance, but Burke smiled a little and nodded.

"Yes, I see her. She'll not come in time to save you."

"Perhaps not," said the other reflectively. "Three, four miles distant—well over a league, eh? But I know her; aye, it's the fighting galleon San Marcos! She went out a day ahead of us to run down two pestilent French filibusters who were ravaging the coast. The same two whom you cozened so neatly, no doubt. So—Here's the blade, eh? The more fool you."

The seaman had returned, and Aguilar caught the rapier thrust at him, and unsheathed it. He looked at Burke as he tested the blade.

"No one to hit me from behind this time, eh?"

Burke drew out his own Toledo. *"En garde!"* he said sharply.

NEXT INSTANT the two blades met, crossed, threw back the sunlight in a dazzling succession of thrusts and ripostes. Now, as at their first encounter, Burke quickly perceived that he was indeed dealing with one who was a master swordsman; if he himself had been the best blade in France, here was one fully as good if not better. The men watched, fascinated, while Malachi peered from over the helm as he held the vessel steady before the wind, straight for that ominous cloud of white canvas rushing closer with each moment.

Try as he might, Burke could not get within the guard of that steel wrist, nor find any flicker of weakness in the glaring violet eyes that met his gaze. Both men fenced coolly, carefully, with as much deliberation as though in a *salle d'armes,* each feeling out the other. Not for long did this last, however. Burke's point slipped in; Aguilar leaped backward with amazing agility—not far enough to escape the lunge that brought out a spreading crimson smear over his heart, but far enough to spoil its force. Then, as though the burn of the wound had maddened him, he attacked with a vicious ferocity that all but attained its aim.

Before this attack, Burke exerted every ounce of his strength, his skill, his own catlike agility. Twice that glittering point touched him, once in the shoulder, once in the upper arm, though neither was a disabling hit. Then, as the mad savagery of the attack died down, his own force was put out in a swift and deadly offensive that, in turn, put Aguilar on a furious and desperate defense.

The white sun smote down upon the two men. Sweat poured into their eyes, their breath was coming in panting gasps as they fought. Burke knew himself tiring rapidly now, for that first mad attack had sapped his strength; but Aguilar was in no better plight.

And now Aguilar, with a swift gathering of every energy, suddenly launched a new attack. Coolness had deserted him, and he panted hoarse oaths as he drove in, his bloodshot eyes alight with blood-lust. Twice Burke seemed lost, and in fact accounted himself lost, but agility each time saved him. Cool enough, he was certain now of the mastery, for Aguilar's fury was increasing, he was forgetting his caution, was going to desperate extremes to reach his enemy.

Then his chance came, in what he intended as a mere feint at disarming Aguilar in order to follow with the deadly lunge in seconds. Aguilar thrust in carte over the arm; Burke parried with the counter in carte, let the other recover, and then abruptly, his wrist reversed, leaned on Aguilar's blade with the edge of his own, driving it away.

Perhaps Aguilar had not expected the trick, perhaps sweat caused the hilt to slip in his hand. Burke himself was astonished to see the other blade go twirling away out of Aguilar's grasp and over the rail into the sea.

A hoarse and terrible cry burst from Aguilar. Then he hurled himself forward, dashed the blade of Burke aside, and in frantic fury caught Burke by the throat and bore him backward, face against face, breast against breast, gripping him so close that the Toledo was useless. Not so the golden hilt, however.

This swept up in Burke's hand, and the rough massy gold smashed into the frenzied countenance of Aguilar—smashed home again and again, cutting skin and flesh to ribbons, until a final blow over the temple dropped the frothing man senseless. Burke came to his feet, as the other men rushed forward, and his voice checked their weapons.

"Back!" he panted hoarsely, threatening them. "Back!"

"Leave us kill him, your honor!" cried one of them. "Sure, it's a mad dog he is!"

"Quiet!" Burke sobbed for breath. "Search him, one of you.

He has letters. I want them."

Neither man had removed doublet or hose. Leaning over the senseless, bleeding Aguilar, whose left face was all a mask of blood from his hurts, one of the men searched through his clothes and rose, bearing two crumpled letters gay with seals—those sent by Don Balthazar. Burke seized them, glanced at them, and thrust them into his pocket.

"Shall we hang him, your honor?" cried out Malachi eagerly from the helm.

"Silence!" ordered Burke. "Eh? What the devil is all this?"

THE SPANISH seamen, poor wretches, were coming forward in a body, babbling with fear. One of them hushed the others, and cried out in terror:

"Señor! Señor don! Put ropes on us, so that it will not appear that we have joined you! She is indeed the San Marcos, and they will hang us if they think we gave you aid!"

Burke looked up and saw the Spanish ship, a towering mass of canvas, so close that he was astonished at sight of her. Even as he looked, her flag went up, and a drift of white broke from her bow, and the *bang* of a gun came to them across the wind. He awakened abruptly.

"Quick, Malachi! Lay close aboard her! You men, don helmet and breastplate swiftly from those soldiers! Seamen to the lines—obey! No harm shall come to any of you! Here, two of you! Get irons from below and put this man in chains. Quickly!"

So it fell out that the great Spanish ship found the little coaster hove to, awaiting her, and rounded in over the dancing waves, a towering cloud of canvas, until she was close alongside. A voice hailed, asking who they were, and Burke leaped to the rail.

"An officer of the Santa Trinidad!' he called back. "We bear a prisoner and letters from Don Balthazar Olivares to Santo Domingo, but have sprung a bad leak and must get back to San Isidro. Can you send a boat to take the letters and prisoner?"

"Gladly, *señor*," came the response.

A boat was lowered from the galleon, and came dancing over the long ocean rollers to the little coaster. Presently a bronzed, bearded officer came aboard and looked about the deck with curious eyes, and saluted Burke as the latter stepped forward.

"I am the vice-captain Hernan Mendez y Pinto, *señor*," he said courteously.

"And I"—Burke returned his bow gallantly—"am Don Diego Ramirez de Sotomayor y Corrubia, and kiss your feet, *señor* vice-captain. This"—he pointed toward the bound, bloody, senseless Aguilar—"is a most renowned and desperate filibuster, one Captain Mayo by name, who had the audacity to attack us at San Isidro. He was defeated and captured by the skill and courage of the illustrious Don Balthazar Olivares, and was being sent by this accursed vessel to Santo Domingo. We have sprung a bad leak; this desperate dog broke loose and almost got away from us, but is, as you see, subdued.

"If you will carry him to Santo Domingo, together with these two letters from Don Balthazar to the governor, I may then regain San Isidro and my ship."

"With all my heart, *señor* don," returned the Spaniard. "This rascal will not escape from us, I assure you."

"One thing I forgot to mention," said Burke, handing over the letters, and signing his men to lower the senseless Aguilar over into the boat. "It seems that the sun has smitten this rogue, so that his mind is turned; or else he tries to play some trick upon us, for he endeavors to make us think, and indeed swears by all that is holy, that he is himself a noble Spaniard. Do not let him impose upon you."

The other laughed lightly and bowed again.

"We are most happy to be of service to you, *señor* don. I regret that I cannot stay, but must return instantly. Our captain is most anxious to regain Santo Domingo ere darkness falls."

So the vice-captain made his hasty though formal farewells, and got over into his boat again, and pushed off, while the marveling seamen stared at Burke and then at the great ship.

A gun saluted them, and presently the little coaster was heading into the north again, while the galleon stood on southward to round the cape.

"The luck of the sea Burkes!" quoth Denis Burke, as he clapped old Malachi on the shoulder and laughed gayly.

"But ye should have hung him, your honor," growled Malachi.

Burke squinted out after the lessening shape of the galleon, and shook his head.

"His punishment is worse than death, for him," he rejoined. "And hasn't he served us well, besides? Answer me that, if ye can!"

MID-AFTERNOON OF this same day found bearded Garf O'Malley on the Madre de Dios in desperate plight. The short hurricane of the previous day, which had blown him off the Hispaniola coast entirely, had shattered all his chances of rescuing Burke, and left him in wild and furious despair. What was more, it left him with smashed bowsprit and foremast gone a dozen feet above the deck, so that his men worked half the night before they could rig enough canvas to get way on the frigate. A sorry wreck aloft, she made for Cape Samana, at the eastern tip of Hispaniola.

Big Garf was like a man stunned. The loss of Burke stung him to the heart, while his own bodily hurts were bad enough; cursing in wild frenzy of bitter grief, he staggered about the deck until he fell senseless. The men were sunk in gloom, despite the riches under hatches. A score had been lost in that mad panic at San Isidro, many were wounded, the heart was clear gone out of them.

With noon, they raised a great headland, and one of the French filibusters recognized Cape Samana; then they saw a sail putting out of the bay and heading for them. This was no other than the Anglesea, an English thirty-gun filibuster, now homeward bound after long raids down the coasts of Caracas. Seeing the crippled Spaniard thus dropped into their lap, the English hoisted their flag and darted upon her gleefully.

Garf O'Malley was brought to his senses, and attempted to get the weather gauge of the other ship, but for lack of headsails moved too slowly. The pirate poured a broadside into his bows and contemptuously bore up to board him, but the frigate reeled and rocked as her full larboard broadside thundered into the Englishman, raking his decks, cutting up his rigging, sending him drifting off to make necessary repairs.

Neither of them noticed a tiny craft that was heading for them. One of the men drew Garf's attention to the little coaster, but he sniffed in disdain and roared at his men to get up preventer stays on the mizzen, weakened by a shot. Before it could be done, the mast rocked and went crashing down. A wild yell arose from the Anglesea, and abandoning all repairs, the Englishman headed up from astern to board the great Madre de Dios.

In vain did O'Malley get the wreckage cut away. In vain did his musketeers open fire from forecastle and poop, while the swivel guns emptied bullets at the deck below. The Anglesea came forging up from astern, flung grapnels, sent men clambering up to cut the boarding mats and netting. Then, locked fast, she poured her men up the high side of the frigate, while Garf headed a desperate resistance.

And all unobserved, unnnoted, the little coaster crept up.

Presently the bronzed Englishmen won a footing on the frigate's deck, made a furious rush, and split O'Malley's men clear in two. Part of them retreated to the forecastle, where with musket and cutlass they made a stubborn resistance; big Garf himself, a bullet in his shoulder, fell back with the others to the quarter-deck.

So thick was the murk of powder-smoke from muskets and pistols and swivel-guns that the light breeze could not lift it, and it hung over the ships in a pall, so that none saw the little coaster slipping in alongside the frigate, on her clear larboard quarter.

Beaten back from poop and forecastle, the English gathered

their strength in the waist, made ready for the final assault. In this brief interim, the smoke cleared away.

AND THEN all men saw shapes come over the larboard rail in the waist—a dozen men, apparently out of the very sea, with Burke at their head, and his voice ringing like a clarion.

"A Burke! A Burke! Up and at them, Garf!"

He hurled himself upon the astonished English, and men died before his glittering blade. O'Malley and the buccaneers thought they beheld a miracle, and sudden wild exultation swept into them. All in a moment, their despair fled away, and they flung forward in a rush from poop and forecastle.

Nothing could stand before the mad fury of that charge. The English were thrown into utter confusion, were borne backward, clustered at the rail in desperate fight. Their captain went down under Burke's reddened steel; they dropped back to their own deck, and after them went Burke and his men. Then panic seized upon those bronzed sea-wolves, and they broke before the rush and the wild Irish yell. In another ten minutes the English filibuster was taken, with all her hold crammed full of Spanish loot.

The wondering O'Malley came close to Burke and felt his shoulders with huge hands, and folded him in a bearlike grasp, laughing and crying at once, forgetting his own hurts. Six feet away, a wounded man half rose from the deck, lifted a pistol, and the ball passed by their heads. As O'Malley leaped on the wounded man, Burke checked him.

"Let be, Garf, let be!" he cried gayly. "Faith, the rascal couldn't harm Captain Mayo! All hands repair ship! Up wi' the canvas, lads, and head for Le Cap, with the luck of the sea Burkes in our sails!"

Cheer upon cheer echoed up, from sound men and wounded alike, and in the glow of sunset two craft headed westward, while behind them the abandoned little coaster rocked derelict to the breeze.

III

SPANISH GOLD

That sunken Caribbean treasure seemed an easy prize to Denis Burke, Irish buccaneer—until his jealous rivals started swarming around it.

CHAPTER I

RESCUED FROM TORTURE

CAPE FRANÇOIS, sweltering and glorious under the long rocky height of Morne Rouge. Le Cap, as it was universally known, immortal and awful refuge of buccaneers, with Tortuga over the northern horizon. Le Cap, roistering, swaggering, magnificent, drunken, miserable, rich with gold flung broadcast, rich with wealth from the plantations of the Plaine du Nord, rich with Spanish loot; the greatest collection of harpies, prostitutes, taverns, in the New World; murder, rape, duellos, of daily occurrence; governed in haphazard manner, swarming with filibusters, buccaneers, rank pirates of all nations under heaven, crawling with vermin and crime—such was Le Cap in 1703, doomed to destruction a dozen times over, yet ever rising from fire and ashes and blood with new virility to become ripe for fresh damnation.

In the harbor lay ships of all sizes and nationalities, a full half being prizes fetched in by buccaneers. From stately Spanish galleon to lowly New England schooner, any might here be found. Indeed, at present were two great ships brought in by Captain Mayo—a captured English corsair, the Anglesea, and a huge prize galleon, both of them crammed with loot. No one knew much about Captain Mayo, but his deeds spoke for themselves. Le Cap was rocking with his name, rioting with his gold and liquor, and the street-girls wore jewels that put to shame the great gems of the rich planters' wives.

While his men caroused and the merchants bought his looted

Half a dozen of the ruffians leaped on Denis Burke.

goods, Captain Mayo and one or two of his friends sat in a wide, cool house fronting the Place d'Armes and the cathedral, a house which Captain Mayo had bought outright with royal gesture; for he, who had known kings and courts, was a homeless man like many another, and Le Cap, while nominally French, was in reality a lawless place that welcomed any man with gold in his fist. Only those who were with him here, and some of the Irish from his crew, knew his real name and his past.

Here was luxury. The house was furnished with royal loot from his two ships, slaves waited on him and his friends, wine ran like water, the planters and officials of the town were entertained at stately dinners, where they ate from plates of gold and silver. But there were no women in this house.

As the liquidation of his loot ran its course, Captain Mayo was bored. Hispaniola was too hot and languid for his Irish blood; he wanted to be at sea again. He had sold the huge Spanish ship, keeping only the Anglesea for himself—a thirty-gun frigate she was, Dutch in the beginning, but cut down for buccaneering use—a splendid craft.

On a hot morning, Garf O'Malley came striding into the

room where Captain Mayo sat bartering with two traders for the last of the looted goods. A big man was O'Malley, bearded and rough of hand, as his nickname "Garf" denoted, with huge strength in his brawny frame. Sailing master to Captain Mayo, he was close as a brother to him besides.

The business was finished at last and the merchants departed. Captain Mayo, slim and elegant in his rippling silks, looked at O'Malley with a whimsical smile on his aquiline, keenly carved features and his blue eyes lightened.

"Faith, Garf, ye look as though there were news in your craw!"

"Aye," returned the seaman, sending a black slave for wine. "When we can talk in private. D'ye know, Denis, these men of ours have kept a close tongue. Drunk or sober, they've breathed no word that you're Denis Burke o' County Mayo. Good lads."

Mayo nodded. "Denis Burke is dead, Garf; let him rest in peace, poor devil! He had a hard life and a useless one. Here's the wine. A health to Cap'n Mayo!"

"With all my heart," said O'Malley.

"Denis," he said, leaning forward when they were alone, "ye've made enemies here."

"Faith, that's no news!" Captain Mayo laughed a little and sipped his wine. "Who?"

"The Frenchman who has those two filibustering craft, Saintonge; and his ally the Englishman, Hardy."

"Bah! Blustering rogues both," and Captain Mayo shrugged indifferently. "True, I had a row with the two of them last night."

"So 'tis said," replied O'Malley, frowning. "They've three strong ships and five hundred men among 'em."

"And not a gourd dollar to their names." Captain Mayo chuckled. "That's why they're so devilish out of temper with me! They've cruised for three months without a capture. Also, I took a poor devil of a Spaniard away from 'em last night."

"So I hear," observed Garf O'Malley dryly. "They've sworn revenge."

"Let 'em swear and be damned to them," and Mayo grinned. "They had picked up this poor rogue in a boat with three others, who were dead. He would not join their crew, and last night they had him spread-eagled on a table in the tavern, about to torture him. I bought his life from them with the dice—wagered a thousand pistoles against him, and won. Why the devil would they want revenge?"

"Hm! Your tongue was none too polite, I gather," and O'Malley chuckled. "It's a wonder ye weren't murdered, ye fool! Don't you know enough to keep some of our own lads around you?"

Captain Mayo laughed gayly. "Never mind, Garf. Those rogues can't do me harm. And that reminds me—the Spaniard said he wanted speech with me. Let's have him in."

"Wait! Devil take it, wait!" cried O'Malley angrily. He brought down his fist on the table. There was a splintering crash. The mahogany collapsed under the blow, wine, glasses, silver goblets going to the floor. Captain Mayo leaned back, laughing heartily.

"Confound it, Garf, will ye leave me no furniture in the house?" He touched his rapier that lay on the bench—a long

Toledo blade, won years ago in France. "There's companion and guard enough, old friend. We'll get Fernando in, eh?"

AT HIS call a black appeared and went hastily in search of the Spaniard. Presently the latter appeared; a tall, thin, grave man possessed of stately Spanish grace, clad in garments Captain Mayo had given him. He bowed to the two, and Mayo waved his hand.

"Come, *señor,* come and join us! Excellent Xeres wine we have here. I believe there was something you desired to see me about? This is my friend, relative, and comrade, Cap'n Garf O'Malley. Your name, I think—"

"Fernando de Ribera y Puertomayor, *señores,*" replied the Spaniard. His features were spare, thinly bearded, the skin tightly drawn over the facial bones. "I owe you great thanks—"

"Which you have now expressed, so it's ended," cut in Captain Mayo. "Here, salvage one of those goblets from the floor—luckily the flask of wine didn't break! Arrange your passage to Santo Domingo, *señor;* I'll pay it and put a hundred pistoles in your pocket, as one seaman to another. For, I take it, you are a seaman as well as a *caballero?*"

"I am," said Ribera, obeying the behest and sipping at his wine. "I also was a prisoner aboard the galleon Santa Margarita. My own ship I fought against buccaneers, six months ago, until she sank under me. I was rescued with a few men. Our admiral clapped me into chains for not having run from the buccaneers instead of fighting them. The Santa Margarita, praise be to the saints, foundered last week in a hurricane. I was flung into a boat with a few others; I think there are no more survivors. I do not care to seek my own country, under the circumstances."

"Good!" exclaimed Captain Mayo heartily. "Then what shall you do?"

"Become a man of wealth, by your help."

"Eh? You mean to join my crew?"

Ribera smiled thinly. "Temporarily. Long enough to show

you exactly where the Santa Margarita lies. She was with the Plate fleet, and she bears the richest of the year's harvest from Peru and Mexico. She was blown far from the fleet, and I know exactly where she now lies. What say you? A fifth to me, the rest to you and your men."

Captain Mayo looked at O'Malley, who was staring thoughtfully at the Spaniard.

"Done with you," he said promptly. Ribera shook his head.

"Wait one moment! You must know why those two buccaneer captains were about to torture me last night. When they picked up the boat I was in, one of the other men was still alive, though he died soon after. Before dying, he talked. They learned something; how much, I cannot say. They tried to make me say more about the galleon."

"Bah!" exclaimed Garf O'Malley, plucking at his gray-brown beard. "To the devil with those rascals—eh, cap'n?"

"Aye. Get out the charts, will you? Let's learn more about this. Where's the spot?"

"We were trying to make Puerto Rico, but failed. The cay is one of a strip, north of San Tomás—I'll show you."

O'MALLEY LUGGED over another table, and on it threw a roll of charts. Captain Mayo spread them out, found the one he desired, and laid it flat. Ribera bent over it and laid his finger on one of the low reefs north of San Tomás.

"Here it is; Piedra Blanca del Mer. A white jutting coral rock. At low tide it becomes an island; at all other times it is a white rock fifty feet long. There are shoals and reefs all around, except to the southwest, from which direction we drove upon it. The galleon struck the outer reef, south of the white rock. It is a huge reef thereabouts, with rocky pools and pits of water."

"If she's on the reef, then she's battered to pieces by this time," said O'Malley.

"She was washed over," said Ribera positively. "Either clear over the reef, in which case she lies in the shallow lagoon beyond, or else into one of the pools of the reef. After our boat got away we saw her lifted and washed on over. Luckily, a current carried us to the southward, and with a scrap of sail we cleared the reefs altogether."

"What do you think, Garf?" queried Captain Mayo. The bearded seaman nodded.

"Not a bad gamble, cap'n. I'd say to pick up a few divers here."

"When can the Anglesea be ready to sail?"

"Day after to-morrow at earliest. We've no water aboard."

"Then get out and find the divers and arrange for water. I'll rouse up our men and get them aboard to-night. Malachi! Devil take you, where are you?"

Old Malachi Halloran, for years his soldier-servant and friend, appeared with a brisk salute. Captain Mayo came to his feet.

"Malachi, find the bos'un. Spread out and order every man of ours you can find to be aboard ship at sunset; they can finish their carouse aboard her to-night. O'Malley, you'd better send out and get her boats ashore. I'll go interview the governor immediately and get out clearance papers for a cruise, and pick up what men I can find on the way. Don Fernando, make yourself at home here."

So, buckling on his rapier, Captain Mayo strode out of the house, a lithe, slender figure; and if there were gray in his hair, the ocean sun had bleached it all to the same fair hue.

Straight to the house of the governor he went, and was at once admitted to the presence of M. du Casse, who ruled the island, or the French part of it, for King Louis. Du Casse, who had previously promised him French letters of *marque,* had them ready and now produced them, laughingly warning him against any buccaneering.

"Spain being our very good ally, *monsieur,* you can only use your cannon against the English and Dutch—that is to say, of course, unless others open fire upon you! In such case, the honor of the flag of France must be upheld at all costs."

Captain Mayo bowed.

"At all costs, *monsieur!* Including a tenth of the plunder to His Most Christian Majesty. We hope to sail day after tomorrow, at latest."

"A glass of wine with you, *monsieur,* to your good luck!" exclaimed the governor. "You are a day behind Captain Saintonge and his friend, Captain Hardy. They sail in the morning, and were but just now here."

Captain Mayo shrugged. "I have nothing to do with them, *monsieur.*"

"See that you don't," said the governor, lowering his voice. "You know their quality, *mon ami;* they are savages of the sea, their crews are the sweepings of Tortuga and Guadeloupe and Martinique. And I have heard threats against you. It would grieve me if such men wrought you ill."

Mayo lifted his glass, a light smile on his lips.

"I assure you, there is no danger, *monsieur.*"

TWENTY MINUTES later, when he entered the Licorne Tavern in search of any Irishmen from his own crew, he came face to face with the two buccaneer captains. Saintonge was a huge, whiskered, burly man of tremendous physical prowess and great brutality; it was told of him that he had a standing challenge to any two sea-rovers who dared to meet him in fight. Hardy was a slender figure, one eye gone and replaced by a patch, his livid, thin features expressive of unspeakable evil; he was garbed all in scarlet, and was girded about the waist with half a dozen pistolets.

A glance told Mayo there was no evasion, short of inglorious and speedy retreat—and no help at hand, either. The two captains leaped up at sight of him; the place was crowded with drinking buccaneers and their women, and a hush stole over the big room.

"So! Our fine gentleman filibuster!" growled Saintonge. "Well met, cap'n. We'd like a word with you."

Mayo eyed him with unconcealed contempt, then looked at Hardy with a slight smile.

"Yes?" He came closer to them. "And on what subject, my two unlucky captains?"

Saintonge swelled with rage. "On the subject of the Spaniard ye cheated us of!" he cried out. "Your men are going aboard to-night, eh? Oh, we've heard! And that means but one thing. Off to seek the wrecked galleon, eh?"

"Look'ee, Cap'n Mayo," said Hardy, unsmiling, deadly as a reptile. "We'll have no interference wi' the wreck. Ye've had luck enough at sea; now leave some one else the pickings."

Captain Mayo shrugged. "I fail to see the force of your argument—"

Saintonge, with a bellow of anger, plucked out his cutlass. Captain Mayo put hand to sword-hilt; but at this instant a man behind him and at one side hurled a pewter tankard with deadly aim. Struck over the ear, Captain Mayo staggered.

Next instant half a dozen of them were upon him, dragging him down.

CHAPTER II

DEGRADATION

THE THREE ships commanded by Saintonge and Hardy slipped out of the harbor that same afternoon, while the search for the missing Captain Mayo was still going on. All three were small, but well armed and crowded with men of all nations and races, and bore French letters of *marque* which nominally saved them from ranking as pirates. There was no distinction of nationality among the buccaneers; England and Holland might be leagued against France and Spain, but this meant nothing to them. They plundered indiscriminately, leaving French shipping alone because French ports gave them shelter. The Spaniards, their chief prey, made agonized efforts to exterminate them, regarding them as sea-wolves and outlaws without exception, whether allies or not.

That same evening after dark, Don Fernando de Ribera y Puertomayor sat in a tavern drinking and talking with the captain of a French brig who was bound for Santo Domingo. The mountains of the interior being occupied by maroons and runaway slaves, there was no overland communication with the Spanish half of Hispaniola. Ribera passed the captain a sealed letter, which the other hastily pocketed.

"You need not try to read it, *señor,*" he said grimly. "It is written in cipher, which only the governor himself can read. Place it in his hands, and he'll at once deliver to you a thousand pistoles. You have everything to lose, nothing to gain, by playing me false."

"Diantre!" exclaimed the Frenchman, with a grin. "I'm sailing at midnight, and in three days I'll be at Santo Domingo. A thousand pistoles, eh? Done with you, and a good gamble."

Ribera finished his flagon of wine and departed.

That night Garf O'Malley, on whom developed command of Captain Mayo's men and ships, sat gloomily receiving reports, all alike vain. Mayo had simply disappeared from human ken. About midnight, however, one of the black slaves crept in, bringing another slave with him, a slave from the Licorne Tavern.

The black, who had scented rewards, told O'Malley a strange story of men drunk and helpless, taken aboard the brig of Captain Hardy when the latter sailed—taken aboard in full daylight. All of them were men of Hardy's crew, it appeared, but there was one man who had been wrapped from head to foot in a cloak and carted off with the rest. The black had observed his boots, which were of soft morocco leather, crimson in hue. When he heard this, O'Malley swore a great oath, gave the black what gold he had about him, and strode into the other room where Malachi Halloran, Captain Mayo's old body-servant, sat in dismal talk with the bos'un and several other men from the ship.

"Found!" exclaimed Garf, his big beard curling savagely about his face. They started up, staring at him. "Found! That devil

Hardy caught him somehow, carried him off. He's aboard Hardy's ship now."

"Aye?" said Bose. "And where's Hardy's brig, then?"

"Where I can find her in a week's time," returned O'Malley. "Every man aboard ship and make ready to sail! Bose, have a boat waiting for me. I'm off to the governor's house."

"At this time of night?"

"Aye. There's a ball going on."

There was a ball indeed, and a very handsome one, but O'Malley plucked M. du Casse from the midst of it, and in twenty minutes had neatly scrivened copies of the letters of *marque* that had vanished with Captain Mayo—safe protection against any French or Spanish ships of war that might pick him up. These in his pocket, he bade the governor farewell and went down to the quays, and so was taken aboard the Anglesea. In five minutes her canvas was being shaken out, and with Ribera's assistance he was laying out his course.

With the following day, when she was off Cape Samana, the Anglesea was flatly becalmed, and she rocked idle to the currents during two whole days, making scarcely a mile of headway, while Garf O'Malley stormed up and down the poop, or sulked gloomily at the rail. What aggravated the situation was that, seven or eight miles closer in-shore, there was very clearly wind enough, for twice they made out the dingy sails of coasters against the green hills. Don Fernando de Ribera was the only man aboard who accepted the matter with cheerful mien; but, as Malachi Halloran pointed out to big Garf, Spaniards were never in a hurry anyway.

So the Anglesea drifted listless to the currents, while Don Fernando eyed the sails of those coasters with gnawing anxiety, despite his apparent equanimity.

Far over the horizon, however, was wind enough and to spare, driving along the two small ships of Saintonge, and the slightly larger corsair of Hardy, the Revenge by name. Aboard this latter, indeed, a very pretty game was in progress.

CAPTAIN HARDY, in his braggadocio scarlet costume and hung with pistols as usual, swaggered about in the waist, in talk with his men. These were a motley crew; Negroes, Spaniards, English, men of all nations, bloods and creeds, and all of them the lowest of the low, scum of the seven seas, very devils for fighting and worse devils in everyday life. Nor were they all men, for not a few had brought along their wenches or women of the port, a fact which in itself showed how low these men were sunk, regardless of all buccaneer discipline. They took good care to obey Hardy, however.

Never had Captain Mayo witnessed such scenes of debauchery as had passed on the decks around him since Le Cap fell out of sight; never had he imagined such scenes possible. Yet he himself was in no very merry plight, being chained to the foot of the mainmast—having indeed spent a full twenty-four hours there. He was stripped to the buff, his fine clothes portioned off among the officers, while Hardy had taken his Toledo rapier and put it in the cabin.

So there sat Captain Mayo, while the men and their wenches pelted him with fruit that had gone over-ripe since it came aboard, and Hardy's one evil eye glared at him. A keg of rum had been broached and was fast being emptied, with the consequences to be expected. When a half-naked mestizo woman slid on the squashed fruit and went sailing into the lee scuppers, a roar of wild laughter arose that went pealing down the wind.

Then, abruptly, the mood was changed. A bawling Englishman heaved up a half-rotted mango to throw at Captain Mayo; but the fruit burst as it left his hand and went slap into the face of Captain Hardy. The latter whirled, saw who had flung the mango, and a pistol jerked up in his hand. To the roar of the shot, the maudlin buccaneer pitched forward, a bullet through his brain. Sudden silence fell, as Hardy glared around with his one eye.

"Ye dogs!" he cried out. "Aye, and I'm one of ye—but ye'd best mind your helm when ye steer athwart of me—"

He hurled a volley of oaths at them, ordered them to heave the dead man over the side, and swaggered up to the chained figure at the mast.

"The great Captain Mayo! Sink me if he ain't a stripped rat, for all his brag!" he exclaimed, and a laugh went up from the men around. "Well, my fine gentleman, with your airs and your loot and your mincing ways—here y'are! And art in a proper mood to talk, eh?"

"Aye," mumbled Mayo, humbly enough.

His once proud air had vanished. Bruised and battered though he was, he had scorned them and had shown it; but now all was changed. Perhaps Mayo had seen that contempt of the rabble around would have only one end, when they became drunk and enraged enough to take his life. Or perhaps the rotten fruit which daubed him from head to foot had altered his mien, as it was well calculated to do. At all events, he sat with head fallen forward on his chest, his eyes no longer striking out with the old keen force, his whole figure drooped in dejection.

Hardy strode up to him and struck him across the face.

"So! You're among real brethren o' the coast now, my fine birdling—a murrain on ye, what a stink it has!"

Mayo's head drooped still farther, his eyes closed. The blow brought no glow of anger to his face. Then, with an effort, he looked up at Hardy.

"The pearls," he mumbled weakly. "The pearls—all the year's take—behind the panel in—in the cabin—"

His voice failed. His head fell forward, and he relaxed limply in his chains.

Hardy started, flung a glance around. None other had heard those words; a huge Negro, his second in command, Manuelo by name, was approaching. Manuelo had taken the lead in subjecting the prisoner to insult, blow and abuse, and now trailed a whip in his hand. He whirled the lash and brought it across the shoulders of Captain Mayo.

"Maybe that'll wake him!" he cried in French, amid a roar of laughter.

Hardy turned to him and made a gesture.

"No more o' this now," he ordered. "Unlock the irons, empty a bucket of water over the fellow, and take him below to the cabin. He's ready to talk."

Manuelo stared at him, powerful black features set in astonishment.

"Him? Talk, cap'n? What about?"

"You fool, d'ye dare to question me?" said Hardy. The huge black shrank away.

"Nay, nay! At once, cap'n."

HARDY WENT below, and there found a shock-headed Martinique lad who served as cabin-boy. Sending the Creole for one of his last few bottles of wine, Hardy tucked tobacco into a long clay pipe from the rack, lighted it, and sank down before the table, scowling. Both he and Saintonge were low on provisions and liquor, For three months they had met with no luck at all. Their men were discontented, and only their personal brutality and unquestioned courage had kept them in command.

Presently Manuelo appeared, shoving along the dripping, staggering Captain Mayo. Hardy could trust the huge black absolutely, and motioned him to a seat. Mayo sank down on the wall settle beside the table, wiping the water from his eyes, and it was quite clear that all the fight had gone out of him.

"Here," and Hardy poured wine into a pewter flagon and shoved it at his captive. "Take this. What a drab dog ye are without the fine trappings! There's a pipe; help yourself to tobacco."

Manuelo, in staring amazement, poured himself rum, his eyes rolling. He knew better than to speak, however, until Hardy gave permission.

Captain Mayo drank, and got a pipe alight with fumbling

fingers. Hardy leaned forward, the one glittering eye transfixing him.

"Now, what's this about pearls?" he demanded curtly. Captain Mayo started.

"Pearls?" he said. "Nay, I know naught about any pearls! What mean you?"

"Hark'e, Mayo," said Hardy, his voice like acid. "Either you talk here and now, or out ye go to the mainmast again, with two whips biting off your hide, and no more chance to talk! This is your last chance. Take it, ye fool."

Mayo darted a frightened glance at the huge black.

"All right, all right," he said hastily. "Ye have the top hand, Cap'n Hardy. In the galleon, they are."

"So Fernando talked, eh?" said Hardy with satisfaction. "The damned Spanish dog! Out with it."

"Not likely!" exclaimed Captain Mayo. "And have you put a knife into me?"

"A pox on ye!" exclaimed Hardy. "Listen. I'll grant ye life in exchange. My word on it! And a share in the pearls as well, if it's kept quiet. Among the three of us."

"Oh!" said Mayo, staring wide-eyed at him. "Ye mean it?"

"Sink me but I do," said Hardy with emphasis, his dark eye all aglow. "After all, I'd liefer have your help than your death. Will ye make the best of it?"

"Aye," said Captain Mayo promptly.

"Good," said Hardy. "Manuelo, lay out the charts. Now, my bucko, trace me where lies the galleon and what ye know about her, first."

Manuelo spread out one of the charts, got ink and a quill, and Captain Mayo, without demur, fell to work, showing where the galleon lay and supplementing the very rough navigating knowledge of Hardy with the proper course to lay.

"Good enough, aye," said Hardy. "See to it, Manuelo! And now come to the pearls. What did he say of them?"

Mayo puffed his long pipe alight.

"The whole year's take of the Mexican fisheries," he said calmly. "A wondrous lot, all bound for the king's treasury. In the main cabin of the galleon, the one that has a stern walk outside, is an oil painting of Santa Margarita, for whom the galleon was named. This picture slides away to show a secret hiding place. There you are."

Hardy looked at the huge black, a light of infernal glee in his black-patched face.

"Swizzle me and sink me!" he exclaimed softly. "D'ye hear?"

"Aye," assented Manuelo, showing his white teeth in a wide grin. "But if the galleon is sunk—"

Hardy swung on Captain Mayo. "How does she lie?" he demanded fiercely.

"Impossible to say exactly," said Mayo. "The Spaniard is certain she's in shallow water, in a pool of the reef. He saw her washed over."

"And we're ahead of your craft, eh?" Hardy's glittering eye narrowed. "Well, I had reason enough to make my bargain with ye, and to keep it. If your ship comes up, there's three of us to take her; and sink me if we wouldn't do it! But we'll have you for hostage as well, my birdling. Now that I've broken your over-proud spirit, ye can bide aft here, for if ye went for'ard one o' my bullies might slit your weazand, and I want to keep ye safe and sound as a hostage."

"It's mortal kind of ye," said Mayo, in a fawning voice. "When will ye raise the Piedra Blanca rock?"

"Lord knows," said Hardy. "In two days or three. We're foul-bottomed wi' cruising, and can't tell about the wind this season. I'll find some clothes for ye. Eat here with Manuelo when I'm done at table, and mind, go not for'ard! I'll not have ye killed."

"Thank'ee kindly," said Captain Mayo, and so meek was he in the saying that Hardy gave him a look of contempt and curled his lip disdainfully.

CHAPTER III

SUNKEN TREASURE

NOW, THERE was no doubt that Hardy hated Captain Mayo with a venomous and deadly hatred, but he was no fool.

He realized quite clearly, now that his head was clear of liquor, that Mayo might be very valuable alive, and of no use whatever dead. The Anglesea would probably follow along to the scene of the galleon's wreck, and while the three buccaneers could certainly overpower her, it meant a nasty fight. But, with Mayo as hostage, things might be otherwise adjusted.

Accordingly, during the following two days, he treated Captain Mayo more as a guest than as a prisoner. He could see clearly enough that he had quite broken the spirit of this man, who, garbed in tattered garments, had never regained his old arrogance, his keenly biting eye, his proud air. Now he slouched about, his head hanging, his shoulders drooping, speaking only when addressed, avoiding the men who jeered at him. There was not much chance for jeering, however, for the tail of a blow swept the Revenge gallantly on her course, the three ships had much ado to keep together, and all hands were engaged with the slovenly rigging and rotted canvas, not to mention the pumps.

The two days wore to a close, and evening came, with Hardy expecting to raise the reefs on the following day.

After a pipe in the cabin, Mayo went out and stood for a long while at the windward rail, drinking in the keen wind, sighting nothing but the stars and the bobbing lights of the other two craft. Presently he went forward to the water-butt lashed there, and drank from the pannikin, then turned aft again, along the bulwarks. He was nearly at the poop when he heard his own name softly called.

"Denis Burke! A word with you, Denis Burke!"

He halted in utmost astonishment, startled and alarmed. Not that it mattered if any of this foul crew did know him—but how did they know? A figure detached itself from the shadows of the rail and approached.

"So ye don't know me, Master Burke?"

"I am Captain Mayo," he said stiffly. "Y'ave mistook the name."

"Aye, likely!" came the response, mockingly. "Ye don't know me?"

Mayo did know her—he had seen her often enough on these decks, a wild, drunken creature, a woman they called Joanna, wearing a sword and pistols like the men around her, but outvieing them in profanity and wildness. A woman unlovely, gaunt and grim of face and body, hair cut short and flying about her neck.

"So it's you, Joanna!" he exclaimed.

"Aye," she said, coming close to him. "But in other days, across the black and dreary years—d'ye remember a lass in Ireland, Denis Burke, a lass who lived in the smithy under the Dungannon hill, a lass named Sheila Halloran?"

Captain Mayo started. "Aye! I remember her well," he said. "But it can't be—"

"It is," said Joanna grimly. "And I knew you again at the first sight of you there in Le Cap, but held my peace. Sheila is dead and buried long ago. I'm a better man than any of these human devils aboard here, Denis—"

"Denis Burke is dead also," said Captain Mayo, and steel leaped in his voice. "D'ye understand that, Joanna?"

"Aye," she responded, with a laugh that was hard and cold. "Why not? Then I'm here to lend ye a hand, Cap'n Mayo, when you have need of one."

"I have need o' naught," said Mayo quickly.

"But ye have," she said. "Well I know you're not the broken, spiritless man ye seem to these swine. Trust me if ye will, and

I'll not fail ye. With cold steel or pistol, I'm better than any except Hardy—he's a devil with a pistol! If ye want to steal away in one of the boats at night, well and good."

Captain Mayo was silent a moment.

"Why would ye do this for me, Joanna?"

"Because you're what you are, and I'd do one decent thing before life ends."

"Thanks," he said softly, and gripped her hard-muscled arm with his fingers for an instant, in a swift pressure. "If any chance offers, Joanna, I'll slip you a word; but no good may come of it. My luck's deserted me."

"Aye, true enough, when ye set up house ashore," she responded in a fierce breath. "Do I not know the old saying, about the luck o' the sea Burkes? And that's your luck, you of the Mayo branch of the family. But good luck or ill, I'm with ye. And here's the open sea and the reefs ahead to bear out the old saying."

She slipped away and was gone.

FOR A long while, again, Captain Mayo stood at the rail, looking out over the night sea where the phosphorescent waters glimmered faintly as they rolled and broke. Wonder filled his mind at this strange meeting with a woman whom he had known in passing so many years ago, so far away, and his heart warmed to the human touch of this derelict.

And there was much in what she said. It was true that he was of the "sea Burkes," as the one branch of the old family was named, and never was there any luck for them ashore, but only out at sea. His own case had proven this. The land brought him ill luck every time, the sea good luck—or perhaps it was that blood told in him, that at sea he was more himself, more capable, more reckless of odds.

"I'll never more set foot ashore, except in passing," he vowed solemnly, in this moment. "Never to live, to reside, to turn my back on the sea if only for a month's time! Aye. Let me see my own ship once more, and I'll stick with her, where I belong, instead of living under a roof ashore and letting her rock idle."

And with this, he turned in for the night, and slept more soundly.

On the following morning they sighted the Piedra Blanca—a white rock which gave the shoal its name. The tide was evidently out, for it was now distinctly a small islet, the surf breaking heavily over the reefs around.

The wind was light, and Saintonge drew up, signalling that he was coming aboard. Hardy, his one eye glittering, beckoned Captain Mayo to one side.

"Hark'ee! 'Twere best for you to go below and stay, in the little cabin. Saintonge is a swaggering brute and would be minded to pass his blade through ye for the fun of it. I'll tell him you're hurt and ill, d'ye mind?"

"Aye," said Mayo.

He went below to the dark and smelly little cabin, and composed himself to wait in patience until Captain Saintonge departed. He smiled grimly to himself at thought of Hardy's eagerness. Saintonge, of course, must know nothing of the great hoard of pearls—Hardy was only too delighted to keep that secret and not share it.

Mayo pondered over the words of Joanna, but could see little hope in what the woman offered. To steal away in a boat was possible, at present, but it would do no good whatever. Later, if the Anglesea did come up, Hardy would undoubtedly clap him under guard to prevent just such a happening. With a shrug, Captain Mayo left the matter to the gods of time and chance. He was convinced that something would turn up—and when it did, then was the time to act. Any planning ahead was impossible. Of only one thing was he sure; that the crews aboard these three ships were very sea-scum, and the world would be best off without them.

After an interminable wait, the Negro, Manuelo, summoned him with word that Saintonge had gone back to his own ship. Captain Mayo went on deck and found all three craft bearing up for the southwest passage into the reefs, with Hardy himself at the helm. Hardy greeted him with a grin.

"He's all for hanging you, but I talked him out of it. We'll raise the wreck any minute now, if she's in shallow water. There's anchorage in yonder."

"But bad ground if you're caught by a blow among the reefs," said Mayo.

"Aye. We'll chance that."

Nearer they swept in toward the reefs, but the channel opened out, plain to see. Men swarmed aloft and sail came in; the two smaller craft of Saintonge followed carefully enough, and presently a hail came down excitedly from aloft.

"Ahoy, cap'n! Off the larboard bow! There she is!"

And there she was, indeed, as the end of Piedra Blanca islet opened out to show her position. A chorus of wild yells went up and was reëchoed from the following craft as they, too, caught sight of her. Captain Mayo, for all the sudden thrill that the sight gave him, stood silent and eyed the scene.

OVER THE foremost reefs had the galleon been swept, exactly as Don Fernando had told. But she was in better situation than he had known, perhaps, or than Mayo had dared to expect. She lay on her starboard beam, wedged solidly in among white-toothed fangs of rock—a reef that was not even awash now, at low tide. The great bulk of her, just rising above the water, showed riven and splintered, masts gone just above the deck—but she was, in the main, quite intact. What was more, she was accessible to boats. The channel which entered the reefs and then thinned out to nothing, would allow the three small ships to come within two cables' length of her, although Mayo strongly doubted whether the Anglesea or any larger craft could enter among the out-flung vigils.

"Another hurricane would break her up," said Hardy. "Just in time, eh?"

Captain Mayo nodded.

Now Hardy snapped out sharp orders. The canvas came in,

the ship lost her way, and all three of her boats were put into the water and lines passed down. The other two craft were following his example. With a small boat in the lead to feel out the passage, the three craft were towed along, approaching the galleon still more closely.

All this had taken time. The afternoon was nearly gone, and the tide was again rising high about the hulk, when the three craft were securely moored, close to each other. A bellow from Saintonge drew Hardy to the rail, and the two decided to go together in a boat to look over the wreck before dark. At this came a growl from the men gathered in the waist, but Hardy swung on them with a torrent of black oaths.

"Silence, ye dogs!" he concluded his tirade. "If ye growl again at me, I'll show ye who can bite, understand? Bose, down into the boat wi' six men. We'll pick up Cap'n Saintonge and visit her.

"The rest of ye bide here, and we'll bring back a keg of spirits, belike."

Presently the boat drew away, and Captain Mayo watched the burly, bearded Saintonge descend into her, then it headed for the reef whereon lay the galloon.

Mayo was not so absorbed in the proceedings, however, as not to observe now what he had noted previously—that the Negro, Manuelo, remained close to him, watched him continually. He smiled grimly at this. So Hardy was taking no chances! But down in the cabin was the Toledo blade which had been plucked from Captain Mayo, and well he knew where the rapier lay in case he had need of it. Hardy had put it away and forgotten it, not knowing its value.

The two captains and the boat's crew straggled over the side of the galleon, for the tide was close to flood now, and they could lay the boat aboard her. At high water, only a portion of her high poop showed clear, and it was obviously impossible to do much work aboard the hulk. The sun was setting when they set off again, loaded down with loot and kegs from the poop-cabins, and Saintonge was set aboard his own vessel before Hardy returned.

ONCE BACK, the one-eyed skipper summoned Manuelo and Captain Mayo to the main cabin, where the prisoner settled down over a pipe with all the assurance in the world.

"To-night at ebb tide," said Hardy, "we're putting a dozen men each aboard her, to get off the hatches and make ready for the work we can only do by daylight. We can't waste time lying here. Cap'n Mayo, the don told you plain enough he'd been a prisoner aboard this galleon?"

Mayo nodded. "Aye. Too bad you let the other man die. He might have known—"

"Eh?" Hardy's one eye glared at him like a live coal. "What other man?"

"The other in the boat when you picked him up. The one that remained alive long enough to tell you about the galleon."

"Swizzle me and sink me! Are ye mad?" demanded Hardy. "There was none other alive in the boat—nor none other dead, either! Don What's-his-name was alone in her."

Mayo frowned. "Somehow, my dear Hardy, I almost believe you're telling the truth," he said reflectively. "Don Fernando informed me that another man with him had told you about the galleon, and that you were about to torture him, when I interfered, in order to learn more exactly—"

An oath of surprise and anger broke from Hardy.

"Why, the cursed lying Spaniard!" he burst forth. "He made no bones about it. Told us of the galleon and where she lay! He never mentioned the pearls, though. As for pricking his skin a bit, that was Saintonge having a little fun. He hates Spaniards, Saintonge does, and cuts up the prisoners a trifle when he has the chance."

"Aye?" said Captain Mayo, more than a little startled by this information. "Why would he lie about it to me, then? Well, no matter. Let it pass."

Hardy growled assent. "The main cabin will be out o' water to-night, when we go aboard. I settled wi' Saintonge that I'd take charge of the work to-night, and he could set the divers going for the lading to-morrow. That suited him, and suited me too. We'll get into the cabin, the three of us, and make sure o' those pearls. D'ye see?"

The eyes of Manuelo rolled delightedly. Captain Mayo, giving no sign of his inward consternation, nodded assent.

"I'd not have the men know you're with us," said Hardy, watching his captive. "Manuelo, pick mostly negars from the crew for the work. Then we'll blacken Cap'n Mayo's face and dress him like the others, and you can take him in our boat."

So it was settled among the three of them. But Captain Mayo, knowing full well that there were no pearls whatever, that his whole story was a fabrication, realized that this night would bring a crisis.

Darkness had fallen, and he was out on deck smoking a pipe, when the gaunt shape of Joanna came drifting past. As he spoke her name, she halted,

"Arrange it," said Captain Mayo, "to get with the boat going aboard the wreck at low tide. Important."

"Aye," said she, and was gone again, as a group of loud-talking men came past.

CHAPTER IV

IN THE SUNKEN SHIP

SO DON Fernando had told Hardy and Saintonge all about the galleon, and his tale to Captain Mayo had been a fine tissue of lies! Why? The query puzzled Mayo deeply and was still bothering him when, toward midnight, he descended into the longboat with Manuelo and a dozen more men, mostly blackamoors of the crew. He was roughly blacked over, wore tattered garments like those of the men, a broken hat over his eyes, and at his side—his Toledo blade.

None had questioned his slipping it out of the cabin or his donning it as Manuelo gave him the clothes and hat. Hardy was probably unaware of it, and cared no jot. But to Captain Mayo the feel of that blade at his side gave new life, new heart, a flooding tide of joy pulsing through his veins.

He crowded into the stern with Hardy and Manuelo, others crowded forward, still others took the long oars and shoved off. At the stroke oar was a familiar gaunt shape, that of Joanna, leaning more powerfully on the ash than any of the men behind her. Manuelo held a lighted lantern at his feet, for the night was hazy, the stars cloaked from view.

In fifteen minutes Hardy laid them alongside the reef near the galleon, for at low tide they could not get up under her bulk. He reached out and touched Mayo and the black on the knees.

"Stay close to me, now, both of ye! We'll go straight to her vitals!"

The other men lit lanterns from Hardy's, and straggled across the slippery reef to the hulk, where lines had been left hanging. Presently Captain Mayo was ascending lithely to the sharply canted deck, the other two following. A hand grasped his arm to help him over, and he saw Joanna standing there.

"We'll be in the main cabin," he murmured swiftly. "Listen. If ye hear aught, join me."

With a word of assent, she was gone. Hardy came up with his lantern, Manuelo followed, and the three, leaving the men to their work, headed for the dripping, splintered entrance to the main cabin. A number of the men were ahead of them, seeking loot, but the voice of Hardy drove them out again. They faced him, sullen and angry.

"Why should ye have the first pick?" said one. "It's all loot to the mainmast, cap'n, and well ye know it."

"Aye," said Hardy, and plucked out one of his pistols and cocked it. "Stand out, whoever it was that spoke! Stand out, and I'll argue it with ye."

They melted abruptly and went forward. Hardy laughed, swung up his lantern, and went on into the passage. He scrambled along the V formed by the wall and deck, for she was lying on her side and the deck rose above them like a wall as they went. And now Captain Mayo bent his wits to what might lie ahead, for unless luck were with him here and now there would be a short and sharp reckoning with the pearl-greedy Captain Hardy.

And luck was not with him, as he saw by the first glance around the sea-dripping cabin, for there was never a picture in sight on the walls.

Instantly he went to Hardy's side, and pointed to the dimness ahead of them, where the cool night air came in through the shattered stern windows.

"There it is—there!" he cried out.

HARDY LIFTED the lantern. Captain Mayo turned, but his foot slipped on the wet planks. He clutched at Hardy, with a frightened oath, and both of them went down with a crash, the lantern falling and leaving them all in pitch blackness.

Not a sound came from Hardy—for the excellent reason that Mayo's left hand gripped him about the throat as they fell. Then his right hand drove in hard, drove in again, before the buccaneer could draw a pistol. The second blow went to the jaw, and Hardy relaxed and lay quiet.

"Cap'n!" cried the voice of Manuelo. "Where are ye, cap'n?"

"Here," said Captain Mayo. "Give me a hand with him—"

Some subtle sense warned the black man. A cry broke from him, a muffled yell of fear and suspicion. Mayo heard him panting, scrambling for the passage to get out of the cabin.

"Joanna!" It was the old crisp, alert voice of Captain Mayo that rang out. "Get him—look out for him!"

"Aye," came a response.

Manuelo cried out again, this time in wild terror; but his voice only served to betray his whereabouts. Captain Mayo heard a wild scramble, a hoarse exclamation, a quick sharp cry, and then silence, until Joanna spoke.

"Got him. What next?"

"Get a lantern from one of the men for'ard. Say that Cap'n Hardy is remaining here until morning; as soon as they get the hatches off, they're to return to the ship. And, Joanna! Do you go with them, for the game's up as far as I'm—

"Go to the devil," came her response, harshly defiant. "With you I stick, for good or ill. Back shortly."

Captain Mayo, alone in the darkness, bent over the senseless Hardy and took the man's pistols. He wrenched the flints from the locks, threw them away, and dumped the useless weapons in a pile at one side. Then he set to work at stripping the man, and did not cease until he was mother-naked, even to the black patch from over his blind eye. With the clothes he crawled to the stern windows, where a great splintered hole was smashed in the ship, and threw them out into the water. He had just finished this when the bobbing light of a lantern appeared, and bearing it came Joanna. She held up the lantern and laughed grimly, stepping over the body of the black man.

"What's this? Stripped him, but not killed him? Run the snake through, I warn ye!"

"Not I," said Captain Mayo. "Tie him up, if you will. The men?"

"Are leaving now. Hatches off and water below. They asked no questions. Tie him up, eh? Why waste the time?"

"It's my pleasure," said Mayo. From his pocket he took a twist of tobacco and a pipe, the stem broken off, and presently had it lighted at the lantern, while Joanna tied up Hardy securely.

"Well?" she asked, harshly. He smiled at her, his incisive features handsome despite their unshaven blur of beard.

"Not well at all," he said coolly. "I saved myself by telling Hardy there were pearls hidden here." In a few words, he made the matter plain to her. "To-night I had to down him or suffer, so I downed him. We can fight it out here, and die like drowned rats, or we can get ashore on the White Rock and take our luck as we find it."

"Why not a boat?" she asked, eying him.

HE SHRUGGED. "I'd rather die quickly than die of sun and thirst. Besides, we'd not get any boat out past those other craft to sea. We'd have to go by channel. They'd be after us in no time."

"No," she said. "You've not watched the sky and water tonight. I have. There's not a breath o' wind. And the boats are moored by the ship's ladder."

"Indeed?" Captain Mayo smiled whimsically. "Could we steal away with one of those heavy boats that eight men can scarce row?"

"By cutting the mooring line," said she, and touched the bloody knife in her sash. "Have you no wits left?"

Mayo started slightly. "Oh! The current, eh?"

"It runs like a mill-race at the ebb tide, out among the reefs to the sea. Each of those boats has a mast, and sail coiled in the bottom. What more d'ye lack?"

Captain Mayo chuckled. "A ship to pick us up."

"Where's yours?"

"Coming," he said confidently. "But Lord knows where she is! Becalmed, perhaps. Garf O'Malley will do his best—"

"O'Malley?" she repeated, a throb in her voice. "Rough Brian himself, is it?"

"Aye, fallen on evil days like your humble servant, and now fellow-captain with me. He'll follow to hell in search of me, and it's like to end in hell, too, the way things look."

"You seem unworried," said she. Captain Mayo shrugged and puffed out a cloud of smoke.

"Soon or late we all die. Why worry?"

"Well, get up and off," she broke out. "We must catch the tide on the ebb if we're to get out o' the reefs. They'll have to come after us in boats if at all. Can ye swim?"

He nodded, and glanced at Hardy, who was still senseless.

"Can't leave him here—he'd drown when the tide comes in. I'll take him out on deck."

"Bah!"

With the irritated exclamation, Joanna stooped and lifted the man's white body easily, lightly, astonishing Mayo by the evident strength of her gaunt frame.

"I'll put a gag in his mouth," she said, "before we leave him."

Then she was gone with her burden. Mayo followed with the lantern, and extinguished it in the passage; but as he did so, he made a most surprising discovery.

Against a door was nailed a large wooden plaque, painted over with a coat of arms and the name of the captain of the Santa Margarita—this was evidently the captain's cabin.

The last flicker of light from the expiring candle fell full upon the name, and it was that of Fernando de Ribera y Puerto-mayor.

CAPTAIN MAYO whistled softly as he dropped the lantern and went on out to the sloping deck of the galleon, puffing at his pipe to get the last benefit of the tobacco. Don Fernando had lied in his story, just as he had told Hardy all about the galleon and then had lied about it.

"Faith, it's strange!" thought Mayo, frowning at the haze-darkened water and sky. "He was no captive aboard here, as he said, but the high captain in person. Why did he lie about it both to me and to Hardy? Perhaps to keep us from clapping a ransom on him, but that's not likely. He didn't seem anxious to get home. In fact, he was coming with us to find the galleon. It isn't like a man of his stripe to want to loot his own wrecked ship and skip with his share of the booty. Hm! Well, that's a puzzle with which I'm not concerned just now. My chief interest is in keeping alive, and it's like to need all my powers."

He perceived that Joanna had offered a very possible solution of their difficulty, and the old keen, high spirit sang in him once again, as he walked along the lower rail to meet her. She had deposited Hardy on the poop, where he would be seen with daylight, and now she stood, stripping off most of her tattered garments, armed only with dirk and sword girt about her.

"No time to waste," she said curtly. "Art ready?"

"Aye," said Mayo. "Make a bundle of your clothes. You'll have sore need of them when the sun comes up to burn us."

Clothes bundled and tied about their shoulders, they slipped down from the galleon's hulk, scrambled across the rocks, and went from the edge of the reef into the water. The lights of the three ships guided them. As Mayo knew, little or no watch was kept by the buccaneers, and as he swam alongside Joanna, he spoke softly.

"If one boat, why not all?"

"One would not be seen, three or four might be," she murmured. "Besides, we'd have to cut the boats from all three ships. What can be done once, can't be done three times, my friend. Don't tempt fate."

Captain Mayo laughed a little, and stroked on, leaving a dim fiery trail of phosphorescence in the water behind. They approached Hardy's ship, which lay closest of the three to the reef, and heard the laughter and oaths of men carousing.

Joanna swam ahead, and merged into the blackness of the boats and the ship's side, and Mayo floated on with the ebb-tide current. Presently a black thing detached itself from the mass, and he knew she had cut out the boat without a sound, without alarm. As it floated out on the current, he came and joined her, catching the gunwale and swimming a little to keep the boat's direction.

Half an hour later, when they passed the other two craft in silence and were out in the channel, they climbed aboard.

"I'd give a good deal to be there in the morning," said Captain Mayo, laughing, "when they loose Hardy, and him in his nakedness!"

"Ye may give a good deal yet, because ye'd not let out his life," said Joanna grimly. "What a fool ye are! No wonder those men of yours love you and swear by you."

CHAPTER V

A SEA DOG'S RUSE

THE SUN came up over a glassy sea—at least, about the reefs and to the northward. There was wind enough to the south, and a light breeze puffing up, but it would be slow in coming.

"Too slow," said Mayo, squinting at the reefs, barely three miles away. The mastheads of the three ships were just visible, as the boat would rise on one of the long, slow rollers. "They'll have boats out after us. If we'd made the wind, we might ha' got clear."

They swung up on another heaving, glassy sea, and an oath came from Joanna.

"Aye, boats! Two of 'em coming out. Can ye step the mast? A puff might help."

Captain Mayo shrugged, but got the mast stepped. They ran up the heavy canvas sail, and it hung lifeless in the hot sun. Captain Mayo laughed a little.

"Where's the luck o' the sea Burkes now, eh?"

She made no answer, but sat watching, each time they heaved up with a sea, the two boats whose oars flashed in the sunlight against the reefs.

"Hardy in one," said she suddenly. "And in the other Saintonge, strap me if it isn't!"

"Oh, yes, he'd like to be in at the death," returned Mayo cheerfully. "I suppose they will pistol us and we'll have no chance at sword-work."

He looked to the south, and sighed a little at sight of the

cat's-paws ruffling over the water, but none of them near enough to stir the listless canvas. Nothing else was in sight, but this meant little. A small boat's horizon is limited to three miles, except when the seas toss her up. The brazen morning sky held no cloud, no promise of wind, unless it should come reaching up from the southward.

The two boats crawled over the slow sea, oars glittering at each stroke. As they came closer, Captain Mayo stood up. He could see Hardy, garbed again in scarlet, and in the other boat the burly figure of Saintonge. The latter swung aloft a fist at him.

"Another twenty minutes," said Mayo, sitting down again. "No wind?"

"Not a breath," returned Joanna. "It's coming no closer—what's that?"

A dull vibration shattered the air.

"Cannon!" Mayo leaped up, held to the mast, stood on the gunwale for better sight. A sea heaved up the boat. "Men are aloft, Joanna—signals! Flags out—listen! More cannon! Something's happened."

Again and again the discharges broke the listless, sodden air. The two approaching boats drew in together, the two captains conferred. Hardy stood on the backs of two men, flung out his arm, pointed. With a sudden sweep and dip of oars, the boat of Saintonge swung around and after a moment that of Hardy followed. Another cannon and another thundered from the three craft. The two boats were pulling desperately back for the reef and the ships, oars dipping fast. Useless canvas broke out aboard the ships.

"Can ye make out anything?" cried Joanna. "Is it your ship coming up?"

"What we cannot see, they can make out clear from the mastheads," returned Mayo, as he searched the horizon. "Aye! By the Lord Harry, there's a scrap o' sail to the south—and another! To the south and west! Can ye see them?"

"Not I," she answered. "My eyes are poor at long work—two ships, ye say?"

"Aye, two, and if—" Mayo stiffened suddenly, for swinging around to the northward, sweeping a glance about the line of sky and sea, he caught the sun on a patch of white, then it was gone again. "And a third coming from the north! What the devil can it mean?"

A sudden sharp cry broke from her, vibrant with urgency.

"Down with ye! Pass me the pannikin—quick!"

CAPTAIN MAYO obeyed, jumping down from the gunwale, catching up the pannikin from the bottom and passing it aft. Like a madwoman, Joanna leaned overside, dipped it, hurled the water up on the canvas, again and again. Then he caught the reason, seeing the cat's-paw rippling over the water toward them. The wet canvas caught it, filled out a little, and the boat moved.

Jumping aft, Mayo went to the tiller, shipped it, ordered her to haul in the sheet. The puff of wind died out, but the wet canvas caught it to the last, and another was following. The breeze had come up, faint enough but sufficient to send the boat along through the water.

The three ships in among the reefs, however, were far from the wind.

Standing up, Mayo gazed again to the south, incredulous, scarce believing that all these craft could be at once converging upon an empty, shunned reef in the sea. Then swift amazement shook him, for instead of two ships, he saw that three were coming from the south, leaning far over to the wind, heading for the Piedra Blanca reef. Turning again, he looked to the north, and a wild cry broke from him.

"I thought so! It's the Anglesea, Joanna—see her new-bent canvas, shining white? Garf overshot his mark and is beating back! She's coming, glory be—"

"Mind your tiller! So is the wind!" called the woman from the bow.

Captain Mayo laughed as he settled himself again at the tiller, and the canvas filled out, and the boat headed around toward the north, heeling over with a surge and hiss of water beneath her keel.

Light as the breeze was, it held steady, and promised to thicken ere long. As they drove along, back the way they had come to skirt the reefs, Mayo saw the three buccaneers laboring desperately, frantically, their boats out towing the three craft into the channel, but they had no faintest breath of wind to help them. And the three ships from the south were bowling up fast, showing a huge spread of canvas that told only too truly what they were.

"Spaniards, Joanna—fighting galleons! Come aft. I'd talk with you."

She came and sat on the after thwart, and he told her what he knew about Don Fernando and what he had learned recently about the Spaniard's tale. She listened without comment, her wild, harsh, scarred features clear-cut and terrible in the sunlight, her eyes fiercely intent.

"So that's the way of it—and he was captain of the galleon yonder, eh?" said she. "Aye, you're dead right; a true-bred *don* he was, and no man to betray his own wrecked ship to buccaneers for gold. Not he! Think ye others were picked up from the wreck, and taken to San Domingo, and have brought the *dons* on us?"

"Not likely," said Captain Mayo. "Not all at once, like this."

"True enough," and she nodded. "Then he told the tale to Hardy and Saintonge and you, eh? Told where the galleon lay. And what was to prevent him sending word from Le Cap to the Spanish at San Domingo, will ye tell me? Ships were going back and forth every day. He wanted to get ye here at the reef, all of ye—"

Mayo brought down his fist on the gunwale.

"Faith, I believe you've hit it! Well, let be. If he's aboard our ship, yonder, we'll soon know the right of it."

"And the *dons* ha' got Saintonge and Hardy gripped beyond escape!" she exclaimed with fierce delight in her voice and eyes, so that Mayo looked at her curiously.

"Ye seem glad of it."

"Glad? I'd like to see every dog aboard 'em hung and quartered!" she cried out. "Not men, but beasts of the lowest, as you should know!"

He nodded, and fell silent.

THE BOAT surged on and on to the thrust of the wind, which freshened every moment. It had reached the three ships now, but gave them no aid, for the boats had to tow them dead into the wind's eye. The boats of Hardy and Saintonge had joined the others. Turning, Mayo saw that the three towering galleons were sweeping along, far asunder, ports down and boarding mats up. There was no doubt now of their intent, and there was no doubt that they would catch their prey.

The Anglesea, however, was becalmed. The wind she had borne with her was gone, the breeze from the south had not reached her yet. Mayo was certain of her identity now. She lay a full league to the north.

"And what would you do," said Joanna, eying him, "if you were Hardy?"

He gave her a flashing, whimsical smile. "He can't run, with his slow craft; can't even maneuver. Those three little ships can't fight three galleons. If he surrenders, he'll be hung or roasted alive or sent to the galleys."

"I know all that," she said impatiently, as he paused. "And what would you do?"

Mayo chuckled. "What Hardy will do. You'll see!"

She spat an oath at him and turned her back. But he remained watching the three little buccaneer craft as they crept out along the channel to their certain doom, and a glint of high excitement lighted his eyes, for he knew what he would see. Dogs they might be, these debased, debauched, diseased brethren of the coast—but when they were at fighting pitch they fought like all the devils from hell. And now their backs were against the wall of death.

The boat drove on across the endless seas, holding ever toward the motionless Anglesea.

Now the three galleons, splendid glittering ships with crosses on their great swelling canvas and the sun glittering on morions and breastplates of the soldiers crowded fore and aft, circled out. One of them, far larger than the other two, held straight for the prey. The others separated, to come in and take the three little ships on either flank. Joanna flung out an arm toward the great galleon in the center.

"I know her, saw her once before. She's the admiral's ship, the Santiago."

She fell silent again, staring, a flush growing in her gray and high-boned cheeks. The boat was now well north of the channel, surging steadily toward the Anglesea, which was just beginning to feel the wind.

Hardy's ship, with the two craft of Saintonge at his heels, was taking the men aboard and setting the boats adrift, as all three of them got the first of the breeze and their canvas bellied. They, too, headed for the north, as though hoping to get the breeze dead astern and make the most of their speed; they were just emerging from the reef, but the great Santiago was bearing down upon them rapidly.

An oath of wild dismay and incredulity burst from Joanna. The three craft, their escape cut off, might have run a little way; but a puff of smoke broke from the galleon, and before the thunder of the gun reached Captain Mayo, he saw the three buccaneers back their topsails and run up a white flag.

The Santiago bore down upon them. Her crew swarmed aloft. Her billowy, snowy, gaudy canvas came off, sail by sail. One of her broadsides could have sunk all three of the little craft, and well they knew it. She lost way, closed in upon them, towering far above the three of them. Her two consorts, surprised by this easy capture, were at a good distance. Captain

Mayo's eyes glittered suddenly.

"Watch!" he cried out, catching a movement of canvas.

The three buccaneers heeled, separated, leaped into speed as their canvas caught the wind. Straight for the huge galleon they darted, hurling themselves at her like terriers at some great mastiff. Confusion became evident aboard the Spaniard. She had come about, and they had the wind of her, and never a gun could she bring to bear except the guns in her stern, which puffed white smoke and cracked out dull reports.

And then they were in upon her, the three of them, smashing recklessly into her, grappling her, their wild and desperate men flooding aboard her with a scarlet speck leading them. Joanna burst into a wild yell, then sank down silent again.

They were aboard her now, every man of them, swarming in at her open ports, over her low waist, clambering up her high poop. And if many a speck fell and was gone, others won their way, and the three little empty ships rocked away, one of them foundering from the mad impact. Muskets and pistols raised a white cloud of smoke, which the wind dissipated on the instant.

The boat rushed on into the north where the Anglesea was tacking to meet her. Once Captain Mayo stood up and waved an arm, and the brig headed straight for him in reply.

CHAPTER VI

VICTORY

WHEN CAPTAIN MAYO stepped to his own deck again, big Garf O'Malley caught him in a huge hug, and men pressed about thickly with cheers and wild delighted oaths, and Garf looked at Joanna, whom he had known well enough as a girl, but he knew her not now.

"And who is this?" said he.

"A friend," said Captain Mayo, and parted the men about

him. He beckoned two of them and pointed to Don Fernando de Ribera, who stood watching at the rail. "Seize that man, put him in irons. Quickly!"

So they did it, and the Spaniard was rushed from sight, and Captain Mayo hastily went aft to the helm. Some one thrust a cup of wine into his hand, and he drank it off, then his eyes struck out at Garf O'Malley with a great laugh.

"Stations, Garf! All hands to the guns! Eh—it's you, is it?"

He found Joanna there beside him, giving him a hand with the great helm, and her grim eyes smiled at him. Garf caught his arm, looked at him anxiously.

"What would ye do, cap'n?"

"Give me the trumpet and get the guns double-shotted."

So Garf obeyed, and Captain Mayo roared his orders forward, and with ringing cheers the men leaped to the lines, and to guns and muskets and powder-kegs. And Captain Mayo held the Anglesea hard over, meaning to come down at the three locked ships in a single long tack.

For locked they were. The proud Spanish flag had fluttered down from aloft, and the Santiago was taken. The two other galleons came driving in on either side of her and grappled; the pikes and morions went pouring aboard her, where a speck of scarlet held command on her high poop and the burly Saintonge on her forecastle, and her swivel-guns spat crowded bullets into the Spaniards swarming aboard in the waist.

"They took him, by the saints!" cried out Captain Mayo. "They took him—and now the other two have them nipped! What a fight it is!"

"Nay," said Joanna, looking into his face. "What a fool it is to be heading for them, when ye might be over the horizon while they cut each other's throats!"

Captain Mayo laughed. "Ye forget, Joanna, that I was in the trap myself. Steady, now!"

The brig bore down upon the grappled ships, the two remaining little buccaneer craft drifting past her, empty and deserted, not a soul left aboard them—even the wenches had gone aboard the Santiago with pike and musket. Now, in the galleon's waist, Mayo saw armor and musketry, and the flash of swords, as the Spaniards strove to down the wild men who held forecastle and poop, but ever they were beaten back.

"Doubleshot the guns, Garf!" roared Captain Mayo. "Give her every gun at the waterline as we pass by!"

Few, if any, engaged in that wild and desperate battle paid any heed to the brig so swiftly running down upon them. And soon enough, the three great gilded high poops shut her out from their sight, as Joanna held her steadily toward them, sweeping up from the stern, laying her alongside the galleon on the larboard side of the Santiago, a biscuit's toss away.

THEN ONE frantic and terrible cry pealed up from the Spaniards, but it was drowned in the roar of guns. Double-shotted were those guns, and the balls tore into the galleon, tore the bottom out of her, knocked great holes gaping at her water-line as the brig surged past her. Then the men to the lines again, and about came the brig, handling perfectly, and in against the side of the galleon that had grappled the Santiago to starboard.

The grapnels were flung, the ships crashed together, and over the high galleon's side went the men of the Anglesea, with Captain Mayo and big Garf heading them. Back upon their own decks were pouring the Spanish men, but they were too late to stop that rushing tide of steel. It struck them, split them apart, and from poop and forecastle poured down the ragged remnants of the buccaneers to smite the foe in the waist.

Saintonge died there, with a pike through his gullet. Captain Mayo came face to face with a stately Spaniard in full armor, whose rapier drove at him with deadly lunge; but the old Toledo parried it and slipped home under the arm, and the Spanish captain was down. For one brief instant Mayo had a glimpse of Captain Hardy, and Hardy saw him, but they never spoke, for a bullet struck Hardy between the eyes and he fell forward and died.

And so, with the noonday sun striking down hot and blazing, the Santiago was cleared and won. Barely in time, too, for the galleon on her larboard side, with the bottom torn out, was sinking and dragging her over, and went down like a stone when the lines were cut.

Aboard the smaller of the two galleons, Captain Mayo sent his prisoners and their wounded. Out of all the buccaneers, not thirty men remained on their feet. Captain Mayo told them and told his own men how they had been trapped here, and then ordered Don Fernando de Ribera led before him.

In chains, they brought up Don Fernando, and his eyes struck around proudly, then gripped upon those of Captain Mayo.

"We know everything," said Mayo. "Have you aught to say, señor, before I hang you?"

"Only," said the Spaniard, "that there is no gold aboard that old hulk yonder—we took it out ourselves, before I came to lead you into the trap."

Yells of execration went up from those around, but Captain Mayo smiled as he met the proud, unafraid eyes of the man.

"You have courage, *señor don,*" he said gravely. "It is a pity you are a Spaniard."

"It is a pity," responded the other politely, "that you are a buccaneer."

"Take him aboard the galleon with the others," said Captain Mayo, "and let them sail home again—"

SO IT was done, indeed, although the remnants of the buccaneers yelled fierce oaths and came near to taking up arms, but that Garf O'Malley and his crew held them in fear. And, then Captain Mayo looked at them, and under his gaze they fell silent.

"You dogs!" he said. "Like men ye fought this day. We'll take this great ship back to Le Cap, and share her together as we won her together, and there's an end of all ill feeling. Are ye content?"

Content they were, and scarce believed their good fortune, and with this all hands fell to work among the wounded, of whom there were many.

But Captain Mayo went back aboard the brig, bethinking him of Joanna. He had seen her nowhere, but presently he came to the helm again and found her still there, gripping the beam and smiling up at him with a strange peace in her dead face. A bullet had struck her to the heart.

So it happened that in San Domingo men spoke of Captain Mayo with awed breath, and Don Fernando de Ribera gloomily pondered how he might meet again with the man who had spared him—and whom he now hated. But into Le Cap sailed the Anglesea and the great galleon her prize, and for many a day the streets ran with Spanish wine, and the taverns and gaming houses were overrun.

Aboard his ship, however, remained Captain Mayo, dreaming a new and greater venture.

IV

BUCCANEER BLOOD

It wasn't the nooses waiting for him in two countries that made Denis Burke want to leave piracy—and Haiti—behind.

CHAPTER I

A FAIR EXCHANGE

M. DU CASSE, royal governor of the French portion of Hispaniola, in this year of war and destruction, 1703, looked from his open window across the harbor of Cape François and frowned as he listened to the trim gentleman before him. Chevalier Renault had arrived only this afternoon, from France. Chevalier Renault commanded The Prince, the frigate now lying in the roadstead, between Captain Mayo's brig and the huge Spanish galleon which Mayo had fetched in as prize, not so long since. Chevalier Renault was a bold-eyed, handsome, confident nobleman.

"My dear chevalier, there must be some mistake," murmured the governor.

"There is none," said Renault. "This Captain Mayo, as you call him, is well known to me. I saw him plainly as I came ashore, and recognized him. He is the man, Denis Burke, formerly a high officer in the Irish Guards, who insulted His Majesty and escaped from France with a good ship. Here are the letters ordering that Burke be seized, wherever found, broken on the wheel, and hung." With his hand, Renault slapped the documents he had laid on the table.

"This Captain Mayo has been of the greatest value to us," said the governor slowly. "You see that galleon yonder? He captured her—"

"We are not at war with Spain!" broke in Renault harshly. "Spain is our ally against England. *Monsieur*, I am astonished by your argument!"

"He is, it is true, a buccaneer," went on the governor, as though he had not heard. "His crew are chiefly Irish and English. They are better fighters than our buccaneers—"

"Scum!" exclaimed Renault with energy. "Filthy brutes, all of them!"

"But useful," said the governor. "It will not be easy to hang this man, my friend. He seldom comes ashore. His audacity is remarkable. He bears my letters of marque, also."

"My frigate can blow him out of the water in one broadside," said Renault impatiently.

"Before it could be fired, your frigate would be lost. You do not know that man, chevalier! He can accomplish the impossible. This matter requires strategy, not force." The governor swung around in his chair. He sighed, for he liked Captain Mayo exceedingly well. The king's orders, however, brooked no protest.

"As you know, chevalier, I am giving a ball to-night for you and your officers. Your sick are coming ashore now. I suggest that you give your entire crew shore leave for the evening. Send them ashore before dark. After dark, certain of them, with a hundred men from my garrison, will come quietly out to your ship. Boats will put out to take other men aboard the Anglesea,

The burning vessel illuminated the harbor.

Captain Mayo's vessel yonder."

The chevalier, very brave in his sky blue and silver lace, frowned.

"I thought you advised against force?"

"Exactly. In ten minutes I shall invite Captain Mayo and his officers to attend the ball this evening. They will be arrested here, in the palace. Many of their men will be seized in the taverns ashore. He is short-handed already, due to his losses in capturing yonder galleon, so that those who remain aboard his ship will be helpless, under your guns. You comprehend?"

The chevalier was delighted. He lifted his wineglass, his eyes shining.

"Excellent, *monsieur!* But you say he never comes ashore?"

"Except on business or pleasure. He will accept my invitation. I'll send it at once."

Hastily writing the invitation, he summoned one of his aides and sent the missive. Then he leaned back and surveyed his guest.

"My dear chevalier, this Captain Mayo is well liked here. He has many friends. He is a gentleman of most admirable qualities. But he is devilish sharp, I warn you! Do nothing that will cause the least suspicion. By no means swing your ship about so your guns will bear—"

"I don't propose to go aboard again," said the Chevalier Renault, with a smile. "I'll send the orders and empty the ship, as you suggest. Most of my men are ashore this moment. A few marines will remain aboard as guard. I will pick those who are to return to-night—"

They fell into earnest, low-voiced discussion.

CAPTAIN MAYO sat in the main cabin of the Anglesea. Before him bowed the governor's aide, and Mayo opened the invitation which the aide had brought to him. Mayo's head lolled forward, his tongue was thickened by liquor. He read the message aloud to his friend and sailing master, Garf O'Malley—huge, bearded, an admirable seaman.

"Bidden to governor's ball to-night, Garf. In honor of Chevalier Renault and his officers," he said, with a hiccough. "Ladies, dice, wine, dancing—Fine!" He looked up at the aide, and waved his hand fatuously.

"Tell M. du Casse that I shall be pleased to accept the invitation. All of my officers, too. An hour after sunset, eh? Good!—Another dozen bottles of this Canary to clear our heads, Garf! And send a dozen ashore with this gentleman. Little gift from Cap'n Mayo."

The French officer bowed his thanks and departed. Captain Mayo met the astonished stare of O'Malley, and a smile touched his sharp, aquiline features. His voice cleared instantly, and his blue eyes were twinkling.

"Are ye blind, Garf?" he said, reaching for a long pipe and tobacco. "He'll go back and say I'm fair drunk. We're in a tight place, eh? The captain of that frigate is Chevalier Renault. Thought I recognized him. He stared hard at me as his boat passed. I was at the rail, if ye mind. Aye! He's just come from France, and now we're bid ashore to a ball!"

A soft whistle of comprehension broke from Garf O'Malley, and his frown cleared.

At the moment, all the Caribbean shores were running red with war and destruction. The English were raiding the French and Spanish islands, these allies were raiding the English settlements. When Port Royal sank beneath the sea overnight, the enemy swept upon paralyzed Jamaica. Buccaneers, gathered from all nations, though nominally under French rule, raided with uncontrolled ferocity,

"The devil!" rumbled Garf. "We've a scant three-score men left, some o' them wounded!"

"Exactly," assented Captain Mayo, briskly. "My real name has leaked out; many of our men know it. This Renault has fetched orders from France to scour every port for me; he was at court when the thing happened. And now the governor invites us ashore, ye see?—Malachi! Malachi!"

The door opened. Grizzled Malachi Halloran, who for years had been Mayo's soldier-servant, entered and saluted. Captain Mayo puffed his pipe and eyed Malachi with eyes atwinkle.

"Malachi, it's a warm day."

"Your honor's right in that," said Malachi.

"It'll be a warmer night, for it may end in hell for some. Pick out the bos'un, and half a dozen more men ye can trust, and give them my orders. None other's to know. Two boats' crews will remain aboard here, with one boat—the longboat. Have her lowered and left alongside, with her oars well muffled. Half an hour before sunset, you'll take ashore all the rest of the men. Ye know that chest of Spanish gold pieces under my berth? Open it up. Give each man as much gold as he can carry. Once ashore, break up into parties among the taverns. Pass the word that Cap'n Mayo has given all hands a night's carouse ashore."

At these startling orders, Malachi's mahogany features changed no whit.

"Half an hour after sunset, you and the others watch our rigging," went on Captain Mayo. "When ye see two lanterns hoisted aft, then muster every man sharp, down to the water front. And not a minute's delay, mind! Tumble into the boats, but make no noise or confusion. Then row out to the French frigate yonder. If any hinder your going, use your pistols."

Malachi saluted and cleared his throat. "You'll be taking the frigate, your honor?" he demanded without surprise.

"Aye. And when the flag goes down from the fort at sunset, hire one of the boatmen ashore to come out here to get a passenger. Mind, now—at sunset! Half an hour later, watch for the two lights. That's all."

MALACHI SALUTED again and stamped out. Garf O'Malley frowned heavily.

"Art mad, Denis? That frigate's crowded with men!"

Captain Mayo, who had once been Denis Burke, smiled lazily.

"Since we left France, old friend, life's been a gamble. I'm gambling now. I take it this invitation ashore is a trap set by Renault and the governor. They'll think to seize me and our men and grab this ship. I mean to take their frigate instead. She's a fine new ship; fast and well armed."

"Eh? But she's full o' men! We've not enough to take her—"

"If my guess is correct, her crew will go ashore. Conscience is a bad guide; Renault will fear to arouse our suspicion, will draw his men ashore. A good part are already there. We'll give up this ship, which has served our turn, and take his."

O'Malley pawed his big beard, uneasiness in his eyes.

"What the devil, Denis! Our gold and our rich cargo—?"

"The best part's already sold; here are the bills of exchange, which will be honored by the money changers in any port." From his pocket, Captain Mayo took a sheaf of papers and tossed them on the table.

"Why give them to me?"

"To keep safely. It's you'll be the captain of the new frigate."

"Devil fly away with you!" roared the exasperated O'Malley.

"What's in your mind, Denis?"

Captain Mayo broke into a laugh. "Why, just this! I'm going to be Denis Burke once more, d'ye mind? Damme if I'll let this dog Renault play me so scurvy a trick without getting well paid for it! I'm going to stop ashore. You'll take the frigate out to sea, and three weeks from to-night come down the west coast of the island and put in at the little fishing port of St. Marc. It's wild country—naught there except a few cattle drovers and fishermen. I'll meet you there, three weeks from to-night."

"You fool!" stormed O'Malley wrathfully. "You'll not stop ashore here. You've proved often enough that there's no luck for you ashore, but only at sea! You're of the sea Burkes, and only at sea will you have any luck—"

"Bah!" exclaimed the other scornfully. "I'm sick of yielding to luck! From now on, I'll make my own luck, my own fortune! I stop here, and I'll stop alone. After serving years with the army in France, think you I can't pass for a Frenchman? And I've plenty of captured papers to prove it, not to mention a valise of gold and jewels I'll take ashore! No more of your blarney, now. Listen to me. I'll give you orders, and God help you if you don't follow them to the letter!"

So, leaning forward, Captain Mayo spoke rapidly, incisively. Big Garf listened, at first in sullen anger, then in gradual comprehension, as he pawed his grizzled beard.

WHEN THE flag was lowered from the fort at sunset, a small boat went out to the Anglesea and brought a single passenger ashore. The town around the shore of the curving bay was riotous with song and loud voices, for the crew of the French frigate, as well as the buccaneers, were ashore. The taverns and the streets were filled with drinking, brawling, shouting men. In from the plantations, scattered along the French portion of the island, had come out-of-work buccaneers, hands, women, owners.

The man who came ashore from the Anglesea was lost in the wild crowd. The shades of evening had crept across the town and the harbor. Half an hour later, two lanterns were hoisted in the after rigging of the Anglesea.

A little afterward, sudden alarm swept the shipping and spread along the waterfront, for it was seen that the Anglesea was afire. Almost immediately there came a great rush of fiery sparks from her after hatch, a tremendous burst of spouting flame that illumined all her spars and rigging. This was swiftly followed by an explosion that shattered every window in Le Cap as her powder magazine went up. A pall of disaster and darkness descended on the harbor. An enormous mushroom cloud of powder smoke settled over everything.

In this instant of appalling horror, no one knew what was happening. No one heard the yells of alarm from the deck of the Prince; no one could see the boats from shore and the longboat from the Anglesea which had converged about the ladder of the Prince. No one saw her upper canvas fall to catch the faint breeze.

Indeed, before the smoke cloud had lifted, before a soul suspected that anything was amiss, she had slid from her anchorage and was standing out for the sea. Then three of her larboard guns crashed out a derisive salute to the fort on Morne Rouge, and in this fashion did Captain Mayo leave Hispaniola forever.

CHAPTER II

SIEUR DE BELLEGARDE

SOME TWO weeks after these events, Sieur de Bellegarde was leisurely riding toward Le Cap, after a fortnight's visit in the south. Presumably, he had just arrived from the Spanish settlements across the island, and he even bore letters from Santo Domingo to certain gentlemen at Le Cap.

No one could have looked less like Captain Mayo—or Denis Burke either. Bellegarde's hair was now black, and a black mustache jauntily adorned his lip. His blue eyes bore the same keen and whimsical laughter as of old, but his once fair complexion was gone; the tropic sun had burned his face to a deep brown. He was clad in rich black velvet, a gold chain glittered at his neck, a gold-hilted rapier slapped his horse's barrel.

Unhurried, he rode through the hospitable, rich, devil-may-care land, where plantations were growing wealthy from coffee and sugar and rum, where visitors were hospitably received, and where the best, if perhaps lawless, blood of France had settled. So, upon a day, he rode up a great avenue of chestnuts to the plantation of M. du Perron, a few miles outside Le Cap, presented a letter from another planter down the coast, and was straightway greeted with open arms. Visitors were literally lords of everything within their sight, for they came rarely and were enthusiastically welcomed. The lazy, luxurious planters and their families liked nothing better than to be visited by guests from the outer world.

Perron, a stout gentleman of fifty, flung his arms about Bellegarde, introduced him to his large family, sent his slaves to make ready a chamber. Then he announced joyfully that other guests would be arriving during the course of the day—namely, a group of officers from the city, belonging to the frigate newly arrived from France.

Bellegarde, being from Santo Domingo, knew nothing of recent events hereabouts and listened with grave interest to the tales of Captain Mayo the buccaneer. He heard some astonishing stories, but none more astonishing than that told him by Perron's eldest daughter, the grave-eyed Felice, as they walked in the gardens that afternoon, after the siesta hour.

"Captain Mayo himself was blown up with his ship," she said. "They say the devil was seen flying away with him; but his men seized the great new frigate in the harbor and sailed away with her. I saw the fire and the explosion when his ship blew up, but I did not see the devil take him. I was in the city that evening, attending the governor's ball."

"Faith," said Bellegarde, "it's lucky for you that Captain Mayo didn't know it! Or else he'd have been there to fly away with you."

"No danger!" and Felice laughed at this. Her laughter was like the ring of silver bells, and in her grave eyes of gray there was a starry glint.

Bellegarde was astounded by the cool, wise ways of her. She was not like the other women in this island.

"He'd have naught of me," she continued. "You see, I'm too old. Past twenty-one, *m'sieu,* and more interested in seeing that the *habitation* is run aright than in love-making."

"That's your misfortune, then," said Bellegarde gaily. "A plantation can run itself, but there must be two parties to a love match. Poor old woman! You'll never be married, then?"

She had told him that she was twenty-one; but Creole girls usually marry early.

"No," she said quietly, and meant it. "The right man never came this way, you see, and my father is easygoing in such matters, and would not force me. So I am doomed to a single life!'"

"Hm! You're not one to be forced," returned Bellegarde. "Yet with all these gallant young officers coming—"

"Bah!" she exclaimed, her eyes flashing. "All they think of is debauching women, gambling, getting drunk! I'll have a man who does things, or none! I'd prefer a buccaneer like that terrible Captain Mayo, rather than a wine-bibbing, empty, swaggering coxcomb. Oh, you well know what I mean! I'll wager you've done things in your time, M. de Bellegarde!"

"I have that," said Bellegarde musingly, "but there's one thing, or maybe two, I've never done."

"Yes?" and she gave him a sharp, eager look. "What might they have been, then?"

"I never dishonored my word, young lady, or betrayed a trust. And on the faith of a gentleman," he added gaily, "I predict you'll have a suitor before another day is past!"

"Oh!" she said, and laughed. "Who is he, then?"

Bellegarde shook his head. "My prophetic gifts don't go that far. I'll look into the future and tell you this evening, if you agree."

Her eyes sobered. "Are you in earnest, *m'sieur?* Can you really read the future?"

"I am in earnest," said Bellegarde. "Most devilishly in earnest!—And I can read the future at times, aye!"

She held out her hand to him.

"Agreed, then," she said as he bowed above it. "After the first dance, to-night!"

BELLEGARDE CHANGED into his other suit, one of plum-colored silk; and buckling on his rapier, went for a walk, to the astonishment of the black slaves, who rarely saw a white man take any exercise. Once away from the house, he scowled and fell to cursing himself furiously.

"You blackguard, you!" he muttered, angrily. "Would ye have no more sense than to be making love to the first woman ye meet? Faith, she's too good for the likes of you, and her thinking you a fine gentleman! What'd she say, now, if she knew you were a rascally filibuster and an outlaw, eh? More shame to you—and you going on forty, to be thinking about a woman half your age! But the devil of it is, she's a fine woman to be thinking about, and she has a liking for you—"

His reflections came to an abrupt end as he strode rapidly along the road. Ahead of him appeared a party of half a dozen riders; the glint of metal, the bright uniforms, told him that these must be some of the officers from the town.

Bellegarde was still thinking of Felice. He had heard that M. du Perron had been a buccaneer in his youth, so it was most like that the daughter had inherited some of the father's lost energy. At this thought, Bellegarde nodded vigorously, and the horsemen came to a halt, looking at him in some surprise.

"Good day, *monsieur*," said one of them politely. "Can you direct us to the *habitation* of M. du Perron, the planter?"

Bellegarde looked up and recognized Chevalier Renault, but the latter did not know him.

"Straight ahead, *messieurs,*" he said, and surveyed them as they rode on. Renault, four infantry or garrison officers—and one man who looked like an Englishman, perhaps a prisoner on parole, for war was taken lightly in these parts.

Bellegarde returned to the plantation at his leisure. Sight of Renault had driven other matters out of his mind; that dark, cruelly handsome face aroused every bit of antagonism within him. Reaching the house, he found the new guests refreshing themselves with wine, and Perron presented him. There was much laughter over their meeting in the road, and Renault gave him a mocking look, not unmixed with contempt.

"*Ma foi, monsieur!* I thought you were a moonstruck poet, the way you walked and nodded! Or perhaps a dramatist constructing a scene."

"Indeed?" said Bellegarde, with his gay smile. "Not at all. It often happens that I have insight into the future, my dear chevalier; and at the first distant sight of you, the prescience came to me that you were a man about to die."

There was instant silence. Renault turned haughtily.

"Do you jest, *monsieur?*"

"Unfortunately not," and Bellegarde bowed as he met the dark, insolent eyes. Hostility flashed between them. "As a friend, allow me to warn you; my prophecies never fail."

Renault smiled in disdain. "I suppose your black arts did not tell you at whose hand I should fall?"

"They did," said Bellegarde gravely. "At the hand of Captain Mayo. I think that was the name revealed to me."

There was a burst of laughter. The general conclusion was that Bellegarde had neatly acted a part, and Renault was quick to resent it. However, the affair passed off. Captain Mayo being dead, as all thought, it was assumed that Bellegarde was joking, and Renault took it in bad part. He was so obviously a gentleman, and a man of parts, that it was impossible to take his prophetic pretensions with any gravity.

Within half an hour, indeed, Bellegarde had made himself exceedingly popular with the other guests. The Englishman was a Sir James Norris, captain of a frigate. He had recently been captured and was now on parole. A bluff, hearty Norfolk man, he had a huge capacity for liquor.

THE SUN down, candles were lighted and they gathered in the salon for an hour of gaming before dinner. The huge ballroom was being made ready for the dance that was to come later, when guests would have arrived from adjoining plantations. Bellegarde played recklessly and lost heavily, for which he cared little. M. du Perron, who was advancing him money in profusion, drew him to one side and expostulated with him.

"My dear fellow, it isn't the money. God knows that is nothing to me! But you display no wisdom in your bets. You throw gold aside as though it were copper!"

Bellegarde clapped him on the shoulder.

"And so it is, *mon ami!* Leave your guests and come to my room for a moment."

With some wonder, Perron excused himself. In the huge chamber occupied by Bellegarde, he watched the latter unbuckle his saddle-bag and take out rolls of gold pieces, then slip into his pocket a flat leather case. Bellegarde, laughing, returned the gold which his host had advanced.

"Come, M. du Perron, were you not a filibuster yourself at one time?" he said, with a wink. "Why not throw gold aside like copper, when my own blood purchased it? Blood is cheap. Come along! I've a fortune awaiting me at Guadeloupe, so why not be amused?"

They rejoined the others. Bellegarde continued to lose heavily, and Renault, who chanced to play opposite, raked in the broad Spanish pieces.

"You must be lucky at love, *monsieur!*" he observed with a sneer.

"True." Bellegarde twirled his mustache. "So lucky, egad, that

I am resigned to lose when I gamble for money. Since you recognize the symptoms so readily, I presume you do not have luck with the ladies, eh?"

"The devil!" exclaimed Renault angrily. "Are you determined to insult me, *monsieur?*"

"A thousand pardons!" said Bellegarde, laughing, and contriving to make the very apology a further insult. "Upon my word, it had not occurred to me!"

Before the matter could go further, dinner was announced.

Bellegarde found himself between Sir James Norris and Felice, at table. It was a feast, rather than a dinner, and washed down with such copious quantities of excellent wine that ere long all tongues were loosened and all spirits high—as the host designed. Of all those at table, Bellegarde alone drank no drop, though only Felice noticed it.

"The Sieur de Bellegarde does not drink our good wine?" she asked in a low voice, giving him a flashing smile.

He met her eyes very gravely. "Not this night, my dear," he rejoined. "To-night of all nights, I keep a clear head."

"For your prophecy to me?" she asked, laughing. He nodded.

"Yes." Just the one word; but it held so much meaning, so much earnestness, that her smiles died before it. She regarded him half-perplexed, half in surmise.

Then, suddenly, Bellegarde turned, for the talk had swung upon Captain Mayo, and Sir James Norris was speaking.

"A pestilent rogue, *messieurs!*" he was saying in his bluff way. "Is he not Irish?"

"Aye," said Renault. "Fair haired, slim, a devil with a rapier. He was Colonel Burke of our Irish regiments, but he insulted the king and fled from France. The ban is out against him. He was to be sent in chains to France, if we caught him. But now he's dead."

"And we also had orders to hang the Jacobite rogue if we caught him," said Sir James.

"Indeed?" queried one of the French officers. "But I understand he had French letters of marque, given before we knew he was Colonel Burke! He'd be a prisoner of war."

"Not at all," said Sir James. "In 1692—that is to say, eleven years ago—it was decreed that Jacobites holding foreign commissions and acting as buccaneers should be proceeded against according to the statute of the twenty-eighth, Henry VIII, and treated as traitors within the 25th of Edward III, if you comprehend our legal wording. In other words, hung."

Sieur de Bellegarde, to whom this information was very interesting, twirled his mustache and smiled, his blue eyes dancing.

CHAPTER III

AU REVOIR

BELLEGARDE DID not meet Felice in the garden until after the sixth dance, for Renault had captured her and he refused to let her go. When at last she joined him in the moonlight, she was flushed and eager, and came running down the path with the grace of a deer.

"Rescue!" she panted, laughing. "Ha! I thought I'd never get away from those officers, but here I am. And now, what of the prophecy?"

"If you like the officers so well, get on back to them," said Bellegarde.

Her silvery laugh rang out again. "What! Angry with me? But I had a purpose in lingering, *monsieur!* I wanted information, and I got it. I'll trade it to you for the prophecy you promised me."

Bellegarde sat with her on one of the garden seats, eying her moodily. "Felice, let the prophecy rest," he said in a low voice. "It bodes you no good."

"So? Let me be the judge of that. Who's to be my suitor? Out with it!"

Bellegarde sighed. "A rascal. His name I could not discern; but he's a man much older than you, an arrant rogue, disgraced, outlawed, a buccaneer who can show his face nowhere. After I saw all this, I looked no farther."

"Oh! But it sounds so interesting!" she exclaimed. "Why, it might be Captain Mayo himself!"

"That scoundrel? He's dead."

"But they don't know for certain that he's dead," she replied. "That's the information I was after! The chevalier says he believes that Captain Mayo escaped with his men, and blew up his ship so that it would seem that he was dead. Isn't that worth while?"

"It has naught to do with me," said Bellegarde dourly.

"Has it not, indeed!" she rejoined. "Do you know what that Captain Mayo should do, if he's really alive? He should go to Santo Domingo."

"Eh? And why?" exclaimed Bellegarde in astonishment.

"Because the new governor there is named O'Donoju, and is of Irish blood. He's going to hire certain buccaneers of note and give them Spanish commissions and send them to rid the seas of all filibusters, buccaneers and pirates. I heard the governor talking about it when I was in the city. He was very angry, because it meant that the business has come to an end; the king's share of the spoils has made him rich, you know."

"Eh? But how the devil could O'Donoju do that," broke out Bellegarde, "unless there were some arrangement made between Spain and France?"

"It's been made," she replied. "That's the very point. France has agreed to issue no more letters of marque to filibusters. I'm surprised you knew nothing about it," she added, "since you have so lately come from Santo Domingo."

"So am I," said Bellegarde dryly. "It'd take an Irishman to think of that plan, sure!"

He was, indeed, dumfounded by this information. That certain O'Donohue families calling themselves O'Donojus, were in the

Spanish service, he knew. Also that there were many other noble Irish names in the service of Spain. But he knew nothing of Santo Domingo, across the island, except that the Spanish there had, once upon a time, nearly caught and hanged him.

In a flash he saw, indeed, that there was the one refuge for Captain Mayo, the one chance for redemption, safety, advancement, fortune. This O'Donoju would favor a brother Jacobite exile. With a Spanish commission, Burke could laugh at further threats from France; and once he had earned that commission, Spain would see to it through diplomatic channels that he would have nothing more to fear from the English.

"Victory and blessings!" he exclaimed in Irish. "It's right you are, little dark rose!"

"What tongue were you using, *monsieur?*" asked Felice, watching his face with a smile.

"That? Oh," said Bellegarde hastily, "that was Hungarian.— I learned it in the wars there, on the Danube. I was merely saying to myself that if I had half your wits, I'd marry a great lord."

"Tell me more about my coming suitor," she replied. He wondered if there was a laugh in her voice. "I'm terribly curious. Is the rascal married already, perhaps?"

"No. He was waiting for you, belike," answered Bellegarde whimsically. "And now, my dear; put my occult powers to the test! The spirits have informed me that he was here among the guests to-night, and that he had left a present for you in the little music room off the salon."

She sat up suddenly. "In the music room! Are you jesting, *monsieur?* A present?"

"So I understood it," answered Bellegarde soberly. "It was— let me see! Yes, underneath the neck of a lute that has a blue ribbon tied about it. Is such an instrument there or not?"

"It is, it is!" she exclaimed, and regarded him wide-eyed. "Come, then! Come, let us test the matter! Luckily, the music room is shut off to-night, and not used. Come along!"

NOW, BELLEGARDE had in no wise intended to accompany her; but such was her vigorous insistence that his wits failed him for once, and he found himself straightway in train, for she caught his hand and fairly dragged him into the house. Laughing, he yielded and accompanied her.

So they came to the music room, a small chamber in which various furniture had been stored out of the way for the night. Felice took a candle from the hall outside, and Bellegarde held it while she crossed to where a lute lay on the floor, under the harpsichord. She stooped, uttered a cry of surprise, and straightened up with a flat leather case in her hand.

"What can it be?" She came back to the candle light and examined it. Then she pressed a spring and opened it; caught her breath suddenly, stood staring.

Within the case was a finely worked gold chain and a jewel composed of a great emerald, with diamonds set in gold around it. She closed the case, turned abruptly to Bellegarde. He saw that her face was white with anger, her eyes blazing at him.

"D'you think I'm some woman of the streets, to be taken with jewels?" she asked in a low voice, so charged with passion that he recoiled a step.

"Felice! What mean you?" he exclaimed, utterly astonished. "Faith, it's no crime to be giving a jewel to the fairest—"

"Aye, but whence came that jewel?" she demanded furiously. "Loot! Spoiled with blood, soiled with shame and murder—"

"Upon my honor!" cried Bellegarde. "It was a present to me! A bishop from New Spain gave it to me personally, for having preserved his life from buccaneers! Think you I'd have given you anything unworthy of you?"

The mask was off with a vengeance, but neither of them paid any heed to the fact. As she met his eyes, Felice changed countenance. Her swift anger died into as quick remorse; and seeing the bitterness that was in him, she put out a hand to his arm.

"Oh, forgive me, forgive me!" she broke out, and he saw tears glittering in her eyes. "How could I know? Indeed, my heart told me from the very first what manner of man you were; but just now cold reason gave it the lie, and I could not resist. You see, I believe you absolutely."

"Thanks, my dear," said Bellegarde quietly, and patted her hand. "But what made you think the jewel was loot, or stained with blood?"

"What?" she exclaimed, searching his face. "Can it be that you have so misunderstood me, so misread my words?"

He saw a quick laugh spring in her eyes and banish the tears, then she reached out and pinched the candle, so that darkness fell upon the room and them both. And now Bellegarde heard her move, and caught her voice, low and merry once more.

"Thanks, my dear prophet, for the gift!" she said. "I accept it with all my heart. What made me think amiss of it? Why, I watched your face when they talked at table of that rascally buccaneer; and I looked at your hair, which has grown a bit since you dyed it. So look to your secret, Captain Mayo! *Au revoir!*"

Then she was gone, slamming the door behind her, leaving laughter like the chiming of silver bells in the room.

Bellegarde groped his way to the hall, but she was gone into the midst of the dancing throng.

He was utterly astounded that she should have pierced his secret. Yet, oddly enough, he was delighted also. He admired her quick brain, her ready wit, her penetration. He knew now that she trusted his word absolutely; and she had come to him, guessing everything, to tell him of the one chance that lay open to Captain Mayo.

TWENTY MINUTES later, he stood alone in one corner of the ballroom, watching Felice whirl past in the arms of Renault, and caught one flashing smile from her. About her neck was the chain and jewel he had given her. Bellegarde had extricated himself from the crowd surrounding him; this courtly gentleman, whose eyes twinkled so merrily, whose nimble tongue and strong aquiline features expressed a perfect readiness to flatter or to fight, had become hugely popular with all.

A black slave approached him, and with a bow handed him a scrap of paper. Bellegarde opened it, and perceived that Felice had not been wasting her time.

"Don Carlos de Alvarado," he read, "who brought the news from O'Donoju, is at Le Cap. He returns to-morrow by ship to Santo Domingo."

Bellegarde started, crushed the paper in his hand, beckoned back the slave. In an instant, he perceived what had been in the mind of Felice. To-night was his last chance to make arrangements with the emissary of O'Donoju, if he would seize this opportunity. The plantation lay only a few miles from Le Cap. He could ride into town and be back within an hour or two.

"Have a horse saddled for me at once," he ordered the slave. "The best horse in your master's stables. I must ride into the city at once. Provide a guide, with another horse. In five minutes, have them ready."

He put a coin into the slave's hand and turned away. M. du Perron, his girth shaking with laughter, was with a group of ladies who had come to the ball from nearby plantations. At a gesture from Bellegarde, he excused himself.

"Well, my friend? You are enjoying our little carefree party?"

"It is admirable," said Bellegarde. "But important business has arisen; I must ride into Le Cap, returning immediately. I have ordered a horse and a guide, with your permission. Pray, say nothing to anyone of my departure. I'll be back before it's noticed. Do you happen to know where I can find Don Carlos de Alvarado, an emissary from Santo Domingo?"

"Let me see—some one mentioned him," said Perron, frowning. "Ah! He is staying at the house of Aguilar, the notary who acts as consul for Spain in the city."

"Thanks," said Bellegarde, and departed hastily.

CHAPTER IV

SAFE CONDUCT

DON CARLOS, who got out of bed to receive his visitor, was a grizzled veteran who stared hard at Bellegarde when the door had closed.

"I do not know your name, *monsieur,*" he said in passable French. "Your business—?"

"Is private, *señor,*" said Bellegarde in Spanish, "and I trust in your honor. I am Captain Mayo."

The Spaniard uttered a low exclamation, and his eyes widened.

"I have heard of your errand here," went on Bellegarde quickly. "I offer myself and my men, and the frigate which I command, in your service. If a commission be given me, I will sail to Santo Domingo at once, and will guarantee to make these seas safe from buccaneers and all pirates of whatever nation. I ask only a full pardon for past offenses."

"By the nails of the Saviour, you have audacity!" swore the astounded Spaniard. Bellegarde swept him a laughing bow. "It requires no audacity, *señor,* to entrust myself to a *caballero* of Spain."

Appreciation lit the eyes of Don Carlos; nightcap and all, he returned the bow gravely.

"Thank you, *señor;* your trust is not misplaced. I cannot guarantee anything, but I have heard your name discussed, and I know that the Conde de. O'Donoju, my master, would be delighted to have you—above all others—take advantage of the new conditions. If you'll come to Santo Domingo, I will at least guarantee you safe conduct."

"Agreed, *señor.* Inform him that I shall be there within a week or two, and give me the safe conduct," said Bellegarde.

Don Carlos sought ink, quills, paper, and presently wrote and sealed the safe conduct. Bellegarde thrust the precious document into his pocket and left.

"And now," he reflected exultantly, as he rode out of town with his negro guide, "naught remains except—to get there! This is Monday. Wednesday night I have a rendezvous with Garf O'Malley. Come hell or tornado, he'll not fail me. But what about Renault? And Felice?"

He questioned the negro guide shrewdly, learning that if he were to reach any point on the west coast of the island by Wednesday night, he must leave the plantation not later than next morning, for he must go by hill trails and across sparsely settled country, the west coast being little occupied. Finding that the man knew these trails, Bellegarde asked his name.

"Jacmel, *m'soo,*" came the response.

"Good. To-night I will buy you from your master. Once at the coast, I promise you your freedom if you guide me well," said Bellegarde. "At sunrise, have the three best horses in the stables saddled and ready, but say nothing of it. You comprehend?"

Wild with delight, the black man promised. As the ball would not be breaking up until sunrise or after, no one would observe his activities.

During the two-hour absence of Bellegarde, Felice du Perron unexpectedly found herself the center of attraction. This night there was a gaiety in her manner, a light in her eyes, a glow in her face, that made a new woman of her. Last but not least, the magnificent jewel at her breast attracted no little comment.

M. DU PERRON, having drunk not wisely but well, took her aside; and on hearing whence had come the gift, laughed in loud delight and departed satisfied, for the gift of a jewel to a fair face was accounted a tribute of all honor. Besides, he liked Bellegarde.

Sir James Norris, however, after dancing with Felice and vastly admiring the jewel, said nothing when he heard who had bestowed it. But presently he beckoned Chevalier Renault into the empty card room and sat down with him over a bottle of wine. Renault laughingly obeyed.

"What!" he inquired. "Do Englishmen prefer drink to such fair faces as we have here?"

Sir James grunted. "Aye, when more important matters impend. You have seen that magnificent emerald worn by Mlle. du Perron, of course?"

Renault's face darkened. He had danced repeatedly with Felice this night, and having met her at the governor's house in town, he had indeed come hither on this visit in order to meet her again, though so far he had had little satisfaction from that meeting, except a few dances.

"Aye," he answered curtly. "A gift from that fellow Bellegarde. Sieur de Bellegarde! I never heard that any of the family were in these parts."

"Well, listen to me," said Sir James. "Some three months ago our squadron picked up a Spanish galleon that had been pillaged by Captain Mayo, then turned adrift with her ship's company. Among them was the bishop of Nuevo Toledo, who visited our frigate and related the story of the taking by Captain Mayo. This bishop was of a great family in Spain, and had much wealth. He told how Captain Mayo had saved his life after the galleon was taken, and in return he had given the rogue—what think you? This exact jewel, no other. He described it in detail, for it was a notable emerald, looted from the Incas in Peru and afterward come to him."

Chevalier Renault leaned back, stared at the Englishman, and swore amazedly. A sudden gleam of fire came into his dark eyes. He sprang to his feet, then sank down again, frowning intently, his face very pale.

"You've hit it!" said Sir James, with a nod. "This Bellegarde is some buccaneer."

"Mort de ma vie!" cried out Renault. "He is more than that, my friend! Now I know why a certain familiarity in his features

struck me! He has dyed his hair black, and grown a mustache! He is brown instead of fair!—by the lord, he is Captain Mayo himself! This explains his insolence to me. Why, curse his audacity, he was mocking me all the while!"

Renault passed into a furious torrent of curses, then checked himself and sat moodily, sipping his wine, an infernal glow in his dark eyes. When the amazed Englishman suggested consulting their host, Renault shook his head, laughed, and stirred into action.

"No, no! Leave Perron out of it. The rogue has imposed on him, and anyway, our host has drunk too much to be a safe confidant. Captain Mayo, eh? Keep it to yourself, my friend. If this night sees his end, you are free without ransom. May I count upon your help?"

"Of course!" exclaimed Sir James. "If you need a rapier, I may say without boasting that I have few equals with small sword or Italian blade—"

"Good." Renault leaned forward. "Look you! This fellow is no gentleman, and is not to be treated as such. He's a pirate, a mad dog, a rogue safer dead than alive. Leave the matter to me and to my friends, and join us when I signal you."

So saying, the chevalier called a slave and sent for his friends, one after another, who had come with him from town. The four officers joined him; and Sir James listened with an occasional nod to the low-voiced conversation, and was well pleased with himself. Indeed, he bade fair to gain heavily by it all, since to be set free without ransom would mean much to him, and he flattered himself that he had very sharp wits.

IT WAS midnight when Bellegarde regained the plantation house, laid aside cloak and hat, and presently got M. du Perron off to himself.

"Peste, monsieur!" exclaimed Perron, half humorously, half in protest. "You're the very devil of an energetic person! You've been to the city indeed?"

"Aye," said Bellegarde cheerfully. "Look you, *monsieur!* I should like to buy one of your slaves, a fellow named Jacmel—"

"Buy him? Do you seek to insult me?" cried Perron. "Nay, take him and welcome! I make you a free gift of him. Eh! That reminds me. You've been making gifts yourself, eh?" And with a laugh, he dug Bellegarde in the ribs.

"So Felice told you? Well, M. du Perron, I have something confidential to say to you," and holding the man's eyes, Bellegarde spoke softly, gravely. "I came hither under a name not my own, for reasons which you may know to-morrow, but which I cannot reveal now. I would cast no dishonor upon you, my friend. I desire you to know that I am going to carry away your daughter to honorable marriage in Santo Domingo,"

Perron's jaw fell. "Eh? Carry her off—*mon Dieu!* Which daughter? I have eleven—"

"Felice."

"Oh!" Perron's face cleared. "I have no objections to that, but about a dowry—"

Bellegarde broke into a laugh. "I desire no dowry, *m'sieu.* I merely wished you to know that I could not take advantage of your hospitality, and that your daughter goes to honorable marriage, to what I trust will be a proud position—"

Perron clapped him on the back, jovially. "Say no more! I thought you were a Spaniard all the while; you have an accent I could not place. Felice, eh? Good! I know you're a man of honor, a gentleman. Can't fool old Perron! You've come to me like a gentleman, and I'll treat you the same way. But what the devil! Has Felice agreed to marry you?"

"No," said Bellegarde, "but—"

The other broke into a roar of laughter. "Then talk to her, and not to me. Carry her off, indeed! Faith, *monsieur*, you have my full permission—if you can! Nay, nay, talk to me no more about it. Do what you like, and may the saints aid you!" With this, M. du Perron waddled away in search of the rum punch. So far as he was concerned the matter was closed, except for renewed laughter.

Bellegarde sought Felice among the throng. Once he came face to face with Renault, who lifted his brows and then bowed mockingly. Again, he encountered Sir James Norris, who puffed out his cheeks and regarded him with angry eyes, so that Bellegarde wondered at the man. However, he at length came upon Felice, claimed her for a dance, and straightway carried her off into the gardens.

Once outside in the moonlight, Bellegarde halted and faced her.

"*Mademoiselle,*" he said gravely, "let us cast off all pretense, if you please. I have just returned from Le Cap, where I saw Don Carlos, thanks to your note."

The light struck her face as she regarded him, breathless, her eyes like stars, a smile touching her lips.

"Oh! Then—?"

"I am Denis Burke, formerly colonel in His Majesty's Irish guards, so-called Captain Mayo. I have a safe-conduct for Santo Domingo, with practical assurance that O'Donoju will welcome me and give me a full pardon, and a commission from Spain. After to-night, the name of Bellegarde is cast aside. I leave here at sunrise, in order to join my men and ship at a certain point on the west coast. It means two days of hard riding through the wilderness."

"So soon?" she exclaimed, and her smile died. "You must go—so soon? But I am glad, so glad, for your sake! I congratulate you—"

Her hand went out, and he bowed over it, holding it within his own for a moment.

"There is something else," he went on quietly. "My purpose in coming back to Le Cap was to seek out the Chevalier Renault and take certain measures with him. This intent I have now abandoned. I have just spoken with your father and told him that you were leaving with me, at sunrise. I have his entire permission to speak with you."

SHE DREW back a pace, swift, startled alarm striking into

her features. Denis Burke smiled a little as he looked at her.

"Thanks to you, life is opening anew," he went on. "You may think me mad, but upon my honor I have not spoken so to a woman before this night! Felice, something passed between us when we met, and grew stronger—a bond of liking, of fellowship, of swift clinging, the one to the other. In five minutes I had known you for years. Neither you nor I have great regard for conventions. A spark was struck, a fire was kindled, and now it's ablaze. I love you. I offer you the future that lies before me, and I lay it at your feet. Will you ride away with me at sunrise, or do you think me mad indeed?"

She was silent for a long moment, staring at him with bated breath, her hand touching the jewel at her throat.

"Mad—yes!" she said in a low voice. "Utterly mad, *monsieur!* To leap at a moment, on which must hang one's entire life! To say one word, suddenly, unexpectedly like this, and on that word to wager all of happiness, of destiny, of home and friends and future.—That were indeed madness! Yes, you are mad."

Burke felt his heart go cold within him. He bowed low to her.

"You are right, Felice," he said in a changed tone. "But such madness is part of me; such impulse, such staking of everything in the world on the turn of an instant, on the choice of a word.—Well, it is my nature! And I've not regretted it."—He straightened up, smiling again, bravely. "I'm sorry you don't see it with my eyes, Felice. I thought you might, though reason warned me against such folly—"

"Wait!" she exclaimed sharply. Then she checked herself, and suddenly put out her hand to him again, and a tremulous smile touched her face to soft beauty.

"Mad! You are utterly mad, it is true," she went on. "But it's a glorious madness, Denis Burke! It's the sort of madness that can come into a woman's life only once; and if she flings it aside, she regrets with tears, all her life after. Yes, I'll go with you.—Love? Ah, how can one be sure in a few short hours? But I'll stake everything on the word, on the moment. If I'm not sure now, then I'll be sure before reaching Santo Domingo!"

Thunderstruck, Burke stared at her, then caught her hand.

"Felice—you mean it?"

Her quick laugh, like the chiming of silver bells, made answer.

CHAPTER V

SOMETHING TO FIGHT FOR

IN THE house again, Burke bowed over the hand of Felice, and the song in his heart was echoed in his quick-ringing voice.

"In an hour, then, I'll pack my few things and be ready," he said. "Since we're going, best be off before sunrise, so it'll not be remarked that we go in company."

"In an hour," she echoed, "I'll come to your room. From the balcony outside, a stairway descends to the courtyard. Our departure won't be noticed."

Chevalier Renault had observed their return. He frowned, as Sir James Norris came to him with a muttered query, and shook his head.

"Not yet, not yet!" he said. "When the time comes, I'll give you the word. All is ready; we await the proper time and place."

Then he advanced quickly and claimed Felice for the next dance, bowing to Denis Burke with his feline grace, and smiling strangely.

"Sieur de Bellegarde," he said, "have you any more prophecies?"

"None, alas!" returned Burke, in his whimsical way. "And mayhap the one I made for you will not come true, *monsieur.* I am not infallible."

"Well," said Renault, "I am something of a prophet myself, *monsieur;* and I predict that ere sunrise you will receive several gifts which you do not expect. Let us see which of us is the better prophet!"

So, smiling and jesting, for he had no mind to give his victim any warning, he bore Felice away in a minuet. Burke believed the man meant that the jewel he had given Felice would be returned to him, and laughed to think of the spite beneath the smiling words, and went out to find Jacmel.

He located the black quickly enough, instructed him to have the horses ready in an hour's time, and told Jacmel of the change of ownership. This done, and leaving the man overjoyed, he came back into the house and devoted himself to the stout and short-breathed Madame du Perron. Since he was departing with her daughter, he wanted to leave her with the assurance of his courtesy, and he accomplished the matter so well that in another ten minutes she was eagerly setting one of her younger daughters to dance with him, and beaming graciously on them both.

Denis Burke, however, watched the clock with vigilant eye.

He was, to tell the truth, like a man transformed. Never had his gaiety been so eager, his wit so sparkling, as on this night. In an hour he had cast off ten years of his life, and a bubbling energy surged up within him, wild eagerness to be off and away. The folded safe-conduct in his pocket inspired him with promise of a new future, the past wiped out, honor and love and happiness ahead.

"Faith, it was destiny brought me here!" he thought, and never noticed how the eyes of the black slaves rolled when he passed, and how some of them had him ever in their sight. "And now destiny leads me on.—Ha! Denis Burke comes back to his own again!"

He realized that Felice had done well in suggesting the method for leaving. The wide balcony outside his corner room was broken by a stairway that passed down the outside of the house down into the courtyard. By this means, the two of them could leave unobserved; and he had instructed Jacmel to bring the horses to the foot of this stairway, or as close to it as might be.

WHEN THE clock showed that the hour was at hand, Denis Burke made his way swiftly to the great staircase, where he had a glimpse of Felice passing up ahead of him, alone. Humming a gay air, he mounted, but he did not see a slave who hurried to the side of Chevalier Renault with a low word.

Swinging along the wide, cool corridor, Burke came to the door of his own room, and entered. Candles were burning on the table, and Burke seized his saddle-bag, meaning to change into his black velvet clothes. He got into the breeches, paused to thrust a few golden coins into his pocket, thought of the safe-conduct, and thrust it inside his shirt. Then, catching sight of a miniature of Felice, framed in gold, that rested on the table, he caught it up with a laugh. For several minutes he regarded it, then thrust it after the safe-conduct until he could find a more secure place to carry it.

He buckled on his sword belt, drew out the rapier, and was in the act of wiping a fleck from the blade when his door was flung open suddenly. Felice, a dark cloak about her garments, ran across the room to him, leaving the door half ajar. Excitement was in her face and voice.

"Quickly!" she exclaimed. "One of the slave women just told me—Chevalier Renault and his friends suspect something! There was some talk about Captain Mayo. We must go quickly—this instant!"

Burke whistled. "So? Then the sooner the better. I'll step out and make sure that Jacmel has the horses waiting."

He crossed to the long windows opening on the balcony, flung them back, and stepped out. There was a stir, a movement. He took instant warning, and recoiled into the room, but too late to escape the blow.

A figure took shape from the darkness, there was a flash of steel, and a cry broke from Felice as the poniard drove home. Burke staggered backward, clutching at his breast, and Chevalier Renault, with two others behind him, followed into the room.

"There's one gift for you, pirate and traitor!" cried Renault. "Ha!—You here, Felice? Know you that this man is Captain Mayo—?"

The others uttered a sharp cry, and Renault whirled. Burke had straightened up, and the rapier whipped out in his hand. He broke into a gay laugh.

"So, my dear Renault, you now try assassination!" he exclaimed. The three men stared at him, aghast. Renault's jaw fell as he looked at the ripped shirt of Burke. One of the officers behind him drew sword with a swish of steel.

"No, I'm quite impervious to steel," and Burke laughed again. "But you're not, my dear chevalier, as I shall soon prove! Felice, out the door—!"

The room door was flung open. In came Sir James Norris, sword in hand, and the other two officers with him. At sight of the scene, his heavy voice rang out.

"Renault! Leave this fellow to me—"

Like a flash, Burke was at him. Norris engaged desperately, frantically. The blades crossed, clicked, hung in air, thrusting, feinting, shimmering in the candle light. Then the Englishman uttered a short choking cry, staggered back, and fell beside the bed with a crash. His two companions remained in the doorway.

"At him!" cried Renault, whose rapier was now out. "Around him, all of you—"

All five came on, while Felice watched, wide-eyed. Burke flung her a kiss, and his gay voice leaped to her.

"Quick! Await me below!"

She darted to the door on the gallery, stepped outside—then remained there, held by the clink and click of the blades. What she beheld was well worth the watching.

RENAULT AND another drove at Burke in fierce assault, a third endeavoring vainly to get at him from across the wide tester bed, the other two waiting, indecisive.

"Well, chevalier, it seems that my prophecy is coming true after all, eh? And yours, I fear, is not. You did not know that I had a steel corselet beneath my shirt, eh? Or the face of a lovely woman next my heart—?"

His cool confidence infuriated Renault. The officer beside the chevalier sent in a low lunge, finding Burke engaged; but like light the long rapier swept the lunge aside, flicked in a deadly riposte, and Burke leaped back as the officer came to his knees and then fell on his face, pinked through the heart.

"Company for Sir James!" he cried gaily. "Pity to let a bluff Englishman take the long road to hell unassisted!"

Renault leaped in. The man on the bed drove down with his blade. For an instant there was a clash of bodies as all three came together. Then Renault, struck over the eyes with Burke's sword-hilt, staggered back, blinded and cursing. Burke whirled about, and the man on the bed screamed terribly as the rapier drove through his body.

But as Burke drew back, there was a spreading smear of crimson on his white shirt.

With vicious energy, Renault attacked again, another officer at his side, the third and last climbing to the bed beside his dying comrade, to get Burke in flank. For an instant, Burke engaged the two blades before him, attacked vigorously, drove them both back—then made a great leap to the bed, just as the officer there came erect.

"Company for Sir James!" laughed Burke, as his blade drove home. He was down again, now on the other side of the bed, toward the balcony door.

He caught a glimpse of Felice outside, and flung her a wave of his hand. "On with you! Keep the stairs clear—"

Then Renault was upon him. Two left now, out of them all, and Renault was cursing like a fiend as he realized it. Burke was out in the open, and the remaining officer circled about to take him in rear, as he engaged Renault's blade.

The chevalier lunged viciously, feinted, lunged again—and

cried out exultantly as a second smear of red crept out on Burke's shirt. But Burke flung him a gay laugh.

"Tut, tut! Never cry quits for a little scratch, chevalier! When I thrust home, the point goes deep—as you'll feel in a moment—"

What with the music and dancing and resounding merry voices below, no alarm had been caused. The two dying men on the bed groaned terribly, and one of them came to his elbow. His blade flicked out on a sudden. Burke, just then evading a rush from the other two, heard Felice cry out in warning. He slipped aside, but not before the point had transfixed his left arm.

WITH AN oath, he drew clear of the feeble blade, leaped sideways, and struck the remaining officer like a thunderbolt. The unfortunate man had not time to parry, scarce knew that Burke was upon him before the rapier touched his throat and he was gone. He coughed horribly and came to his knees, clutching at his throat.

"At last, a fair fight, chevalier!" cried Burke, as he crossed swords with Renault. The latter, panting, attacked him like a madman, throwing caution to the winds.

Under that furious, desperate attack, Burke was forced back and back. His cool smile was gone now. Blood had soaked over his shirt, and a pallor was growing in his cheeks; he was failing, and Renault perceived it with fierce joy.

"No quarter, traitor!" he cried out, pressing on the more. "To the death!"

"Aye!" said Burke, and suddenly laughed and flung himself into a terrific attack.

Then the chevalier perceived how Burke had toyed with him, tricked him, felt out his style of play. No weakness now in that pale, deadly face; no faltering in those icy blue eyes; no hesitancy in the swift, lithe footwork!

Back and back Renault was driven. Sweat streamed down his face, set now in frantic lines. Yet he fought in bitter silence, exerting every trick of play, trying at all costs to get through

Burke's guard. But that wrist was like steel, and the rapier was one with the arm that held it, and Renault saw death before his very face and closing in upon him.

As the two of them passed the body of Sir James, Burke slipped in the blood and fell sideways, heavily, on his left hand. Renault drove down a swift and vicious lunge; but Burke writhed aside from it, so that the sword point drove into the floor, missing him by the fraction of an inch.

As Renault tugged to free his blade, Burke, lying there, lunged up with his long rapier; then rolled aside and came to his feet.

"I am a true prophet, chevalier," he said, panting.

The sword fell from Renault's hand. He took a step, took another, then his knees were loosened and a gush of blood came from his mouth. Quietly he fell forward on his face.

Burke caught up his cloak, sheathed his rapier, snatched a towel from the corner, and the next moment was descending the outside stairs after Felice.

Ten minutes later, three horses pulled up alongside the road. Felice and Jacmel took the towel and made shift to bandage Burke's hurts against loss of blood; none of the wounds was bad or dangerous, otherwise. His bloody shirt cast aside, he drew the cloak around him and chuckled.

"You can ride, then?" questioned the anxious Felice.

"Ride? To hell and back!" he cried. "Look! It was this picture of you that saved me from Renault's poniard.—But alas, the picture is ruined!—However, I'm glad I killed the rogue."

"The picture matters not," she said, smiling at him. "Since you have the reality, why desire the shadow?"

"In that case," said Burke gaily, "you must reassure me before we mount—"

The reassurance duly given, he was in the saddle with a laugh and a spring, and shook his fist up at the moon in wild exultation.

"Luck of the sea Burkes!" he cried out in derision. "What's

luck, then? What's destiny? What's anything? Less than nothing—when a man has something to fight for!"

So he rode on into the west, with the world before him.

V

SPANISH BLOOD IS PROUD BLOOD

"Most men die because they don't think fast enough," was the creed of Denis Burke, buccaneer.

CHAPTER I

IMPOVERISHED NOBLEMAN

IN THE name of honor!—Well, it works various ways. See for yourselves, comrades. Devilish surprising, sometimes, too!...

Belike, you remember the tremendous hurricane a few years back—1703, to be exact? The one that swept the Main and the Carribee like a devil's broom? Aye! That was when it happened. Rather, it was right after the big wind...

Captain Mayo was heading for Hispaniola, by the long way around. In Spanish eyes—and in English—he was plain pirate. In French, he was something worse, for the French had learned that he was no other than the Denis Burke, once colonel in the Irish Brigade, who had snapped his fingers in the face of Louis XIV, and then taken to the sea. So, capturing a fine French frigate in Le Cap, Captain Mayo went aboard with Felice da Ferron and sailed for Hispaniola.

He never reached there, however.

True, he had every incentive. He and Felice were to be married at Santo Domingo, and the governor was to give him a Spanish pardon and a commission, whereunder Captain Mayo would settle himself firmly and put down piracy. All of which went by the board when the hurricane intervened.

On the second day of it, bearded Garf O'Malley came swaggering into the main cabin, where Denis Burke sat talking merrily with Felice as the ship rolled. O'Malley was more than a brother to Burke, and he was the best seaman ever out of Galway town.

"I'm glad it's you'll be having the deck this night, and not me," said O'Malley, as he got into dry clothes behind the door of his own cabin.

"Why so?" asked Burke. "The blow is quieting, by all seeming."

"Aye, it's a lull—but the kind that fetches round more wind. By night-fall you'll see the sky emptying—and maybe for days and days on end."

Once again Denis Burke laughed his gay laugh.

"Well, what of it? The ship's sound, new, well found. She's just from France, with stores and goods! We've enough Irishmen aboard to man her, if not to fight her, and we've the luck of the Sea Burkes behind us.—Why worry?"

O'Malley came out of his cabin, braced himself, and stuffed tobacco into a long clay pipe as he eyed the two before him.

"Aren't you two in haste to be married?" he demanded.

"One place will do as well as another," said Felice with a laugh. Her father, M. du Perron, had been a buccaneer in his day, and she had his spirit.

O'Malley's grim eye warmed at her smile, her dancing eyes, her quiet confidence. He turned to Burke.

"Denis, ye fool," he said, "don't ye know we can't reach Santo Domingo now? We're far out of our course. Lord knows where

"One move from you and she dies!"

we'll be blown! And except Santo Domingo, there's no safety for you or for us.—Chiefly, none that's safe for you."

Burke shrugged. "Bah! Fate is what you make it. .Most men die because they don't think fast enough! Accept what comes, think fast, act faster—and destiny is yours! So no more croaking—"

A thudding of feet, and Malachi Halloran, who had been Denis Burke's soldier servant and now was his chief gunner, came bursting into the cabin.

"Come you back above, Garf!" he shouted excitedly. "There's a wreck ahead of us, and we'll be striking her if ye give us no orders!"

Not Garf alone, but Burke and Felice were on deck in another moment. The high bows and stern of the Prince, as the frigate was named, were well above the water, but the seas swept her lower main deck intermittently, so far without damage. Dead ahead, as she bore down with the wind, showed a less lucky craft. She was down by the head and sinking fast. Men were clustered in her rigging.

Impossible to give help? Yes, rankly impossible. Therefore, Denis Burke did it. He got lines to her, made fast at risk of sending his own ship down when the wreck plunged. The hapless men came aboard, though not all of them. Some were shaken off into the gulf. Some weakened, gave way. Some were crushed. Thirty men and an officer got aboard before the wreck plunged and the ropes were cut. The rest went down. And the hurricane came three minutes later—a blast out of a cold hell. The frigate was lifted, tossed, blown away and away, in a smother of foam that raced up the dark rim of the ocean.

An officer and thirty men. The Vicomte d'Hendaye, a dark, grim-faced man; also a *capitaine de vaisseau,* serving in the navy of His Most Christian Majesty. At a time when lieutenants commanded frigates and captains ordered squadrons and fleets, a captain in the French navy was distinctly somebody.

There was, among the rest of the thirty men, one named Perouse. A buccaneer; a fierce, bold-eyed rascal, who had acted as pilot aboard Hendaye's vessel. Burke questioned him that night.

"She was a sloop of war, *m'sieu,*" said Perouse. "Sent from Le Cap to pick up M. d'Hendaye. His frigate was lost a year ago. We just learned that he was alive at the mainland. The rascally Spaniards there held him prisoner—"

"What?" exclaimed Burke. "But Spain and France are allies!"

The buccaneer grinned. "Who cares about such things at the edge of the world? And they did not let him go, either. He escaped—by help of Indians. Our sloop picked him up.—And you, *m'sieu?* A buccaneer, eh? Well, ship me and those thirty men. You can use a few more honest filibusters aboard here!"

So it was agreed.

HENDAYE DID not show himself until next day, being near to death from sheer exhaustion and suffering. He was, none the less, a man of iron.

Worse and worse became the hurricane, yet the frigate weathered it well enough; blown on, she crested the seas interminably. Hendaye shared watches with Burke and O'Malley, and proved himself an able man, a fine officer. None the less,

O'Malley fell foul of him, none knew how; and ere the blow died down, they hated each other.

Each blamed the other that last day, when the top-hamper was wrenched over and the frigate left a splintered wreck under lower rigging alone. Still, it was Hendaye who set the men to work, set the wreckage out as a sea-anchor, made things shipshape, after a falling block had laid O'Malley in the scuppers.

With the next day, the wind had blown itself out and the sun returned to sight. The Prince was lifting on huge, swelling seas, but the hurricane was gone. And the battering of those seas had done things to the frigate. Alow and aloft she was in bad shape. However, she still swam, after a gale that had left few other living ships in these waters.

Burke took stock of her, got the gear and rigging in shape to set out a rag of canvas, set gangs of men at the pumps, and then turned to see Hendaye step out of the shrouds and join him. A glass was over the officer's arm and a wry grimace on his lips.

"Well, M. le Capitaine! Know you where we are?"

"Hardly," said Burke, with a shrug. "No more than yourself."

"But I do." And Hendaye laughed, extending the glass. "Go aloft, look west by south, and you yourself will know. That is, if you've heard tales of the Main! For here's a landmark none can miss. And before ye set a course, let me have speech with you."

He went below, this grim man.

Denis Burke swore amazedly. The mainland? America itself? Impossible! Yet he mounted aloft, and with the glass he made out land, where Hendaye had directed him. And more! A mountain like a sugar-loaf, with two others beside it. The three Sugars, by the Lord Harry! Best-known landmark on the whole Main! And not fifty leagues north of Santa Barbara, the little haven!

Ere sunset, Perouse had confirmed the matter. Then came Malachi Halloran to where Burke stood in talk with Garf O'Malley, on the quarterdeck.

"Your honor, there'll be lashings of seams opened in that storm," he said. "Do what we may wi' the pumps, the water gains. It comes in heavy, forward."

"Break out the spare mainsail," said Denis Burke. "Pass it under the bows, with a line from either corner, and leave it there. The water pressure will hold it so, and it will stop the leaks for a bit."

Malachi saluted and strode off.

Garf O'Malley met Burke's gaze. "Well, Denis? What's yonder at the Main, except hanging? But we can head nowhere else; she can scarce swim now, and she needs repairs and caulking urgently."

"Head for the mainland, of course!" Burke turned, as he saw Felice approaching. "Ah, mistress! Enjoying the sunlight, are you?"

"Well enough," she answered. "Go below, Denis—aye, and you, Garf!—Go and talk with the *vicomte.* I've had speech with him, and it would interest you, too."

"My soul to the devil," said O'Malley roughly, "if I want to pass a word with the likes of him!—It's hard to keep my hands off him. Sorrow the day he came aboard us!"

Denis Burke broke into a laugh. "None the less, come you down as Felice orders!"

So they obeyed. But O'Malley muttered that the Frenchman had done too much talking with Felice, these last few days of storm. Denis Burke laughed again at this, though he was soon enough to find that it was no matter for laughing.

THEY JOINED Hendaye in the main cabin, with wine set out and long pipes alight, and he said his say bluntly enough. He asked if they had heard of Santa Barbara.

"Aye—but vaguely," said Denis Burke, smoothing back his hair and smiling a little. "No man knows it well. They say part of the Plate fleet assembles there each year, and the Spanish keep down all knowledge of it."

"It is little more than a castle dominating the river-mouth and haven," said Hendaye. "The harbor is good, but small. The Spaniards send their choicest treasures thither from the west coast, "instead of to Panama. The roads are more secure, the castle is strong, and the affair is rather secret ...

"Each year, two galleons come to Santa Barbara, pick up the royal treasure, then join the Plate fleet at Panama. Few know of this. The mule trains of treasure come across to Santa Barbara under strong guard.—The treasure is expected there on the first of next month. The galleons arrive two or three days later."

"Eh?" exclaimed Burke sharply. "And how do you know all this, my dear *vicomte?*"

Hendaye smiled in his grim fashion, his thin lips like an old, pale scar. "It's there I was a prisoner until so recently," he said. "For months I was there. I know every inch of the harbor and the fort. With such a ship as this, with such men as yours, the right man could be in command of Santa Barbara when the treasure arrives from the mines. And I think you're the right man!"

Burke's eyes narrowed reflectively, as he puffed at the tobacco. "Hm! The first of the month ten days away, eh? And with a fair wind, we'd reach there in a couple of days."

"And a huge treasure for the taking!" said Hendaye.

Burke eyed him coolly. "Is that all ye can see in it? Gold, eh?—But there's another thing. You're a king's officer. Would ye share with buccaneers in robbing the Spaniards, allies of France?"

"Aye," said Hendaye grimly. "Did they not hold me prisoner, for fear I'd tell about their damned treasure plans?—Well, talk it over. I'm for a breath of air."

He went out on deck. O'Malley met the flashing, eager eye of Denis Burke, and swore. "I see you're tempted, eh? If we had a place to careen the ship, at least, it would pay us for the work of driving out the dons!—Hark, Denis. Think ye this *vicomte* knows of you? Does he know the price King Louis has set on your head?"

"Apparently not," said Burke. "He's a Norman, a man of action rather than an idle courtier. Perhaps he has stuck to the sea most of his life. A nobleman, but devilish hard up, like many another."

"I'd not trust him this side of hell!" growled O'Malley.

"Then trust me!" cried Burke, with his gay laugh. "Besides, Felice has been talking with him. It was she who urged him to speak with us.—Eh?-—She thinks it worth while."

"Then it's settled," snapped the rough seaman, and came out of his chair. "We'll have a breeze with sunset, and the canvas in shape to bear."

CHAPTER II

THE WAY TO THE FORT

THEY WERE more than two days in raising Santa Barbara, for the winds were light and baffling, the water ever gained on the pumps, despite the sail under the bows, and the frigate handled sluggishly.

During these days, Vicomte d'Hendaye was much in company with Felice, who liked him well enough. To her brave, level eyes he showed his best side, and he could be courtly indeed at will. Besides, he had done things; he had fought the redskins in Canada and the English on Hudson Bay and the Spanish in Brazil, and he had tales to tell.

Denis Burke paid no heed. For one thing, he had his hands full. The new men had to be whipped into shape and had to get a taste of his stern discipline. Nor did it occur to him that this clear-eyed girl who had won his heart, whose beauty and power drew at his very soul, might waken the same feeling in other men. Had he thought of it, Burke would have laughed in pride at her ability to sway men's hearts.

Further, he drew charts and obtained from Hendaye a most

detailed knowledge of Santa Barbara. The Spaniards had held its very existence a secret, so that it appeared on few maps; but when he comprehended everything, Burke hummed a gay air. With a hundred and fifty men, thirty guns, and his own audacity, he would have cheerfully attacked a squadron, let alone one small fort.

There was no town. Normally, the place had only a skeleton garrison. Its position, on high ground, with heavy guns commanding the river mouth and the little harbor, was impregnable. Each year, a large escort of troops arrived with the treasure, acting as garrison until the Plate galleons departed. Two of these galleons should arrive soon, according to Hendaye.

Even Perouse, the pilot, knew naught of Santa Barbara. The mainland he knew, however, and brought them in close to its blue shape. Mountains and jungle lifted ahead, and low islets along the coast. Burke hoisted the English flag, for it was well known to all the Indian natives of these parts as that of Spain's great foe, and therefore their friend. It was close by here, said Perouse, that his sloop had picked up Hendaye.

Sure enough, before sunset a *pirogue* set out from the shore with three men in it, making signals. Presently one of the brown men came aboard and greeted them in Spanish; he had but one foot. The other was lopped away, and all his body was criss-crossed with deep scars. Hendaye greeted him with delighted recognition; this was one of the Indians who had helped the *vicomte* escape.

He was given a gun and other gifts.

Burke asked about Santa Barbara.

"A few hours' sail, *señor capitán.* I have been there, as my body shows.—Other ships? None there." The Indian peered at him sharply. "If you need help against the Spaniards, I have some dozens of warriors!"

Burke glanced inquiringly at Hendaye, who nodded. "They are brave men, *m'sieu.* The Spaniards oppress them cruelly; if they can kill one Spaniard, they are content to die. Good allies, and true men also."

"Good!" Burke turned to the native. "The day after to-morrow, bring your men to Santa Barbara. If you see the English flag above it as a signal, you will know that the place is in my hands. If not, go away again."

So the Indian departed with his gifts, and Burke sailed southward.

AN HOUR after sunrise, the frigate, under shortened sail, was standing in for the harbor entrance, hoisting the French flag.

It was quite obvious to all that she was French; further, that she was battered and not far from sinking. Informed by Hendaye of the usual signals, Burke saluted the fort with four guns. Two made reply, to which he answered with three. Naturally, the Spaniards could suspect nothing amiss, and had naugh to fear from a half-sinking ally.

The one landing was a boat-platform, directly below the fort, and guarded by a battery of brass guns. When he had surveyed the place Burke passed his glass to O'Malley and turned to Felice with a smile.

"Well, my dear, in an hour's time you will be mistress of a fair castle!" he said gayly. "So wish me luck. Garf, is everything ready?"

"Aye," replied O'Malley. "Hendaye is biding out of sight."

"Then I leave the ship in your charge. When I wave my arm, go ahead."

The frigate surged in past the battery and rounded to, a hundred feet from the boat-platform. One boat that had escaped the hurricane was lowered. Denis Burke, wearing the attire of a French officer, descended into the boat with a dozen men. From the castle broke brave movement; helms, pikes, morions were glinting in the morning sunlight. A number of officers and guards left the gates, coming down to the waterside.

Burke's boat drew in, and the Spaniards drew up on the boat-platform to receive them. In their midst was a stout *caballero,* magnificently attired. Burke perceived that he alone seemed to be of any rank; the men around him appeared to be hard-bitten adventurers, failed of fortune, or soldiers of no rank.

Upon mounting to the platform, Burke was greeted with a ceremonious bow from the stout gentleman. He returned it in the most courtly fashion imaginable. Once again he was the old Denis Burke, the courtier and friend of kings; and the stately Spanish tongue sat fluently upon his lips.

"*Señores,* I am the Marquis de Rien, capitaine de vaisseau," he exclaimed. "I bear letters and certain confidential instructions from your viceroy at Vera Cruz. With whom do I have the honor to speak?"

"With me, *señor don,*" said the stout *caballero.* "With the governor of this place, Don Jaime Muriata y Gonzalez, hidalgo of Spain, knight of the Order of Alcantara, who bids you welcome. We were astonished that you seemed to know the signals and the approach to the harbor!"

"The viceroy sent a pilot with me from Vera Cruz," said Burke. "But first, there is a matter in which you may be pleased to assist me. On the way hither, I captured an English ship and took some fifty prisoners. Unluckily, I have no quarters aboard for them. I must either kill them or turn them loose ashore, and neither course is to my taste. If you have any use for the rascals, I shall be delighted to give them to you!"

The stout Muriata, who had great girth but little wit, was delighted at this.

"*Por Dios,* nothing could be more opportune!" he exclaimed. "I am hastily building new slave barracoons under the walls, on the other side of the castle. These prisoners can relieve my brave fellows of this distasteful labor. Our Indian slaves are all dead. These low English can take their places, eh?"

"Excellent!" approved Burke, with a laugh. "I'll signal my lieutenant to send them ashore under guard. You may leave them in chains, as you prefer. They are yours, and welcome! Hang them all, if you like!"

Burke turned and waved his arm to the frigate and the watching O'Malley.

A STIR broke out aboard. Another boat dropped into the water.

The Spaniard was overjoyed on two counts. Not only would these prisoners take the place of slaves, but when the treasure galleons came he could send the prisoners along to Spain as evidence of his own prowess. So he bade Denis Burke up to the castle at once.

Burke demurred, begging to await the landing of the prisoners, and talked fluently with the governor and his men. The Spaniards were delighted with him; his ready smile, his gay wit, his soldierly tongue, charmed them. He used the politest of expressions, and knew their tongue perfectly. He called the hidalgo Don Jaime, and not Don Muriata, as other foreigners were apt to do.

He himself admitted that he was an intimate friend of King Louis. He had even heard mention at Vera Cruz that Don Jaime was shortly to be appointed governor of all Cuba. What with one thing and another, he contrived to make the time pass most pleasantly to all, until the boats drew ashore.

Indeed, Burke rather repented him of what was going forward, though there was no help for it now. He found Don Jaime a very perfect, if rather stupid, cavalier, filled with all the devilish pride and honor of a true hidalgo, but none the less a fellow to be rarely liked. And it was quite plain that Don Jaime liked this handsome Frenchman, who wore his gold-hilted rapier with so gallant an air.

The prisoners, all in chains, were landed, under guard of Perouse and a number of Frenchmen. Don Jaime sent them on up to the fort, bidding his own men come forth to relieve the French guard. He and his men inspected the English captives with huge curiosity, and such of the Irishmen as knew English speech, broke into it. The boats, meantime, went back to the frigate, to bring more men ashore openly. The crisis was now at hand.

The file of chained captives went on up to the fort. Don

Jaime, taking Burke's arm, puffed up the ascent after them, sending his escort on ahead. Then, approaching the gates, he halted and turned to his guest.

"*Señor,* I believe you mentioned certain private instructions from His Excellency the Viceroy, for my ear alone?"

"Yes." Denis Burke watched the last of his men pass through the open gates, and smiled. The two men, Spanish gentleman and pseudo-Frenchman, were standing alone. "These instructions, Don Jaime, are that you should surrender yourself and your castle to me. I am no Frenchman, but a buccaneer—Captain Mayo, of whom you may have heard. As I took that frigate yonder, so I am now taking your castle—like this!"

From beneath his cloak he drew a pistol and fired in the air. Then he whipped out his long rapier and regarded the stupefied Don Jaime with a thin smile.

Already, O'Malley was coming ashore in the boats. At the pistol shot, the supposed Englishmen in the castle threw away their chains and produced dirks and pistols, while their French guards turned on the amazed Spaniards.

Within half a minute the latter broke in every direction. Some were slain in the courtyard, others on the walls. Those who surrendered got quarter, but some chose to fight things out even to the death. There was no possibility of escape, and none tried. Either they surrendered or died fighting.

Stout Don Jaime, with a roaring bellow of shame and fury, drew his sword and hurled himself on Denis Burke. The latter met his attack, smiling. A moment later the gold-hilted rapier sent his sword twirling a dozen feet away.

"Ah, you foul dog!" burst out the Spaniard, his eyes blazing. "Devil take you—slay me and be done with it! End my disgrace, dastardly buccaneer!"

Burke laughed a little and sheathed his rapier.

CHAPTER III

PROCLAMATION OF TREACHERY

OF THE ensuing events might be made a great tale. Denis Burke held Santa Barbara like an open net, into which swam the fish all unsuspecting. In truth, not since Morgan sacked Panama had such noble and diverse plunder come into the hands of buccaneers.

First came the two galleons, sailing proudly into the tiny harbor, somewhat earlier than expected. They were no whit alarmed by the presence of the frigate there; she had just been careened, and was under repair. Their commanders and officers and noble passengers came ashore right eagerly. The castle gates opened for them, and closed upon them again. Then the guns of the battery, of the castle, and of the frigate, opened upon the two hapless galleons. These, as needs must, straightway surrendered.

Two days later, Indians brought word that the convoy was coming; three hundred mules laden with gold and silver, and two hundred soldiers of Spain as guard. Burke was already making ready. The smaller galleon had been stripped of her guns, which went ashore to strengthen the fort. Her cargo went into the other and larger galleon, and she was made into a prison ship. All the captives were sent aboard her, with the exception of Don Jaime, and the Conde de Lucar, a spare, dark man, commander of the larger galleon. These two refused to give any parole.

Burke, finding that both were of great families in Spain, held them for ransom. Temporarily, he placed them in a cell of the castle, and so left them.

Now came the convoy, marching to the land gate of the castle; pikemen and arquebusiers, veterans of many a war; the mules and their tinkling bells making an apparently endless file. Half the escort was in the courtyard, the other half still outside, when the cannon was turned upon them. Indians assailed their flanks, and a storm of musketry shattered them. There was little fighting. They had no chance whatever, and they surrendered at discretion.

That same night, Denis Burke put all his prisoners aboard the stripped galleon, with food and water, and let them take her whither they might list. Some fifty slaves he had set free. English, many of them were; others were French. These joined his force. The Indian slaves took to the woods, with the Indian allies, to whom Burke gave powder and muskets.

Evening, then, found all done, when he joined Felice and Garf O'Malley, and the Vicomte d'Hendaye in the handsome room of the late governor. Under Malachi Halloran, a few of his own Irish were on guard. In the courtyard, the remainder were carousing wildly with the French and the freed slaves. Their shouts and songs lifted to those in the room, where supper was just over.

"Well, all's done!" said Burke, sipping wine from a great silver flagon. He eyed the others with a frown. "Sink me! Why so glum, you three?"

"Somewhat is yet unsettled," growled O'Malley, and Hendaye gave him a grim smile.

"Oh, devil take your private quarrel!" cried Burke. "If you two rogues break into a fight, I'll put you both in chains.—Aye! My word on it! So keep out of trouble, until we reach Santo Domingo, at least!"

At this, the two men and Felice alike stared at him.

"Eh? You're not going there, surely?" she asked, gravely enough. "The governor there might have welcomed you before, but now, after what you've done here—"

DENIS BURKE broke into a gay laugh, and his eyes danced at their puzzled wonder. Reaching for the tobacco jar, he began stuffing a pipe with the weed.

"Here's the way of it," he explained. "O'Malley, you'll take the great galleon to Le Cap, along with the Frenchmen we shipped and some few of our men. You'll take half the gold, unload it at Le Cap, and take bills of lading for it. All in your own name, mind! You'll have no trouble, for the French are not after you. Then fetch the galleon around to the other side of Hispaniola, and you'll find me waiting at Santo Domingo."

"And how the devil will ye get there?" demanded Garf O'Malley.

"In the frigate, of course!" said Burke, chuckling. "With the other half of the gold, which I'll turn in to the Spanish governor at Santo Domingo. M. Hendaye will come with me, since I'll need his testimony."

"Wait, Denis!" broke in the girl anxiously. "After what's passed here—"

"That's just the point, my dear," said Burke. "Already they want me in their service, and after this stroke they'll want me more than ever. I'll have half the gold, to buy a pardon. Also, this fortress here, in which I'll leave a garrison."

"What?" cried O'Malley. "You mean to hold this place? You're mad, Denis! The Spaniards will drive you out with fleets and armies!"

"Think you so?" Burke laughed a little. "Let them try! No, now you have the truth, and my purpose. Felice, my dear, will ye come back here with me, after we're married at Santo Domingo?"

"With all my heart, Denis!" she answered happily.

"And you, Garf?" Burke glanced at the bearded O'Malley. "Now you're a rich man, ye may go home to Ireland again."

O'Malley fingered his beard and glanced at Hendaye, his eyes aglitter. "That remains to be seen," he answered. "When do I leave wi' the galleon?"

"As soon as the gold's put aboard her," said Burke. "I'll set some of her guns and powder ashore, too. Ye should get off to-morrow evening."

"Good enough," said O'Malley.

Later, when he and Felice du Perron were alone before the embers of the fire, Burke found her eyes very thoughtful, and a bit anxious.

"Denis, I mislike those two silent men!" she said at length. "They watch each other like wild beasts. We'll have trouble of it yet! Hendaye—" and she paused.

"Well, what of him?" said Burke.

"I don't know. He's pleasant enough, yet he's deep; and he has a dark soul," she made response. "He has the air of one who waits his time."

"Aye—true!" Burke's eyes danced. "Those two men hate each other. The end of it will be that O'Malley kills the *vicomte.* Wait and see! They'll fight it out at Santo Domingo, and welcome. Meantime, they'll be separated, so let it pass. Will ye walk out on the roof and look at the stars?"

They passed up the stairs and out, and Burke thought no more about her words.

WITH MORNING, there befell work and to spare. The freed slaves, and the French recruits under Perouse, were enough to serve as crew for the galleon. They were told off aboard her, and the work of landing her guns and powder in large share, and of lading the gold aboard her, was begun. Perouse was chosen by O'Malley to serve as lieutenant of the craft on the way to Le Cap.

Toward noon, Perouse came ashore to arrange about the gold that was going aboard. As he came through the castle, Hendaye encountered him in the courtyard and drew the man into his own chamber. Closing the door, the *vicomte* set forth wine and silver cups.

"We have talked more than once together," said Hendaye, meeting the bold, fierce gaze of the buccaneer, "and our thoughts run in the same channel.—Eh?"

Perouse emptied his goblet, and laughed. "Aye, *m'sieu le vicomte!* We feel alike toward these devils of Irish. Not to mention their leader. He acts more like a king than a buccaneer chief!"

Hendaye nodded. "That's not all. He's sending O'Malley, with you and the galleon and half the treasure, to Le Cap—or so 'tis said! If true."

Perouse started slightly. "What mean you by that, *m'sieu?*" he demanded quickly. "Is it not true?"

"Bah! This man called Mayo is wanted everywhere by France. He's a deserter, a traitor, with a price on his head! Would such a man send gold into French hands, think you?"

Perouse drew a swift breath. "Not likely. What does he scheme, eh?"

"I've learned his real plan," answered Hendaye. "Instead of sending half that treasure to Le Cap, he's only sending silver in the chests. All the gold and the jewels remain here with him. He's keeping the two Spanish lords here, meaning to ransom them and the castle. Then, with this ransom, and the best part of the treasure, he's a made man!"

"Pardieu!" A sudden savage flame leaped in the features of Perouse. "The same trick Harry Morgan played his men, eh? Cheat us of our winnings and skip out, eh? That's why he's taking the powder and the heaviest guns out of below-decks of the galleon!"

"That's why. Pulling your teeth," said Hendaye, and sipped his wine as the other swore great oaths. "Come, Perouse! You know me well.—What would you, and the men under you, think of changing captains?"

The filibuster whistled softly as he met the grim, hard eyes. "So that's it! My answer is—aye! Count on me, *m'sieu.* As for the men, they'll be glad enough, once I've passed the word among them. They know you for an officer—a nobleman—out of the royal navy."

Hendaye smiled at this, and leaned back in his chair. He began to speak carefully, with great deliberation.

Perouse listened, nodded, and presently an admiring torrent of oaths broke from him. "Name of the devil, M. d'Hendaye! But can you accomplish it?"

"I can," said Hendaye quietly, "if you'll do your share."

"Count upon me," answered Perouse with decision. "I'll answer for it! We'll not be ready to sail before midnight at the very earliest. About this Captain O'Malley—"

A terrible light flashed into Hendaye's eyes. "Be ready an hour after dinner; at nine of the clock! A man will shout the message from the boat-platform. Do not miss it. After you bring O'Malley ashore, have a score of our men ready to follow you, then get the gold and load it aboard. No one will know. There will be no alarm, no fighting."

Perouse uttered a hoarse, incredulous laugh. "Then, *m'sieu,* you will be a worker of miracles! Subdue such a man as Captain Mayo, this leader of buccaneers, without a fight, without an alarm? *Diantre!* It is past belief!"

Hendaye merely smiled thinly, but with so fierce and deadly a light in his eyes that Perouse, as he presently departed, hurriedly crossed himself.

By mid-afternoon, Denis Burke had completed the division of the treasure into fairly equal parts. This done, and half of it safely aboard the galleon and the other half temporarily stored in the castle, Burke left O'Malley to take care of the galleon. He himself had pleasure to take.

JOINING FELICE, he gave his eager attention to this castle of which he had become master. Felice was no less eager and delighted than he, for she shirked no detail of what must soon or late happen if she were wed to such a man as Burke. Guns must roar, but it was in her blood to be pulling the lanyard when they roared, if possible.

So together they went over every inch of the place, planning batteries, disposing of the heavy guns from the two galleons, and guarding against the future. Burke was confident that the Spaniards would accept his terms only too gladly, since he held them in a cleft stick. And once back here in the castle, with or without a Spanish commission, he had the world before him.

With a modicum of care, the place was absolutely impregnable. The walls were thick and solid. The sole approach from the land side was entirely commanded by the guns, and further, by two batteries that he planned. The sharp descent to the water, like the tiny haven itself, was equally under the castle guns. Within the place was an excellent well of water. Even an army would find this a very hard nut to crack.

"And if things go wrong at Santo Domingo," said Felice, thoughtfully, "we can stop in at Basse Terre or at some place where you're quite unknown, ship a few more filibusters, and come back here with enough men for anything!"

"Right! But things won't go wrong," said Burke confidently. "I'll leave Malachi Halloran here. He could hold the place against a fleet and an army at once."

"And what will be the end of it all, Denis?" she asked calmly, meeting his gay eyes. "In case the Spanish will make no peace with you?"

He looked up at the green hills beyond the jungle, and laughed. "Then we fight and die—a little sooner than otherwise! Does the prospect displease you, my dear?"

She pressed his arm. "I'm content with life or death, Denis, so that you be at my side. We'll play out the game together, as it comes.—Eh?"

"Yes," said Burke quietly. "But fear not! Spain will buy my sword, and I'll serve her better than Morgan served England! This castle is ours; we'll hold it for Spain—or despite Spain, as she may choose. Devil a bit do I care which!"

"Agreed, then!" she said brightly. "But, Denis! What about those two prisoners we saw in the cells? Will you leave them here?"

"No; take them to Santo Domingo. They're not suffering, in any case."

IN THIS statement, Denis Burke was wrong, for once. The two gentlemen of Spain, fast locked in one of the castle cells, were keenly suffering from shame and mortification of spirit, if not from bodily ills.

The Conde de Lucar, a court gallant who had warred against the Moors and was a soldier of note, did not spare blame on his companion. To this, Don Jaime retorted fiercely enough. It was quite true that Don Jaime was directly to blame for everything, since he had allowed Burke to cozen him and to take the castle. On the other hand, Lucar had walked into the trap without a blow struck, and had lost his galleons like a simpleton. By this time, however, both of them had wearied of vituperation, and were now sullenly resigned to their fate.

In the heat of the afternoon, when all except the guards and those at work on the ships were seeking relief from the hot sun, a shadow moved before their cell door. It was the Vicomte d'Hendaye, who stood at their door and spoke softly but earnestly.

Don Jaime was the first to comprehend that their visitor was not jesting. He stirred his stout person, and went to the door, staring at Hendaye.

"By the Saints, *señor,* this is a strange thing!" exclaimed Don Jaime, his heavy-set features against the cool bars. "Why, you are this man's lieutenant!"

Hendaye's pale gash of a mouth twisted in a thin grimace. "I am not," he said flatly. "I am an officer, a nobleman of France. This man is not only a filibuster, but he is a traitor to France—a deserter, and worse! He and his buccaneers have served my purpose. Now I shall rid myself of their dishonorable company. You are true *caballeros,* hidalgos of Spain. You can understand my actions!"

Don Jaime blinked at Conde de Lucar, who was scowling fiercely and biting his huge mustachios. Then he looked again at Hendaye.

"Well, that is true," he responded in a mild voice. "My family is of the *viejos Cristianos,* from the old Gothic line. And all men know the house of Lucar! Yes, it is true that we are gentlemen."

"And you do not love this buccaneer?" said Hendaye.

"No!" cried out Lucar savagely. "It is certain that we do not love him! He treats us like common felons!"

"Well, you shall question him about that to-night," said Hendaye. "I will send a man to free you. He will come sometime this evening. Follow him to the governor's room and be ready to assist me as I may require. Is it agreed? Upon your honor?"

Don Jaime bowed at the bars, in his stately Spanish fashion. "Go with God, *señor!*" he responded reassuringly. "You say that you will set us free—without ransom? *Madre de Dios!* Who could say no to such generosity? My friend and I are *caballeros.* We are of knightly blood, like yourself. It is true that we have lost everything except honor, and therefore we appreciate your position all the more."

Hendaye smiled again and departed. In these two men, whose hatred of Denis Burke was deep and real, he had gained allies of vast importance.

THE ONE chamber in the castle furnished with any luxury was the governor's room. This was a very large room off the main reception hall. Comfortable seats. Tapestried hangings. An enormous fireplace, much needed during the cool, damp nights of this season. Also, the room was very convenient to either gate of the castle. Denis Burke liked the big room.

The evening meal was over. A fire of mahogany logs, slow-burning, hot, had been built in the fireplace. Burke, lighting his pipe from a candle, was giving Malachi Halloran orders in regard to keeping the castle during his absence. Garf O'Malley was at work aboard the galleon.

Felice was sitting by the fire, cutting up some fine Genoa velvet which she was designing for a gown. Hendaye, who had been sitting in talk with her, frowned a little and rose. She was pleasant enough to him, but not as cordial as before. No fool, this girl.

As he left the room Hendaye cast a glance at the little chests ranged beneath the windows, along one wall. In those chests lay the half of the gold that Burke meant to put aboard the frigate. The silver bars were stacked out in the courtyard. Hendaye glanced at these, too, as he emerged. Close by, as though awaiting him, lounged a member of the galleon's crew.

"The time is come," said Hendaye to him unconcernedly. "Go down to the boat-platform and call to the galleon. Say that the captain wants Captain O'Malley ashore. As you pass the guard at the gate, tell them to admit O'Malley and any others who may come ashore from the galleon."

With a nod of comprehension, the man took his departure. Hendaye went back into the corridor that led to the governor's room. Here he met Malachi Halloran, who was coming out to set the guard for the night.

"O'Malley is coming ashore to seek the captain," said Hendaye. "Will you have a cresset lighted by the watergate?"

"Aye," said Malachi, with a dour nod, and passed on. He had no love for the *vicomte.*

In the corridor, near a small door that opened into the powder room, there was a niche. Here was a statue of the Virgin, and below it a lamp that lit the corridor. Hendaye passed on to the door of the governor's room, stood listening for a moment at it, and caught the voices of Felice and Denis Burke from within.

Then, smiling, he came back to the niche and stood waiting there. He fingered a long poniard with a jeweled hilt, part of the loot which he had appropriated. After a time he looked up suddenly, as the outer door opened.

Big Garf O'Malley, bearded, impetuous, appeared. He was alone. He strode swiftly forward, impatient to learn the cause of this summons. At sight of the Frenchman waiting there in the passage his face darkened. Hendaye, however, quietly lifted a hand and halted him.

"Wait! You know what has happened? They told you about it?"

"Eh? No! What mean you?" demanded O'Malley.

Hendaye glanced around, with an air of mystery, then pointed to the powder-room door, half behind the other man.

"The proclamation! There, on that door—"

Astonished, O'Malley swung around. Hendaye plunged the

poniard into his back, wrenched it out with savage ferocity, was about to drive home a second blow. But O'Malley collapsed and fell on his face without a sound.

The Frenchman kicked open the door of the powder room, dragged his victim inside before the blood could rush out over the stones.

CHAPTER IV

THE SWORDS OF GENTLEMEN

WHEN THE door of the governor's room opened and Hendaye appeared, Denis Burke paid no heed. He was busy lighting his pipe at one of the candles on the table.

Hendaye crossed the room to where Felice sat, near the fire, with her velvet goods. As she glanced up, he stepped swiftly behind her chair. Then, with one hand, he caught her by the hair, pulled back her head suddenly, savagely. With the other hand he held the bloody poniard against her throat, touching her white skin.

"Quiet, Burke!" he blared, his voice blending with her quick, startled cry. "Quiet!"

Burke leaped to his feet, then stood petrified, not daring to grasp his own gold-hilted rapier on the table before him. The grim and terrible face of Hendaye, the dagger at the throat of Felice, held him paralyzed.

"One move, one shout from you, and she dies!" exclaimed Hendaye in a firm voice. "Aye, much as I love her and desire her—she dies!—My dice, Burke, and I've thrown a main. Not a move, mind you!"

Burke's first thought was that the man had gone mad. The blazing eyes, the excited features of Hendaye, supported this thought. Then he saw the blood on the poniard, the red smear on the throat of Felice. There had been killing already!

"Careful, Felice!" he said. "And you, *vicomte!* What means this?"

"Enough!" Hendaye's harsh laugh rang out. "Dog of a filibuster, you've played the great lord long enough! Now you're toppled from your high estate. The galleon is mine. This treasure goes aboard to join what's there already—and you with it. Then I follow, with this woman."

For the first time, the possibility of a plot flashed across Burke's brain.

"You're mad!" he cried sharply. "*Vicomte*—whose blood is on your blade?"

Again Hendaye laughed fiercely. He pressed the poniard against the white throat of Felice. She sat motionless, not speaking, her dilated eyes fastened on Burke.

"The blood of your rascally Irish lieutenant, O'Malley!—Mad, am I? Mad enough to know that you're wanted for desertion, for traitorous acts, Denis Burke! Mad enough to hale you back to France in chains, aye! Not a move, now! Not a move, unless you want to see her die!"

As the last words sounded, a scrape of booted feet came from the corridor. Denis Burke, livid with fury, dared not move. He was more securely tied by the peril of Felice than by any bonds, and Hendaye knew it well.

Then the door was flung back, and into the room strode Perouse, behind him half a dozen of the Frenchmen.

Perouse halted at sight of the scene, comprehended it and uttered a laugh of approval.

"So you managed it, *m'sieu!* Good!"

At these words, Burke knew that Hendaye had turned the French and the others against him. He had only the Irish on whom to depend now. And O'Malley—murdered! No madman here, but a crafty rogue who would stop at nothing. A groan broke from Denis's lips.

"By heaven, if you harm her I'll have you drawn apart by horses!" he cried.

"Find your horses first—and catch your man," sneered Hendaye. "Ready, Perouse! Navy style now, my lad. Set a man on guard outside, to stop any entry here except to our own men. Then go down to the prison cells. Bring those two Spanish prisoners here to me. Say it's by the captain's orders. Now, the rest of you men! Start getting those chests out of here and aboard the galleon."

The men fell to work, and Perouse strode out of the room.

DENIS BURKE still stood stunned by the baseness of the treachery. With every moment he saw more clearly the extent of this calamity.

Then Felice spoke to him, unhurried, softly. "Think not of me, Denis! Let him kill me—"

Hendaye jerked back her head, the steel halting her words. Burke ground his nails into his palms until the blood came. His face was like death. Fury and dismay tore at his spirit. Yet he stood there helpless.

"Listen to me, you dog," spoke up Hendaye. "Back to France you go, dishonored traitor—and in my care! Well I know that this woman's life is more to you than gold or galleon. One false move, one shout, and she dies as that fool O'Malley died. Hurry up with those chests, men! Ah, there are the other men now."

Others of the French and the freed slaves came into the room. The little chests of gold and treasure were being rapidly carried forth. Denis Burke bit his lip, but he held his peace.

Again appeared Perouse. At his heels were stout Don Jaime and the lean, dark Conde de Lucar. These stopped short before the scene that greeted them; Burke, agonized, helpless, a mortal pallor bedewing his face with sweat; Hendaye, holding back the girl's head, his bloody poniard at her throat. All plain enough to their eyes.

"Come, *señores!*" cried out Hendaye, exultantly. "Here is your prisoner! This dog of a filibuster is now in your hands. You are his guards. Take him aboard the galleon and keep him there until I come." He turned to Burke, toward whom the two Spaniards advanced. "Go with them, *señor capitán!*" he cried mockingly. "Unbound, as you are, between them—good friends, for all your men to see! Perouse follows, his pistol ready. If you speak with your men—if you give alarm by word or look or act—Perouse fires his pistol. Into you or into the air, no matter! I'll be waiting here. At sound of a shot, this woman dies. You comprehend?"

The sweat stood out on Burke's face as he comprehended how craftily, how shrewdly, this man had planned. He knew that Hendaye, whether or not he desired Felice for himself, would kill her in an instant if necessary. He was playing a wild, desperate game, in which she was only a pawn—desirable, true, but only a pawn.

"Now," went on Hendaye, taking a loaded pistol that Perouse handed him, "you and I, Doña Felice, will remain here until these others are safely aboard my ship! Then we follow them. And unless you remain submissive, unless you accompany me freely, I will fire my pistol. If that happens, Captain Burke, aboard the galleon, will die on the instant! Look to it, my good Perouse!"

The latter nodded. Felice, as Hendaye relaxed the grip on her hair a trifle, met the tragic eyes of Denis Burke. She seemed calm enough—desperately, terribly calm.

"Where is O'Malley?" demanded Perouse.

"In hell!" Hendaye laughed. "If you seek his body, it lies in the powder room.—Off with you, now! Take your prisoner aboard, *señores!* Give them poniards, Perouse, and if need be answer to the guards for them as you pass. Remember your pistol!"

Perouse swaggered to the door, flung it open. The dark Conde de Lucar fingered the dagger which had been given to him, walked close to Burke, looked him in the eyes.

"Well, *señor* buccaneer! Come!"

A sound, half groan, half sob, broke from Burke. Then he obeyed. Only too well did he perceive the devilish ingenuity of

Hendaye's treachery. He himself dared nothing. He must pass among his own men silently, go aboard the galleon, yet make no sign. Hendaye, in a pinch, would murder Felice without a qualm. And when all this was done, she would come aboard in like manner, lest Burke be murdered.

So, between the two Spaniards, and followed by Perouse with pistol ready and a gay air on his lips, Denis Burke passed out. Across the courtyard, his own true men on every side, staring, yet unaware of anything wrong. Out the gate and down to the boat platform. There, the last of the treasure was going into a boat. Perouse's men were ready at the oars. On out to the galleon, which was blazing with lights. Her canvas was being lowered in readiness to depart.

When Burke came over the rail, a low mutter of oaths and curses reached him from both the Frenchmen and freed slaves. They hated him, not only for his stern discipline, but for the lies which Hendaye had spread about him.

ONCE ON that deck, Burke knew himself a lost man, beyond any hope of rescue. O'Malley was dead. Malachi Halloran was somewhere ashore, perhaps sleeping. The frigate lay across the harbor, dark and empty, suspecting nothing. He was marched aft between the two Spaniards; and Perouse, at their heels, gestured toward the main cabin, opening directly off the main deck, in the bowels of the great after castle.

"Watch him, *señores!*" Perouse cautioned the Spaniards. "The stern windows are open. If you hear a shot or an alarm ashore, kill him instantly."

Don Jaime put his dagger at Burke's back. "March, accursed dog!" he exclaimed fiercely. "By the Saints, I'll kill you with the greatest of pleasure if you give us an excuse.—March!"

Perouse, seeing them pass into the cabin, lifted his voice and sent ashore a bellow for Hendaye to come. It was picked up and passed on by men at the landing.

Lanterns burned in the main cabin, and the three who entered were not alone. Men were coming in and out, bearing the treasure chests. These were lowered through the open hatch of the lazaret, in the cabin floor.

Other men were breaking out powder. The powder-room was in the corridor, outside the main cabin, for all the guns remaining aboard the galleon were being loaded for action. Burke, standing at one side between the two Spaniards, dismissed all hope. Even if he should, by some miracle, get out of this trap—even if he got ashore—he could not hope to pursue this galleon with the frigate and recapture her. Hendaye could outsail, outfight, outrun him, with this splendid galleon.

The stripped, working men taunted Burke as they passed, flung jibes and jests at him, spat upon him. He stood grimly unmoved, however. His eyes blazed at them, speaking the despair and fury that was in his heart. Presently the treasure was stowed and the lazaret closed. From alongside came the voice of Hendaye. The stern windows of the galleon opened on the stern walk, above the rudder, with the water not ten feet below.

As the last of the men trooped out, Felice came into the cabin, with Hendaye. Her face was very white, but her level eyes were unafraid and calm.

Hendaye regarded them with a laugh, and showed Burke's gold-hilted rapier that he had fetched along. He extended it to Don Jaime.

"Here, *señor*, a worthy weapon for you! We sail instantly. Take care of this rascal until we're out of the harbor and I'm free. Felice, into this cabin with you!"

From this main cabin opened other sleeping-cabins. Hendaye threw open one of these doors. Felice met the gaze of Denis Burke, and at his nod she obeyed the order silently. Hendaye closed the door upon her, turned the key, leaving it in the lock.

"Good!" rang out his voice. "*Señores*, in half an hour I'll be free to take this rascal in charge. Well I know that your hatred will guard him more safely than any of these men under me! Then we shall consult together as regards the future, and a most honorable disposition of this ship and the treasure, as well as your own good selves."

He bowed to the two, and they returned his bow. Burke wondered just what game Hendaye was playing with them. That he meant to part with the galleon and the gold was hardly possible. Don Jaime balanced the gold-hilted rapier in delight, and Hendaye swung out of the cabin and slammed the door.

On the instant, the Conde de Lucar swung around and faced Burke. "*Señor,* you may guess that we bear you no love," he said darkly.

"Granted." Denis Burke, guessing that the man meant to kill him on the spot, as Hendaye might have foreseen, laughed lightly. He looked into the dark eyes, unafraid. "I am at your mercy."

Don Jaime chuckled, strode over to Felice's cabin and unlocked the door. At his call, she came out, staring at the three. Don Jaime bowed to her, with profound grace, despite his stoutness. Up above, feet were trampling the deck and orders were being passed. The Conde de Lucar, after a bow to Felice, turned again to Burke. "*Señor capitán,*" he said proudly, "we knew nothing of what was proposed, when we were brought to your presence ashore, there. It is true that you are an enemy. But *caballeros* of Spain do not lay violent hands upon women, nor do they murder helpless men."

"No, no!" put in Don Jaime, puffing out his cheeks, as the astonished Burke met his eyes. "We do not love you, *señor,* but before God, we prefer an enemy to a traitor! I beg you to believe that we had no hand in this affair, and no knowledge of its details. The blood of Spain is proud, *señor!* We have humored this rascally *vicomte,* rather than see you and this lady murdered. To you, dear lady," and he bowed again to Felice, "we offer knightly service. We kiss your hands and feet. We place the swords of gentlemen at your disposal!"

"Aye," said Lucar curtly.

Don Jaime, turning, handed Burke the rapier.

Now, for a moment Denis Burke stood as though stupefied.

This unsuspected gallantry flung him into the utmost astonishment. Then he suddenly came awake, realized that it was all true, and a flash leaped in his eyes.

"Aye, Spanish blood is proud blood, indeed!" he exclaimed. "Gentlemen, there is no time for words.—I offer you my respect and friendship. Of that, more later. Can you swim?"

"I once escaped the Moors by swimming," said Lucar.

Don Jaime, amazed at the question, merely nodded assent.

"Quick, then!" Burke gestured to the open stern windows. "Drop into the water and swim ashore. We'll follow you. First, I have a small matter to settle.—I pray you, do not argue! Once the anchor is up, it is too late! Go now—quickly!"

"Right," said Lucar. He bowed to Felice in his grave fashion. "You will excuse us, my lady? Come, Don Jaime!"

They passed out to the stern walk and were gone.

CHAPTER V

FAREWELL TO THE ASSASSIN

NOW FELICE came quickly to Burke, caught his arms, broke into a laugh.

"I can't realize it! I never suspected that they would help.—But what can we do now? I cannot swim. We cannot get ashore—"

The old, gay laugh on his lips, Burke leaned over and kissed her, then straightened up. His eyes were dancing; all his keen features were in a glow, an eager sparkle.

"No matter! Go on deck at once. Find Hendaye and bring him here—alone if possible. Tell him some story, anything you please! Lure him here. My soul to the devil, if I don't pay him out for murdering Garf O'Malley!"

She argued not nor protested, but turned and went on the errand.

Burke leaped into action. He knew that any pursuit would be folly; he might escape, but Hendaye would be gone. He swore it should not be.

He darted to the powder room. Once the boats were stowed and the anchor taken in, the galleon would be out of the harbor. It would be too late then. He rolled out a half-emptied powder keg and spilled the black grains quickly. They made a thick train along one wall of the passage, around the main cabin, and so to the stern windows. The keg was emptied. He lifted it out to the stern walk, then took down a lantern and set it there by the window.

Up forward, Perouse was getting sail on the galleon, although as yet her anchor was not out of the mud. The Vicomte d'Hendaye was high on the poop, sending his orders along the deck. There was no alarm ashore, and now he saw himself quite secure.

Then the *vicomte* saw Felice, hastily running to him. She seemed in no fear of him, though she cried out as she ran. Amid the noise and confusion, he could make nothing of her incoherent words, but it was clear that something had happened in the cabin below.

So, passing word for Perouse to get the anchor in at once, the *vicomte* followed her back down to the main deck, and so in at the cabin entrance. Hendaye strode after her through the passage, and came up with her as she entered the main cabin. He caught her hand, seeing only her face before him as she turned, in the entrance.

"What is it, dear lady?" he exclaimed. "Be not afraid! Now you are free of that dog of a buccaneer—"

"Not yet!" said Burke, and slammed the door shut.

Hendaye whirled about and saw him there, rapier in hand. He saw the Spaniards gone. There were but the three of them alone. Then he uttered a shout, and clapped hand to sword.

Burke did not move, but spoke aside to Felice, his eyes on Hendaye the while. "A powder keg is outside the open window," he said to the girl. "Throw it over, then jump after it. The keg will support you until I come. Go—go quickly!—Well, my dear Hendaye? Shout all you like. Your men will hear nothing, thanks to the confusion above. So you murdered poor O'Malley, did you? Well, then—die!"

With that Denis Burke attacked, carefully, grimly, deliberately. He knew Hendaye to be an excellent swordsman. As the blades clashed and clung in air, Felice went to the stern window. She passed out to the stern walk, indeed; but there she waited, eyes fastened on what was passing inside.

It was well worth the seeing, for Hendaye fought as never in his life before. Features set in desperate fury, he set all Burke's science at naught. He fought, indeed, like a madman. Inside of a minute his breath was coming in gasps, sweat was bedewing his face. Yet he had not touched Denis Burke, and the latter was smiling slightly into the traitor's dark, bloodshot eyes.

Relentless, implacable as fate itself, Burke's gold-hilted rapier played about the *vicomte,* turned him, forced him back. As a dog turns sheep, now leaping at this one to head him off, now sending that one into a certain opening, so Denis Burke worked his enemy into a certain position. The long rapier glimmered and clashed, licked about the doomed man, beat away his steel.

Hendaye's face was set in hard lines; but presently his eyes became dilated, filled with terror. He realized that Burke had some set purpose in his mind, and he dreaded what it might be.

SUDDENLY BURKE laughed and drew back slightly.

Hendaye now stood directly before the closed cabin door.

"Murderer!" cried out Burke. "Take your reward!"

The rapier leaped in like a tongue of death. Hendaye parried desperately. Burke's body uncoiled like a spring. He disengaged. Faster than light the thin rapier seemed to lunge of itself. Denis Burke sprang back and stood panting, empty-handed.

Hendaye let fall his own blade with a clatter. Through his body, and even piercing the stout door behind him, was the rapier. A frightful spasm contorted his face.

Burke caught sight of the girl outside. "Felice! Off! Swiftly!"

Her figure vanished. Burke heard the splash as she followed the keg into the water. The galleon had just begun to move over toward the harbor entrance.

Burke picked up the ready lantern, and from it took the burning candle. One last look at the contorted face of Hendaye.

"Farewell, assassin!" he exclaimed.

Then he lowered the candle to the powder train. There was a faint *pouf!* Whereupon he hurled himself backward into the water. Even as he went under there was a terrific explosion from the very bowels of the galleon.

AN HOUR later the governor's room in the castle witnessed a strange sight. Burke, still dripping wet, stood watching the couch before the fire. O'Malley lay there, two men skilled in wounds working over him.

Felice appeared, freshly clothed. She advanced to Burke's side. Don Jaime and the Conde de Lucar, in dry garments, came in and stood silent.

"Faith, your honor, he'll pull through," said one of the two men. "The poniard reached no vital spot—and it's tough he is."

Burke's face lit up.

Malachi Halloran came striding into the room. A fierce exultancy shone in his face, as he halted with a salute.

"Your honor! The galleon's ashore on the point, and burning."

"No matter," said Burke. "Gold is gold, even if it be melted!"

"We ha' taken a score or more of the Frenchmen, your honor."

"Give them a boat, food and water, and turn them loose."

"Aye." Malachi grinned at him in delight. "We've got that scoundrel Perouse in the courtyard, unhurt."

"Hang him!" said Burke curtly.

With a salute, Malachi was gone.

Burke turned to the two gentlemen of Spain. His quick, warm smile flashed out at them. "*Señores!* I have a proposal to make. The treasure can be salvaged, Conde de Lucar. I shall hand it back to you and send you to Vera Cruz. I ask you there to seek out the viceroy, and obtain a pardon for me. I offer to hold this place from the crown of Spain and to rid the seas of all buccaneers and filibusters. Don Jaime will remain here in command, for most of my work will lie at sea; but none the less, Santa Barbara will be mine. That may compensate you for what loss you have borne."

A flash of joy in his dark face, Lucar bowed gravely. "*Señor*, you have my word! As it happens, the viceroy is my uncle. I answer for his reply!"

Then the two Spanish gentlemen went out to the hanging of Perouse.

Denis Burke looked into the eyes of Felice and drew her to him.

"So, my princess—the future grows clear after all! And instead of a buccaneer, you'll have an honest man for your husband, praise be!"

"All wandering comes somewhere to an end, Denis," she answered softly.

H. BEDFORD-JONES

BEDFORD-JONES IS a Canadian by birth, but not by profession, having removed to the United States at the age of one year. For over twenty years he has been more or less profitably engaged in writing and traveling. As he has seldom resided in one place longer than a year or so and is a person of retiring habits, he is somewhat a man of mystery; more than once he has suffered from unscrupulous gentlemen who impersonated him—one of whom murdered a wife and was subsequently shot by the police, luckily after losing his alias.

The real Bedford-Jones is an elderly man, whose gray hair and precise attire give him rather the appearance of a retired foreign diplomat. His hobby is stamp collecting, and his collection of Japan is said to be one of the finest in existence. At present writing he is en route to Morocco, and when this appears in print he will probably be somewhere on the Mojave Desert in company with Erle Stanley Gardner.

Questioned as to the main facts in his life, he declared there was only one main fact, but it was not for publication; that his life had been uneventful except for numerous financial losses, and that his only adventures lay in evading adventurers. In his younger years he was something of an athlete, but the encroachments of age preclude any active pursuits except that of motoring. He is usually to be found poring over his stamps, working at his typewriter, or laboring in his California rose garden, which is one of the sights of Cathedral Cañon, near Palm Springs.

Bedford-Jones has written stories laid in many corners of the earth, but among his most popular tales were the John Solomon stories which started many years ago in the *Argosy*.

17080839R00138

Printed in Great Britain
by Amazon